where
love lies

where love lies

a novel

RAZ TAL SCHENIRER

GREENLEAF
BOOK GROUP PRESS

Published by Greenleaf Book Group Press
Austin, Texas
www.gbgpress.com

Distributed by Greenleaf Book Group

For ordering information or special discounts for bulk purchases, please contact Greenleaf Book Group at PO Box 91869, Austin, TX 78709, 512.891.6100.

Design and composition by Greenleaf Book Group and Mimi Bark
Cover design by Greenleaf Book Group and Mimi Bark
Cover image used under license from ©Shutterstock.com/Welry

Publisher's Cataloging-in-Publication data is available.

Print ISBN: 979-8-88645-153-5

eBook ISBN: 979-8-88645-154-2

To offset the number of trees consumed in the printing of our books, Greenleaf donates a portion of the proceeds from each printing to the Arbor Day Foundation. Greenleaf Book Group has replaced over 50,000 trees since 2007.

Printed in the United States of America on acid-free paper

24 25 26 27 28 29 30 31 32 33   10 9 8 7 6 5 4 3 2 1

First Edition

For Alma and Romy

The nice girl loses an important protective mechanism when she assumes that life is fair, or that Prince Charming will always protect her.

—SHERRY ARGOV, *Why Men Love Bitches*

I

The Princess

Tel Aviv

Chapter 1

What does it mean to take control of your life?
Does it start with drinking green juice in the morning and end with a sleep meditation at night? Or is it something bigger than that? Does it mean you're free to be yourself without the burden of a raised eyebrow? Or does taking control of your life mean doing what's in your heart, even if you're bound to hurt someone you love along the way? Maybe it's saying yes. Yes to sex, yes to stretching out like a starfish on satin sheets with the breathlessness of love's endless potential, yes to tangled limbs and dewy mornings, yes to more wine, yes to dessert, yes to youth, yes to life.

These were the thoughts that circled my mind as I sat alone watching the sunset on Tel Aviv's Gordon Beach, my toes nestled in the damp sand, the crisp blue water of the Mediterranean Sea glimmering with each subtle wave. Only a month before, I was throwing back tequila shots in carpeted basements with my high school friends, the Connecticut suburbs our playground of experimentation. And now, here I was, dropped onto a beach in a foreign country, with nothing but the smell of the ocean to comfort me.

I could officially say goodbye to initialed L.L.Bean backpacks and oversized college sweatshirts, goodbye to driving around Greenwich in my best friend Julia's Range Rover Sport looking for a McDonald's drive-through, goodbye to smoking weed behind the bleachers, to drinking warm vodka out of plastic water bottles, goodbye to all of that. It was time to say hello to Tel Aviv's Tamara Juice Bar fruit smoothies, to tahini dripping down the forearms of people standing in line on Frishman Street, hunched over a pita overflowing with falafel; hello to the Levinsky Market, where teenage girls and boys sat on the sidewalks to smoke cigarettes; and hello, of course, to the unimaginable: joining the Israeli army, against my will. Tomorrow. Talk about losing control.

Just a few minutes before, I'd bought a bottle of Sancerre to drink on the beach, and the clerk at the liquor store—a man in his fifties in a yellow-stained white T-shirt and a beer belly peeping out from underneath it—had a gaze so sharp I felt like he was undressing me with his eyes.

"Who's the lucky guy?" he asked, a lit cigarette hanging from the side of his mouth as he scanned the wine bottle and handed it to me with a few paper cups hanging loosely from its neck.

I could barely hear him over the yelling on the television behind him blaring a Maccabi Haifa soccer game. "Oh, come on!" he yelled at the screen.

I laughed nervously, a drunk-in-the-back-seat-of-an-Uber-at-three-o'clock-in-the-morning laugh trying to make light of the driver's idiotic jokes. *You're so hilarious, a real comical talent. Just don't rape and murder me, please.*

"What, are you alone?" the clerk said, his eyes back on me. "What's a nice girl like you doing drinking a bottle of wine alone? You sure you don't want any company?" He scratched his stomach.

As if.

"Oh, no, I'm meeting my boyfriend," I lied and turned to walk out of the shop. The idea of a man waiting for me at the beach was enough to send his attention back to the game.

Alone. I needed to be alone. I wanted the wine to wash away this feeling of doom, of not knowing where I was going to be when the sun rose the next morning, the same way the waves washed away the tracks in the sand. I needed to hear my own thoughts, without the constant interruption of my parents' opinions. *Open your mind, Ella. Think of the army as an experience. You'll thank us in the end.*

I had snuck out of the house a few hours before, without telling them where I was going, shutting the door behind me and leaving the two of them sitting together at the kitchen table drinking tea with mint leaves, their relationship the epitome of what a marriage was supposed to be, at least to spectators. I had imagined the beach as the perfect escape from the stuffy apartment we had temporarily rented, with its creaky electric blinds and worn-out hardwood floors, but now, the humidity made me feel even more smothered, not to mention that it was seriously ruining my hair. I breathed in deeply, but the air didn't fill my lungs the same way the Connecticut breeze did, and at that moment, I missed home so much. Here, the wind stood still, and while the swishing sound of the waves was meant to calm me, sweat sprinkled down the backs of my knees, and sand stuck to my skin in all the wrong places, so it was impossible for me to appreciate the setting. My only company were the beach bugs disappearing into the sand, digging their heads deep down, ignoring the world around them. I wished I could do the same. I looked to my left at a young couple making out a few feet away from me, their mouths seemingly stuck open, their tongues grossly at war. *Ew,* I mouthed to myself, but inside they made me feel only more single and alone than I already was.

An entire month had passed since that dreadful Wednesday afternoon when our three-story Greenwich home was packed up and emptied. Boxes lined the entrance, and the smell of fresh paint lingered in the air. Before my mother stepped out the front door for the last time, I watched her look back, lean over, and kiss the wall of the home that had fulfilled her American dream. From the time of having to sneakily buy a slice of pizza she couldn't afford in the littered streets of south Tel Aviv to her years of owning a three-story suburban house in America—*America*—my mother had admired the land of the free, and I knew her heart broke at the mere thought of going back to where she had come from.

When we landed at Ben Gurion Airport in Israel, a part of her stayed behind, and so did a part of me. I spent each day in Tel Aviv lying in bed, drinking chocolate milk from a small plastic bag, a common way to drink it in Israel, hoping my mother would stop cleaning the apartment maniacally and tend to me, which she never did. She was so invested in her own sorrow that she put me on hold, with nothing else to do than dread the future.

And boy, did I dread it. In what universe was I, Ella Davidson, expected to know how to prepare for army service? I was born in Israel—that was true—but my parents and I moved to the United States when I was just a baby, before I could even crawl. I had no patriotic connection to Israel; if anything, I felt like an all-American girl. Would there be anything to eat? Did they have gluten-free options? Did I seriously have to wear a uniform? Where the hell was I going to sleep? And the question that didn't stop haunting me: How was I going to get out?

"Ella, you're worse than Kim Kardashian when she lost her diamond earring in the ocean," my sister Natalie said as she stood at the entrance to the bedroom we now shared, leaning on the wall of hand-painted pink peonies.

"Get out!" I said, throwing the empty chocolate milk bag in her direction. Wise beyond her thirteen years, Natalie was the introverted, less-emotional one of the two of us, although she, too, was dealing with her preteen life having been turned upside down.

"There's people that are dying!" she yelled from the hallway, quoting Kourtney Kardashian. I grabbed the pillow beside me and smothered my face into it, muffling a scream.

At least here, at the beach, I could look out at the ocean and remember that it was bigger than me, bigger than the nightmare my life had become. I had felt insignificant from the moment the plane landed in Tel Aviv, and here, watching the waves break, the white foam disappearing against my toes, I was tiny, which somehow seemed to minimize my problems. If I was tiny, so were they.

I felt the tears well up behind my eyes, and I inhaled the saltiness of the sea in an effort to relax. I needed to surrender. To let go. To accept my fate. And what better way to let go than to break down? I took another sip of the wine, my tears mixing with the alcohol. Unless I was going to pull a Virginia Woolf and drown myself in the ocean, there was nothing I could do to stop tomorrow from coming.

As I tried to accept my fate, a runner sprinted past me, flinging sand all over me and into my paper wine cup. I spit the sand out and wiped my face with my Reformation sundress. *Seriously? With the wide expanse of space on this beach, he had to run close enough to kick sand into my face?*

"Asshole!" I yelled after him. Was I that insignificant? I felt invisible and ignored, and there was no worse feeling than being ignored by a gorgeous guy. I closed my eyes and sighed quietly, cursing the world for snatching away the last few moments of my mope session. It was bad enough that I was going to be waking up before the sun the next morning and getting on a bus to an army base in the middle of nowhere. Did the universe really have to send over a sexy, sweaty runner to make me feel even worse?

All of a sudden, the runner turned around and ran back toward me, his golden hair bouncing up and down, his tall frame magnified with each stride. He was annoyingly handsome, hotter than I'd initially thought. The dewy hour of sunset highlighted his cheekbones, stepping stones to his hazel eyes. I rolled mine.

I thought I heard him mumble "sorry" under his breath in Hebrew, but I couldn't really tell. "What?" I said.

"I'm sorry," he said, this time in accented English. "I didn't see you there."

"You didn't see me?" I waved my hands in the air. "You need glasses, then. I'm sitting right here."

He knelt down to look at me, his AirPods still in his ears. I practically fell backward when his eyes locked with mine. In a matter of seconds, I was lost in the yellow specks of his irises. It was like the world around us had stopped. Even the waves seemed to silence, and I could hear him catch his breath. My mind wandered to him panting like that on top of me. I shook my head. His eyelashes were so long they almost looked fake, and his smile was so straight and white and bright that I felt my tongue gloss over my own teeth in insecurity. He had a tiny birthmark on the side of his neck that resembled a heart, and I imagined where other birthmarks hid. His shoulders were broad, in stark contrast to my fragile frame, and he had a deep golden tan—probably from all those runs on the beach past other girls lost in thought.

Why did he have to see me like this, with my shoulder-length brown hair tousled and ratty from the beachy wind and my eyes puffy from crying? Why couldn't we have met a few months before, when my life was normal, when I was perfectly put together, strolling through Greenwich in my Burberry trench coat without a care in the world?

I watched as his eyes glanced over my face, the look behind them softening when he noticed the tears welling up in my eyes.

He held out his hand for me to shake. "I'm Liam," he said.

"Ella," I said, regaining my composure.

When my hand touched his, I felt my blood surging through the galaxy of my arteries, rushing all the way down to my toes. Handshakes weren't supposed to be felt in the toes. Or in the stomach, or between the legs, if we're going to go there. His touch didn't stop in the palm of my hand like it should have. It hit me like a lightning bolt, waking up even the idlest nerves in my body. I watched in slow motion as he ran the hand I'd touched through his hair.

"Hey, you okay?" he asked.

I glanced down at my feet again and looked back up at him. The sincerity of his voice and the gentle look on his face made me pity myself even more, and I started choking up.

Liam bit the inside of his cheek, like he was working up the courage to say something. "Listen, I owe you a drink," he said. He lifted his chin and nudged his head toward the sandy wine cup. "There's a cool place around the corner. Want to go?"

I shook my head.

"Come on, get up," he said when I couldn't come up with a reason not to. It sounded like a demand, despite the way he smiled when he said it.

"What? Now? No, I can't," I said.

Liam slipped his hand into the pocket of his shorts and pulled out a coin. "Heads or tails?"

"Um, heads?"

He flicked the coin into the air and slapped it into his other palm. "Tails it is! I win. We're going."

I laughed. "No offense, but I want to be alone," I said, enunciating each word slowly, like I was speaking to a child. He couldn't be gorgeous *and* smart, could he?

He reached out his hand. "I don't take no for an answer," he said, even slower than I had, half-mocking me. *Are all Israeli guys this aggressive?* "Come on, just half an hour. Let's go."

"Fine," I said, the wine hitting me as he helped me up. I brushed the sand off my Louis Vuitton tote bag and threw it over my shoulder. "Half an hour."

We walked toward the boardwalk, the fluorescent lights revealing the crinkled corners of his eyes. His phone screen was cracked, and his shoes were so worn I had to look twice to make sure they weren't Golden Goose sneakers. But with my manicured nails and overplucked eyebrows, I felt free in the aura of his carelessness. I looked over at the restaurants we were walking by, trying not to show him how interested I was in what this evening had to offer.

When we reached the bar, Liam spoke to the hostess in Hebrew, and I felt a sudden sense of relief at being able to understand the language. Back in Connecticut, my parents made it a rule to speak Hebrew at home so that my siblings and I wouldn't forget the language. I understood everything, but my accent was thick and my vocabulary minimal. Another reason added to my mental *Why I Will Never Survive the Army* list.

We stepped past a neon sign that read "The Pineapple Bar" into a dim, yellow-lit room with an exaggerated amount of pineapple décor. There were pineapple-shaped seat cushions and pineapple wallpaper. Even the hostess wore a pineapple scrunchie in her hair. She sat us in the corner at the only available table, and though the bar was full of people, as soon as Liam started talking, they blurred and faded into the background, only sharpening his image.

"Let me get a bottle of—" He turned to me. "What was that wine you were drinking?"

"Sancerre," I said.

He shook his head and pointed his thumb toward me. "What she said."

I laughed a real laugh for the first time that month. I liked how confident Liam was in his unfamiliarity with French wine. I glanced over at him. He was staring at me.

"What?" I asked.

"Nothing," he said.

"What?" I asked again. *Do I have a piece of food stuck in between my teeth?*

"Nothing. I just—I didn't realize how beautiful you are," he said. He took his phone out and tried to snap a picture of me.

"Not so close up!" I said as I turned my head. I heard the click of the camera. At least he only got the back of my head. I rolled my eyes. *Is that the best he can do?*

The waiter brought us our wine, and I eyed the Corona the blonde girl at the next table was drinking out of the bottle.

Liam noticed. "You want a beer?" he asked.

I shook my head. I used to go to bars in Westport using Julia's older sister's ID, listening to immature college guys spend hours talking about themselves as I sipped a Corona with lime. Liam was nothing like them. He was a man, and his intimidating demeanor gave his compliments more weight. He had deep-set eyes, and I hated to admit that the mystery behind them excited me. I was used to having everything laid out on the table, but with Liam, I realized I'd have to work to peel back each layer.

"Do you have a girlfriend?" I asked, the wine loosening my lips. With the half bottle I had downed at the beach and now another glass, I felt my muscles relax. Finally, the tension disappeared into the pineapple universe.

Liam laughed, adjusting himself on the barstool so that he was facing me. "You don't hold back, do you?" he said, fingering the stem of the glass.

"Well, do you or not?" I asked, surprised by my own straight-forwardness.

"No, I don't. I'm not the girlfriend type."

"Not the girlfriend type?" I repeated. "Oh, so you're one of those."

"What's that supposed to mean?"

"You're one of those. You know. The good-looking, tough guy with issues. The one who's been heartbroken in the past and needs fixing. The one who's 'better off alone,'" I said, using my fingers as quotation marks.

"If only my life were that simple," he said, calling the waiter over with the swift motion of his hand. My heart dropped. He was going to ask for the check.

"We'll have another bottle," Liam said, without asking me. *Have we really already finished this one?* "And a large pizza. I'm hungry," he said.

Finally, a guy who ordered for me. American guys were constantly worried about what I wanted, how much, how little, but Liam made me feel like he knew what was best. For both of us. I was annoyed at my own relief. Wasn't I a feminist? A decision-maker? The daughter of two educated, liberal parents? I wasn't used to letting go, to letting somebody else take the reins, but after a month of lying in bed, feeling like each day was a battle of survival, I was pleased to be *taken* care of instead of *taking* care.

The waiter, a redhead who couldn't have been older than twenty-one, with freckles splattered across his nose, returned fifteen minutes later with the pizza and the wine bottle. He poured a tasting of the wine into Liam's glass. Liam nodded for him to keep pouring.

"What's your favorite sex position?" Liam asked me with a straight face, the waiter smirking as he overheard.

I swallowed so hard I almost choked on the single slice of pizza I was letting myself eat.

"I'm not going to answer that," I said, shaking my head. I wiped the corners of my mouth with a pineapple napkin. "I don't even know you." I had been intimate with only one person in my life, Ethan Santos, my high school boyfriend who'd moved to Connecticut from Madrid two years before.

While technically I was considered inexperienced, Ethan and I had experimented with each other the way only horny teenagers could, expanding each other's sexual worlds, pushing them to the limit. I let him watch me sit around naked while we studied for midterms; I gave him blow jobs under the desk during his math private tutor sessions on Zoom; I let him fall asleep inside of me. The openness we felt with each other was a sacred space of trust and, more than that, of immaculate wonder.

Liam placed both of his hands on the tabletop. "Okay, you want to know me? I'm Liam Levine. I'm twenty-five years old. My mother's from Australia; my father's Moroccan. I'm originally from a small town up North, but now I live here. My mom has Alzheimer's; my dad's an abusive asshole who refuses to pay for anything since the divorce, so I work to take care of her medical bills. I work in—"

Oh, God, no. Enough. When I'd snuck out of the house that evening, it was for the sole purpose of escaping. I had promised myself that I would let nothing and no one interrupt me. I even left my phone at home, throwing it on the couch before opening the front door. I didn't want to hear the problems of a guy I would never see again, no matter how attracted to him I was, not only because I wanted to enjoy one last night of freedom but also because Liam's issues made mine seem shallow and trivial.

"Reverse cowgirl," I said, interrupting his monologue. Liam squinted his eyes in confusion. "Your question," I said. "My favorite position. It's reverse cowgirl."

Before I had time to think, Liam leaned in, his lips a centimeter from my mouth. I could smell the garlicky scent of pizza sauce on his breath. I closed my eyes, expecting him to kiss me, but when I opened them, he was still there, a centimeter away, not touching me. "Mine, too," he whispered before pulling away.

"So what's your story, cowgirl?" he said between bites of another slice. He had eaten more than half the pie, leaving only two beautiful, shining slices of cheesy goodness on the tray. The alcohol had heightened my appetite, but I couldn't possibly eat more than one slice on a first date, regardless of whether I saw a future with him. "Why were you crying on the beach?" he asked, as if we didn't just experience the most sexually charged moment in the history of my life.

God, he is so sexy.

I didn't feel like telling him my story, especially after he fake almost-kissed me. How embarrassing. Who said I even wanted to kiss him in the first place? Plus, from the little I'd learned about Liam's hard-knock life, his serious problems minimized my own in a way that made me look spoiled and pathetic. Liam's mother was battling Alzheimer's, and I was sobbing on a beautiful beach because my family had moved out of the Connecticut suburbs into an apartment in Tel Aviv overlooking the ocean? I had no choice but to justify my tears with a few white lies.

"I live on the Upper East Side," I said, "and believe it or not, I'm in medical school. I'm only here on a break before my residency starts." I was slurring my words.

"New York City?" Liam said, his eyes widening; finally I had impressed him. "I've always wanted to go there, to walk around Times Square, to visit the Statue of Liberty, to have a picnic in Central Park."

"Sounds like your very own American Dream," I said.

He shrugged and pointed to the window of the bar that faced the water, where a row of yachts lined the dock. "That's my dream. To have enough money to buy a yacht. I don't care what I do or where; I just want to make money doing it."

"You shouldn't do something for money. You should do what you love, and the money will come," I said, repeating a quote my father loved.

"Easy for you to say, Miss Louis Vuitton. You wouldn't understand what it's like to think about money, to check the price tag before you swipe Daddy's credit card. Not everyone has everything handed to them on a silver platter."

My jaw fell open so wide it almost hit the floor.

"You are such an asshole," I said, pouring myself the last of the wine, secretly amused. He was wrong. I had it all, and now, my world was falling apart.

"This is the second time in one night you've called me an asshole. I might have outdone myself," he said. I could tell by his smile that his lips started feeling looser, too, his eyelids heavy. "That's all you're eating?" he asked, looking at the half-eaten pizza slice on my plate.

"I'm so full," I lied, rubbing my slushy, wine-filled stomach. Liam promised we'd only be there for half an hour, but when I looked at the pineapple clock on the wall, it was already past midnight, and we were the only ones left in the bar.

"You probably go to fancy Pilates studios and wear matching workout clothes, don't you?" he said.

I wasn't used to feeling like I had to prove myself around people. Maybe it was the wine, but the ruder he became, the sexier he was.

"What's with you thinking you know everything?" I asked.

"Your eyes give it away. You look like a girl who hasn't had a taste of real life yet," he said.

"Based on what notion, exactly? You don't even know my last name. You don't know how old I am. You have no idea what I've been through," I said.

"Well, I know your favorite sex position," Liam said. "I think that's enough."

Liam stood up to go to the bathroom, and I was left staring at the pizza in front of me. "Fuck it," I said out loud to no one in particular. I inhaled the last two slices, my mouth overflowing with mozzarella cheese and saucy dough. With my mouth still stuffed, I called the red-headed waiter over to pick up the empty pizza tray before Liam came back.

Chapter 2

The day my life was turned upside down, Julia and I sat scrolling through TikTok on the pink-skirted faux-fur couch in my bedroom while half-watching *Say Yes to the Dress* and contemplating the pros and cons of a breast enhancement.

"Look at her boobs," Julia said, pointing to the slim bride on the flat-screen TV mounted onto the wall. "They're so hard they practically hold up the dress."

I looked up from my phone and shrugged. "I feel like hard boobs are better than saggy boobs," I said, squeezing my own with my free hand.

"My boobs are too small to ever be saggy," she said. "I want a boob job. I need one." She rubbed her glossy lips together, still pouty from the lip injections we'd snuck off to get three months before. Julia wasn't effortlessly beautiful, but she knew how to pull herself together, and that's all that mattered to high school guys, which meant it was all that mattered to us. Her auburn hair didn't get oily, so she got away with getting only one blow-out a week, and with heavy black eyeliner and a dab of blush, she turned heads.

"I'd get a boob job with you," I decided. I looked up at the clock. "It's already after six and our makeup's not even done. Ethan and Brian are picking us up at eight, which means we have less than two hours to get ready for the game. Tonight's the night. I have to look *perfect*."

As a senior in high school with a serious boyfriend who also happened to be the captain of the hockey team, it was officially time to lose my virginity. While the first time I gave Ethan a blow job was in the closet at Jared O'Connor's garage party, I wanted the actual act of sex to be romantic, to be a night neither of us would forget. "Your eyes shine brighter than the stars," Ethan said to me the first time we made out in the back of his pickup truck.

"You're corny, and you're lying," I answered.

"I might be corny, but I swear," he said, his almond-brown eyes staring into mine, "*te amo.*"

Julia perked up and walked over to the other side of the room, past the pink velvet rug that matched the comforter on the bed. "It's about time. You've made Ethan wait for, what? Five months already?" she asked, looking at me through the reflection of the vanity mirror on the desk.

"Six and a half," I said under my breath.

She shook her head. "We're seniors in high school. I don't know how you do it. He's so Latin and hot. I wouldn't have been able to wait a week."

"I know, but we've done everything else," I said.

"Did you shave?" she asked.

"This morning, not yesterday. No stubble," I said.

A light bulb went off in Julia's mind. "I'm adding that one to the Goddess Rules!"

She opened the glittery Moschino notebook resting next to the polka-dotted desk lamp and added another rule to it, the pink feathers on the tip of the pen dancing back and forth as she scribbled. "*Always be smoothly shaved but . . . never childlike*," she said aloud.

At the beginning of junior year at Greenwich High School, Julia and I had started a list of rules we picked up from life in the Connecticut suburbs. They were the rules to getting the guy you wanted, and since following them, there hadn't been a single guy—from *the* Ethan Santos to Julia's ex, Mitch Pollack, the gorgeous, green-eyed nerd in Algebra II—that we couldn't snag. It was like the Goddess Rules were our very own Pandora's box of answers to surviving girlhood, a locked safe only the two of us knew the code to. We'd hear the rules in the most unexpected places, from a conversation with my father to an Instagram story or a side remark on Miley Cyrus's new podcast. The last Goddess Rule we added—*Men want some meat to hold on to, but watch what you eat*—was a sentence we overheard a mother say to her daughter while waiting in line at Costco just as the daughter was biting into a hotdog. Julia and I only had to exchange glances to know that a rule was worthy to be added.

If I had to draw a map of the rules Julia and I had learned growing up about what it meant to be whatever it was guys wanted, it would look like a confusion of lines zigzagging back and forth, doodles in the margins, exclamation points and upside-down question marks everywhere, with a crown at its inevitable center. I stood over Julia's shoulder and watched as she added another rule to our list.

THE GODDESS RULES

Sit up straight, but don't look like you're trying.

If an opportunity doesn't present itself, create it.

Be yourself, but not overly honest.

Laugh at his jokes, but not too loud.

Discuss your accomplishments, but never before he does.

Look youthful, but not childlike.

Be experienced, but not slutty.

Don't complain, but say what's on your mind.

Wear makeup, but don't wear too much.

Do your hair, but be natural.

Be skinny, but not boney.

Be curvy, but not fat.

Be smart, not right.

State your opinion! But don't be aggressive.

Wax your legs. Your arms. Your face.

Pluck your eyebrows, but keep them thick.

Cook and fold and clean until the house is spotless, but don't be a housewife.

Never be a housewife.

When you look good, you feel good.

Be a feminist, but don't keep your last name.

Make him work for it, but keep him satisfied.

Have a career, but put your family first.

Men want some meat to hold on to, but watch what you eat.

And now, *Always be smoothly shaved, but never childlike.* We had no idea what the world wanted us to be; we just knew we wanted to be it.

———

"Girls! Dinner! *Bo'u le'echol,*" my mother interrupted from downstairs. She knew never to speak Hebrew around my friends, but Julia was more than a friend; she was a sister, so I didn't care.

"Be right there," I yelled back, sliding open the closet door.

I turned to Julia. "What should I wear?"

What outfit was I going to describe to my future daughters when I regaled them about the night I lost my virginity to their father? There was no point in contemplating; Greenwich High School girls had their own football game uniforms that Julia and I had no business changing: black leggings, high socks and Birkenstocks, and a school sweatshirt with a boyfriend's name on the back. Since Ethan was on the hockey team, I took pride in wearing the oversized sweatshirt he gave me, with not only his name and lucky number (13) on the back but a beautiful, envy-provoking word written in yellow-and-black capital letters right on the front: CAPTAIN.

Julia and I had only forty minutes to scarf down our dinner and fake interest in my parents' conversation before Ethan and Brian would show up in a toy-red pickup truck, the unmistakable bulge of dipping tobacco in their mouth as they waved us over.

We sat in the camel-colored leather dining room chairs tucked into the mahogany wooden table and stared at the hand-painted Middle Eastern decorated plates before us, overflowing with purple cabbage salad, bright red *shakshuka*, and *schug*, a spicy green paste made of hot peppers and fresh garlic my mother made from scratch.

If Ethan's going to be tongue-deep in my throat tonight, I'm not eating that.

"Honey," my mother said with a devastating smile, "we have something we want to tell you." She looked over at my father. My parents had been acting strange lately, and my mother had been avoiding eye contact with me, even after she came home from the gym, when she was usually in one of her annoyingly uplifting moods. My father had even been texting me random motivational sentences all week: *Just one positive thought in the morning can change your whole day* and *Keep on keeping on!* Being so consumed with choosing between Big Apple Red or the Thrill of Brazil OPI nail polish for the basement party Julia was going to throw, I didn't think much of it. But now, as I sat across from them, I tried to imagine what they were going to tell me. Was my mother pregnant again? She was already forty-four, but things could happen, right? I wouldn't be thrilled to have a baby crawling around the house, but Julia and I would be off to college next year anyway.

My father shot a glance at my mother, but she didn't meet his gaze. Instead, she continued fiddling with the napkin on her lap, folding and unfolding it absentmindedly.

"Sweetheart, my crown jewel," my father said. "I have good news, and I have bad news. Which do you want to hear first?"

Julia and I looked at each other in confusion, her perfectly penciled eyebrows burrowed against her forehead. "The good news?" she answered for me.

"Well, the good news is that you're looking at the new department head of plastic and aesthetic surgery at Assuta Hospital," he said with a goofy laugh, pointing to himself with both forefingers. He kept talking. "Assuta—you know, in Tel Aviv." He could tell by my clueless nodding that his words still hadn't registered in my brain.

"Honey," he continued, speaking more slowly now, "we're moving to Israel. The whole family—me, you, Mom, Natalie, Jake, Emma. We're even bringing the cat. And don't worry, Julia can come visit anytime you want. We spoke to her parents. The two of you will meet at least twice a year, winter and summer."

I sat there in silence, the weight of his words slowly sinking in. A sudden dryness gripped my throat, and I could barely swallow.

"The bad news," he said, "is that you're going to have to put college on hold for the next two years."

College? On hold? What was going on?

"What are you *talking* about?" My voice came out louder than I expected. "We're moving to Israel? I'm not moving anywhere."

My father's lips continued moving, beads of sweat forming as he talked for what felt like hours.

"So when you . . . when you said you were proud of me for getting into Columbia *and* NYU, when we visited the campus and celebrated my near-perfect SAT math score at Nobu, you were just being *nice*? When you ordered those extra pieces of fatty *toro*, and we toasted to my future with champagne and black caviar, it was all . . . fake?"

I looked over at my mother, hoping she would say something. Instead, she just sat there silently, once again going along with whatever crazy idea popped into my father's mind. "How long have you known about this?" I said, my voice shaky. I tasted salt on my tongue and realized I couldn't stop my tears.

"Relax, Ella, relax," my father said as he walked over to my chair. He tried putting his arm around me, but I pushed him away.

"I don't know who you think I am, but I'm not some extension of you and your decisions. I'm my own entity, and I'm not moving anywhere, Dad. You can't make me leave. I'm an adult, and I swear to God, I'll do whatever it takes to stay here."

"There's something else," he added, ignoring my pushback.

"Now's not the right time, honey," my mother said, resting her hand on my father's shoulder.

The room started spinning, slowly at first, and then gradually picked up speed until I felt as though I could barely find my balance in the chair. I glanced at Julia, whose face had turned white as she messed around with the red *shakshuka* sauce on her plate.

"*Not the right time for what?*" I screamed. "There's more?" Suddenly, the honk of Ethan's truck beeped for Julia and me to come outside, but the atmosphere in the room didn't budge.

"I'll tell them to leave," Julia whispered.

So much for losing my virginity, I thought for a split second before realizing that what was happening right here in this living room was even bigger than that.

My father handed me a manilla envelope that had been sitting on the granite countertop. I had noticed it earlier that morning, but my eyes skimmed over it without realizing this very envelope would change my fate forever. Now I tore it open, noticing the seal had been tampered with as if someone had already opened it.

ISRAEL DEFENSE FORCES

For Miss Ella Davidson,

You have been selected to join the Israel Defense Forces Intelligence Corps.

Please arrive to the Bakum base at 6:00 a.m. sharp on the day of your scheduled enlistment.

Have a safe and influential service, soldier.

Aaron M. Shulman,
Israel Defense Forces Chief

Chapter 3

Accepting my enlistment into the Israeli army didn't just happen. I didn't wake up one morning to find that—*poof!*—my Louis Vuitton Pochette Metis had magically transformed into a stiff M16 rifle or my Adidas Samba sneakers had morphed into combat boots that were so tight they slowed my blood circulation. It all happened gradually, like a frog in a pot of water slowly being brought to a boil.

There was the initial shock of learning that I was moving to Israel in the first place, followed by the understanding that Israel had a mandatory military service for both men and women, which meant that anyone born in the country and living there had to complete a two-year army service. Next, there was the second, much more serious freak-out of realizing *I* was in that criterion, that instead of popping Adderall and sipping matcha lattes at Ralph's while studying medicine at Columbia, I would have to become a real-life army soldier. Then, of course, there was the hysterical crying and screaming at my parents for forcing me to move to Israel, begging them to let me live with Julia's family, and an eventual tear-filled breakup with Ethan, followed by the grim realization that I had no choice, that I *actually* had to move away and join the army. And finally, there was the utter disbelief at the situation, the bursts of cackling laughter at the ridiculousness of how my life had, over the span of six months, turned completely upside down.

My mother had served as an officer in the army, as did my Israeli aunts and uncles. Like every Israeli, that period in my mother's life was a rite of passage, like going to college or snagging a first job. Most Israelis didn't see their army experience as the nightmare it was to me because they had grown up talking about it, preparing for it, even looking forward to it.

But as the date of my enlistment grew closer, I realized I was doomed.

"What can they do if I just don't show up?" I asked my mother.

She said I'd end up in jail.

"If I could, I would take this pain away from you, my love. I'd go instead of you," she said, her voice cracking. My mother had loved her life in America, but she sacrificed that life and stood beside my father when he decided we were moving to Israel for good, fighting to keep our family together. I was jealous of Natalie, Emma, and Jake, still young enough to linger in that phase in life where it doesn't matter where you are or where you're going; the whole world fits in your living room.

In the shower, two weeks before my service was set to begin, I came up with the idea of going on a hunger strike, like Gandhi, until my parents promised to call the military manager or whoever was in charge and exempt me from the mandatory service rule. My parents had gotten me into this mess, and, since I barely knew how to read or write in Hebrew, they had to get me out of it. I spent the first day of the hunger strike refusing to eat until that night after everybody in the house fell asleep, when I snuck into the kitchen, practically inhaling the spaghetti Bolognese my mother had prepared for dinner. My parents must have noticed half of the pasta in the pot missing the next morning because they ignored my continued efforts to scare them through fake-starving myself.

"Am I even allowed to bring a suitcase?" I asked my mother as we sat on the apartment floor in Tel Aviv, filling my bubblegum-pink suitcase to the brim.

"Well, it's only the first day. You'll say you didn't know," she said.

————

Only twenty minutes from civilized Tel Aviv was the *Bakum*, an army base where all soldiers were processed before being sent out to their specific bases spread out all over the country, from the inner city to the outskirts to the southern-most point of Eilat and beyond. It was the morning after my night out with Liam, and even though I'd taken two Advil before bed and managed to sneak in a few good hours of sleep, I still woke up to enlistment day feeling like I was going to die. I was sick the entire car ride there, a mixture of nerves and the bottles of Sancerre we'd downed, squished in between my siblings in the back while my parents sat silently in the front.

"Don't take everything so hard, honey," my father said, looking at me through the rearview mirror. "The whole world isn't on your shoulders."

But it was. My body felt heavy, stress sinking into each cell. All my life I had grown up to believe I had agency, and here I was losing control of the life I worked so hard to create. Julia was gone. Sunday night football evenings eating chicken wings with Ethan, gone. Senior prom pictures and getting drunk in a cheesy limo, gone. Life as I knew it was officially over.

When I arrived at the army enlistment desk, I waited in line with the other soldiers and their families until it was my turn to hand over my life to the Israeli army. Without looking up from her desk, a soldier with and French-manicured nails asked for my photo ID and enlistment letter. My mother handed her the paperwork, and still not looking up, she wrote down my nine-digit ID number on a yellow sticky note.

"This is your name now," she said in Hebrew as she handed it to me. We followed the rest of the families into the *Bakum*. There was a falafel stand at the far-right corner where soldiers-to-be could buy pitas and coffee. *What do they think this is, a town fair? Who could possibly be thinking about food at a time like this?*

In front of us stood a line of coach buses. "What's with the buses?" I asked, barely able to speak.

"That's part of the process, my love. You get on the bus, you wave goodbye to your family, and they take you to a different base to pick up your new army equipment. Don't worry. Just follow the crowd," my mother said. She rubbed the locket necklace around her neck, a habit she had whenever she was nervous.

"Ella Davidson." I heard my name and ID number called over the loudspeaker, and I was surprised to feel a rush of relief wash over me. It felt like I was leaning over a cliff, about to bungee-jump off of it. Staring down at the endless abyss just elongated the suffering process. I wanted to jump already, even if it meant jumping to my demise. I followed the other soldiers to the bus, barely saying goodbye to my parents, the deep anger I had for them bubbling up with each horrendous moment that passed. I tried lifting the suitcase up into the bag compartment, but it was so heavy it barely budged. On my right was a short, bulky soldier with a fresh buzz-cut guarding the back door of the bus, his hands behind his back, his chin lifted up.

"Um, excuse me, sir," I said in accented Hebrew, waving at him. He turned to look at me. "Can you help me with this, please?" I pointed to the suitcase. "It's really, really heavy."

He ignored me and looked in the other direction, lifting his chin up again and waiting for the rest of the soldiers to get on the bus.

Okay, then. Rude!

A blonde girl with enormous boobs that almost popped out of her tank top squatted down to help me. "You take that side," she said. I thanked her until she sincerely asked me to stop. We stepped onto the bus together, and as I walked by the soldier that refused to help me, I glared at him, holding my phone in my hand. "You know, it's not very polite to ignore people when they ask for help," I said.

"You know," he mimicked me, bobbing his chin from side to side, "this is the army, not a Hollywood movie."

I clutched my phone and purse to my chest and sat in the first row of the bus, right behind the driver. Through the dirty window, I watched as my parents stood a few yards away, squinting in an effort to catch a glimpse of me through the tinted windows. I smiled at them, my heart beating through my chest while I calculated how the hell I was going to get out of there.

———

I spent the majority of the three-hour bus ride from Tel Aviv to the army base hung over, applying an anxiety tactic I'd learned on YouTube called the hovering technique. Like the dreadlocked yogi in the video, I took twelve deep breaths with my eyes closed and imagined I was hovering over the situation as opposed to experiencing it. It seemed to work. *Breathe in, hover, breathe out, hover.*

Now, on the bus with twenty-nine other female soldiers chattering with one another, I was officially screwed. There was no turning back. I didn't speak to any of the soldiers, not because I was a snob, but because I knew that if I opened my mouth, I'd either throw up, start crying, or both. Plus, a female commander who reminded me of *Gossip Girl*'s Blair Waldorf sat silently next to the bus driver, exerting an authoritative air that made it clear she was in charge. And then she stood up and held out a wooden basket. "Phones in here," she said as she walked the length of the bus. Along with the other soldiers, I threw my phone into the basket. That was it; even my phone didn't belong to me. Staring through the smudged window at the perpetual dryness of the Middle Eastern desert swooshing by, my American life seemed like a fairy tale, worlds away.

You are not you anymore, I kept thinking.

After one absurdly short break at a gas station, where all of us slipped in and out of a single handicapped bathroom, we finally came to a stop at the army base, in front of what appeared to be a highly secured gate. It was like arriving at a maximum-security prison, with armed soldiers at every corner and an intimidating barbed-wire fence stretching endlessly in both directions. I had imagined driving up to a building resembling a summer camp, with ugly, white-painted benches and coolers full of popsicles near the entrance, maybe a few soldiers hanging out smoking cigarettes. But this was nothing like that. This army base, called the Mifrasit Army Base according to the sign hanging above the gate, was nothing more than an enormous expanse of desert sand littered with tents and small trailers. At first glance, it looked more like a trailer park than an army unit.

We stepped off the bus with our bags and stood in a U-shape in the desert heat, the sun beating down on us, the sweat behind my knees dripping down to my heels. Hot, thick air filled my throat like smoke. A female commander stood before us. She looked like a super-model—almost six feet tall, with mocha-tan skin and striking blue eyes. Her voice was high-pitched and feminine, the cadence of her speech rolling back and forth effortlessly. Like all of the commanders, she wore dark green, yet on her it barely looked like a uniform. It was more like a choice.

"Ladies, congratulations. If you didn't catch my name by now, wake up. I'm Commander Mia. Take a look around, because this right here is *home* for the next two years. And for the next six weeks starting today, you'll be in intense boot camp, so no, you won't be going home until it ends. Stop asking me. Once the six weeks are up, you'll be going home every weekend, so man up until then, okay?" She stopped to blow her nose, and the blonde girl and I exchanged looks.

"Now, what are you dimwits going to be doing here?" Commander Mia continued. "Well, first, you'll go through basic training within the framework of fourteen various courses in which you'll learn physical strengthening and empowerment."

She sounds like an actress reading from a script, I thought.

"Next, you're going to face challenges both physically and mentally, but you will overcome them with great satisfaction."

Eye roll. The only satisfaction I could have used was a seventy-five-minute foot massage at the Plaza, equipped with essential lavender oils and a fresh green tea spa pedicure.

"You will learn how to give, how to contribute to others, how to stop thinking only about your selfish selves, and, despite how out of shape you are right now, by the end of these two years, you will acquire the greatest possible title on earth: army soldier."

Who is this woman? Does she not have a life? Why would she choose to continue her army service as a commander instead of pursuing a career as some Olympic athlete or Victoria's Secret model? Is she a masochist? I tried to imagine what Commander Mia was like at home, sprawled on the couch with her boyfriend, drinking red wine and scrolling through Instagram, but I couldn't. She had to have an interesting life outside of this base—she looked smart and cool enough. Commander Mia's nails weren't painted, but they were clean, and although her hair was in the mandatory army ponytail, I knew a beachy-wave blowout when I saw one. Under different circumstances, we could have even been friends.

She didn't look like the other female commanders I saw lurking around the Bakum, with their baggy uniforms and bushy eyebrows, and not just because she was naturally spectacular. She was also well kept—and intentionally so. If Julia were here with me, she would be thinking what I was thinking: Commander Mia was obviously hopelessly in love with someone at the base, someone she was seeing every day; otherwise, she wouldn't be looking this good. Why else would she stay in this shithole? I was willing to bet my life on it.

Commander Mia led us to the changing area, where duffle bags with our ID numbers written in black marker were waiting for us. Inside each bag was a dark green army uniform a few sizes too big, a green belt, a black backpack, two canteens, a beret, warm gloves, an overused dark green fleece jacket, a dark green winter jacket, and black combat boots that were nothing like the Doc Martens I expected them to resemble.

We followed Commander Mia from the bus to one of the trailers at the farthest end of the enormous desert expanse, past dirt-ridden tents held up with broom handles, past soldiers practicing formation, each step taking me farther from the exit and deeper into this place I couldn't leave for the next six weeks. Every so often terrible thoughts snuck into my mind until I forcefully brushed them away. *Where am I? How did this happen? How is it legal for people to treat other people like this?* When I stepped into the trailer—if a room with a curtain for a door, one minuscule window, and eight bunk beds can be called a trailer—I watched as the other girls with whom I would share this space raced to grab the beds closest to the power outlets and farthest away from the curtain entrance.

"Mine!" a girl I didn't recognize said as she slammed her duffel bag onto the bed in the far left-hand corner.

The white tile floors were littered with dirt from the soles of black army boots, and if you took the time to notice, dust bunnies floated along the corners of the room. The room wasn't clean, and it smelled like the whiff of garbage that used to sneak into my nostrils when Ethan and I made out behind the bleachers next to the trash bins at the end of the school day.

"The bathrooms are located in Segment C2 of the base, a fifteen-minute walk from here," Commander Mia said, the sweat on her face only adding to her natural J. Lo glow. "And don't leave your trash lying around. The trash room is the next one over," she said, gesturing to the right with her thumb. "Lucky you," she added sarcastically.

So that's why it stinks in here.

In a matter of seconds, each girl had claimed her bunk bed, while I stood there pathetically, still in shock. There was only one bed left: the top bunk farthest from the power outlet and closest to the curtain door. I could tell that if I stuck my arm out even an inch, the ruthless desert wind would graze the hair on my arm. The blonde from the bus set her bag on the bottom bunk beneath mine.

"Are they gonna give us time to shower tonight, do you think?" I asked her.

"Shower? I heard they don't let you shower for the whole first week so you feel as disgusting as possible," the blonde answered. "That way, you're so desperate to feel human, you'll do whatever they say."

I climbed to the top bunk and tried to make myself feel something like optimism, but instead came a wave of such intense unease that I felt a dampness under my armpits and noticed two sweat stains forming through the uniform. *Ew.* I was a soldier. Hanging on the wall beside me was a two-inch-by-two-inch mirror the commanders must have forgotten to remove from the girls that stayed here before us. I caught a glimpse of myself in that tiny mirror and barely recognized the worn-out face looking back at me. I wanted to hide inside of the oversized uniform already swallowing me up.

"Hey, 'Merica, what's your name? Do you talk?" the blonde girl asked, snapping me out of my pity party.

My heart lurched. "Yes, I talk. I'm Ella."

"I'm Anna. Listen, Ella, if you don't stop looking like you just landed here from Mars, they're going to eat you alive."

When you pretend to be confident, you become it. My father instilled that sentence into our brains as soon as we could talk, but I was so drained I couldn't even find the strength to pretend.

The mattress on the bed was yellowed and thin, and I thanked my mother for the pink satin sheets she insisted I bring with me. I wanted to call her, to hear the pity in her voice when she'd say, "Oh, sweetheart," but the commanders had taken our phones away before we started the trip to hell, so I was screwed. I wanted somebody, anybody, to feel bad for me. Didn't the universe realize what a tragedy this was?

As the girls opened their duffel bags, a Bach symphony of zipping sounds filled the room. Unzipping my bag, I carefully took out the items my mother and I had packed together. There was a set of fleece kitten pajamas; one pair of fuzzy socks I used to take with me on plane rides; a long-sleeved thermal shirt for the weekly desert hikes my mother had warned me about; twelve, yes, twelve, pairs of Victoria's Secret lace underwear to make me feel like myself underneath the uniform; my favorite Marc Jacobs Daisy perfume; a leg rest; and a cute sun hat I wouldn't get to wear because the only hats allowed were part of the uniform given to us by the commanders. Along with the pink satin sheets was a matching duvet cover, a down-filled comforter, two pillows, and enough deodorant to last six months. Since my mother warned me that coffee was served only once a day in the morning and I drank at least seven cups daily, I brought miniature packs of instant coffee I could empty under my tongue to prevent a withdrawal headache. I brought a heatless hair curler, a pair of Swarovski-crystal-studded pink flip-flops for the shower, and my favorite Charlotte Tilbury highlighter. I'd also packed a green tea face mask, gold-plated under-eye patches that promised to decrease puffiness, lavender shampoo and conditioner for the showers I naively thought I would enjoy, and a quick-dry towel. There was a thermometer, a lip gloss keychain, a first-aid kit, a Swiss army knife, the compass my father gave me that I had no idea how to use, Nora Ephron's *Heartburn*, Joan Didion's *Slouching toward Bethlehem*, and, of course, the Goddess Rules.

Before leaving the house, I'd thrown in two sixteen-ounce Fiji water bottles and a bag of Cheetos for emergencies.

I gazed at the pile of items on the bunk bed. No matter how American and privileged I was, here in the army, I was just another soldier like everybody else.

I organized the mountain of things on the shelves beside the bed and threw the rest of the items into the bag that hung off the edge. My lips were so chapped I attached the lip-gloss keychain to the inside pocket of my uniform, despite the direct command to remove any and all makeup (this was medical; my lips were in danger), and put the sheets and duvet cover, the pillows, and the leg rest right on the bed. When I was finished, the bed looked like a Disney Princess hotel room suite against the backdrop of a jail cell.

"Soldiers! One minute and twenty-five seconds until you are outside standing in a line with your hands behind your back!" Commander Mia yelled into the megaphone.

Isn't a megaphone supposed to yell for you?

"What are you looking at?" she barked at me.

I hopped off of the bed and watched as the other girls readied themselves. I adjusted my ponytail, tucked my army shirt into my pants, tightened my belt, and stepped out. My toes were scrunched inside the boots, and I could feel the nails on my big toes cracking already. In a straight line, we marched outside, and I looked around at the seemingly endless desert surrounding us. I longed for familiarity, for something I recognized as my own. I missed snuggling with my father on the couch watching *Curb Your Enthusiasm* while my mother baked her famous spinach-feta *burekas*.

"What are we waiting for?" Anna whispered to me, as if I had a clue. Her face was almost freakishly symmetrical, with honey-brown eyes and a plump, babyish pout. Were all Israeli girls this pretty up close?

"Ladies, listen up. You are now going to meet your officer. When your officer arrives, you must salute respectfully on my count," Commander Mia said, demonstrating a proper salute.

One of the girls at the front of the line raised her hand. She was chubby, with a sweat mark covering her lower back.

"Soldier, speak," Commander Mia said.

"Can I tighten my bun?" she asked.

"No. Your commander is arriving now. On my count, salute at one."

Before I had time to wipe the sweat trickling down my own back, I saw, from far away, the outline of a tall, broad-shouldered man walking toward us. With each step he took, the desert sand, the smoldering heat, and the deceiving serenity of the sky all muddled into one incoherent image. I squinted harder and harder as he walked in our direction, and I felt a pang of familiarity. His stride, the way his blonde hair bounced under the beret, the way each step he took burst with intention, and the confidence radiating from him were enough to stop any girl in her tracks . . . to stop any girl sitting on the beach, drinking wine. Familiarity rose up inside me like lava about to erupt.

I know that walk. He stepped closer.

I know those slanted eyes. Another step.

The dewiness of his skin. I had felt it.

And then, when he was just a few feet away, *the heart-shaped birthmark.* *Liam.*

"Three . . . two . . . one," Commander Mia yelled.

I saluted.

"Good afternoon, soldiers," he said after he saluted back to us. "I'm Officer Liam Levine. I'll be your direct officer for the rest of your service. I am your eyes and ears. Your mother and your father. From now on," he said as he pointed at us, "you belong to me."

The girls shuffled among themselves, no doubt excited to see such a handsome male officer leading a sea of young women.

I stood there, sweating profusely. What were the chances that the guy I met on the beach the night before was now in charge of me for the next two years?

He stuck his hand into his pocket, pulled out a folded piece of paper, and read each soldier's ID number out loud. In return, each soldier saluted and yelled out her name.

"204-439-005," he said finally, when he reached mine.

"Ella Davidson," I yelled back loudly, with purpose. I was here, and I wanted Liam to know it. I watched in what felt like slow motion as Liam lifted his eyes from the paper and met my piercing gaze. I imagined flashes of the night before rushing through his mind.

Liam's eyes widened as he instinctively covered his mouth with his hand and coughed into it, a failed attempt at concealing his surprise.

"Water, Officer?" Commander Mia asked him, a look of suspicion on her face. She looked at me and then back at him and then at me again.

Liam snatched the water from her hand without looking in her direction and stared deeper into my eyes with each gulp. *Maybe,* I thought as the familiar rush of feminine power washed over me, *this hellhole isn't going to be as bad as I thought.*

Chapter 4

Could I really have a relationship with an officer in the Israeli army? Maybe there was a God after all. What could be better than dating my own officer? If I decided to pursue Liam, I could say goodbye to the worst parts of the army: cleaning the eggplant machine at kitchen duty, guarding at the earliest hours of the morning—hell, to guarding at all. Forget bathroom duty, which I'm sure Liam wouldn't make me do once my tongue slipped into his mouth. A warmth washed over me and then another thought: *Meant to be.* I wanted to talk to Liam, to get a sense of what was going through his mind, although the look of utter shock on his face when he first saw me meant he didn't know I was going to be his soldier, either.

Was it a good kind of surprised, though? Why was Commander Mia looking at me like that? *God, Liam is much sexier in uniform.* The dark green color complemented his tanned skin, and he had a tick where he kept licking his wet, thick lips. The same lips that had been a centimeter from mine the night before. How had I not noticed how truly breathtaking he was at the Pineapple Bar? He wasn't as striking in workout clothes, but I could work on his wardrobe, at least for the two years I would be stuck in this nightmare. If I was being honest, it wouldn't *not* be exciting to fuck him all over the army base.

My phone vibrated in my hand, cutting off my thoughts. "Hello?"

"Hi, sweetheart," my mom said, and the familiarity of her voice brought tears to my eyes.

"I miss you so much. I can't stand this place," I said. My chest tightened.

"I know, sweetheart, but give it time; just give it time," she said. I heard the evening news playing in the background. I could almost taste my mother's *maamoul* cookies, feel the creamy date filling sticking to the roof of my mouth.

"Time?" I was crying again, trying to keep my voice down so I wouldn't interrupt the other girls in the room during their single hour of contact with the real world. "Time is what's been snatched from me, *Ima*. I was supposed to be . . . to be . . . to be drinking Don Julio reposado in a frat guy's dorm room right now, not here, practically held hostage in the . . . army," I cried. "They're making us stand outside all the time—in the sun. Do you know what I look like right now? And the showers—there's no hot water; it's not even *lukewarm*, Mom. It's freezing. Can you believe I'm carrying a gun around? A gun! What the literal fuck? No, seriously? How could you let this happen?" I was sobbing now. "I have a bruise on my hip bone from the M16 hitting against it when we walk. I just want to go home."

"I know, I know. I had a hard time in the army in the beginning, too, until I met Daddy," she said. I rolled my eyes. The last thing I needed was to hear their love story for the thousandth time. Suddenly Commander Mia stormed into the room. "*Shaat tash* is over! Hand over the phones," she yelled, holding a basket.

"I have to go; I love you," I whispered to my mother.

"I love you more," she said.

I stepped off the bunk bed and dropped my phone into Commander Mia's basket. Before I could climb back up, she switched off the light, leaving my eyes struggling to adjust to the pitch-black desert darkness. "Lights out. If I catch any of you talking, you'll have double bathroom duty tomorrow. I mean it."

————————

My father and mother met in the Israeli army. One summer morning, when my mother was guarding the Israeli-Lebanon border, my father, a medic, ran into her booth with his hands up, blood dripping down his arms from stitching up a wounded soldier. She helped him wash up, and as he drank the last sips of water left in her flask, lifting his head up toward the clear blue sky, she pointed to his nose hairs and laughed. A year later, she was helping him pluck them out before their wedding, and twenty years after that, they were still married, with four kids by their side. This story was so much a part of my life that no matter what happened, no matter how often my parents fought, I was always comforted by the notion that they had once been madly in love, nose hairs and all.

My father, Ben Davidson, was the only child of two emergency room doctors who worked all day and all night. He spent most of his childhood at his best friend Raphael's house so that he could escape the loneliness of walking into an empty home and the growling of his stomach when he opened the refrigerator door to nothing but an old carton of milk.

Raphael's family became my father's second home. But Raphael's father beat his mother; he broke her dishes, broke her arm, broke her two front teeth. Even after he split her lip open, she stayed. A day after my father's fifteenth birthday, he and Raphael saw Raphael's father through his bedroom window dragging his mother by her hair down the street in broad daylight. Raphael, scared of his own shadow, buried his face in his hands, paralyzed. That's when my father ran outside in a sudden rage and beat Raphael's father so brutally that he sent him to the hospital for two days. Raphael's family never talked about the incident after that, but it was clear that my father was no longer welcome in their home. He didn't tell his own parents what he had done and went about life as if it never happened.

My father went back to living with his parents in a two-bedroom apartment in Bat Yam, a small city outside of Tel Aviv with the highest crime rate in the country. After school, he worked as a pizza delivery guy, taking notes of the secret pizza recipe until he saved up enough money when he was eighteen to open up his own tiny pizza place, Benny's Pizza, which became the most popular corner pizza place in the city. Six months later, he shut the place down, joined the army as a paratrooper, met my mother, married her, and a year later, brought me into the world.

By then, we lived in Tel Aviv, in a series of different apartments on sunny streets: Dizengoff, Rothschild, Yirmiyahu. Then, when my father was denied admission to one of the most prestigious Hebrew medical residency programs that worked with Yale University hospital, the American Dream bug planted itself inside his mind.

"If they won't help me get there," he told my mother, "I'll do it myself." After saving up and applying to Yale on his own, he was once again turned down.

My parents sat on the hardwood floor of our Tel Aviv apartment and applied to eighty-two different medical residency programs in America. *Eighty-two.* He was denied admission from every single school except one, a tiny private hospital in Greenwich, Connecticut. A few months after we moved to America, the program was shut down because of a lack of funding, but by then, my father had barged uninvited into the office of the chief of plastic and cosmetic surgery at Yale University and demanded a job until he got one. That's how he officially became a Yale New Haven Hospital physician.

The night he signed the contract at Yale, the medical team went out to a Japanese hibachi restaurant nearby. My father snuck into the bathroom to call my mom.

"Maya, you won't believe it! There's a chef right here at our table cooking the food in front of our eyes. He throws food into your mouth for you to catch it! One day I'll take you here," he promised her.

From then on, my father worked late nights in green scrubs splattered with blood as a resident at Yale New Haven Hospital while my mother taught Hebrew to high school students at Yeshiva High School in the next town over. I used to wait to hear the sound of my bedroom door creaking open and my father's soft footsteps enter before he hugged me in his scrubs with a worn-out smile. Only after he kissed me on the forehead could I sleep in peace.

On Saturday mornings, my mother worked overtime as a private tutor, and my father and I danced in the living room to Marvin Gaye until the album ended, and he played it all over again. He picked me up and spun me around and asked me again, and again, "How much do I love you?" I was hypnotized by the way his blue eyes changed color in the light, by the strength in his arms when he held me, by the way he moved his hips to the beat of the songs. He made me feel like I was a prize, a treasure, a crown jewel.

We lived in a big, red barn, the oldest house in Greenwich, built in the late 1640s by a Puritan minister who had come from England to flee religious persecution, but to me, it was a modern castle. When my father unlocked the front door for the first time, I could barely wrap my mind around the enormity of it; the airiness of the living room, the great green expanse of the backyard, the elegance of the indoor balcony overlooking the den. Worlds away from the tiny one-bedroom apartment in Tel

Aviv where I snuggled in between my parents on a sagging mattress, this creaky, old barn was my own private palace. The first property my parents ever owned since immigrating from Israel ten years before to the rural suburbs of Connecticut, the barn was more than just a place for us to live—it symbolized the success in achieving what my parents had worked all those years to attain: the American Dream.

I met Julia then, in third grade. After I saw the house she lived in, with her elevator and outdoor waterslide, her nanny and private cook, her seemingly endless collection of American Girl dolls, I started hiding behind the boxwood bush in my front yard whenever I'd wait for the bus with my father so the other students wouldn't see where I lived. "What a shame," he used to say, shaking his head.

Although my first language was Hebrew, and the unspoken rule in our home was *Hebrew only*, since my parents didn't want us to forget our mother tongue, I was in love with the English language. I had grown embarrassed by Hebrew—the guttural phonemes and thick reverberations that came from the very back of the throat—and refused to speak it, especially when my American friends came over.

When I reached high school, on Friday evening dinners, when my family sat around the table, the smell of vegetable soup and chicken schnitzel sneaking up into our nostrils, I'd remind my parents of what friends were coming over on what days that week, and there, I'd lay out my own house rules: "No speaking Hebrew—not even with each other. No Hebrew music, no Hebrew jokes, and no Israeli food." It wasn't that *I* didn't love being Israeli—I did, just not in front of my American friends. I didn't want to ruin what I had worked so hard to build—the ease of blending in, of being like everyone else.

My parents decided to make life easier on us by giving my siblings and me distinctly American names: Ella, Natalie, Jake, and Emma. That's what my little siblings were to me: NatalieJakeandEmma, their names blurring into one all my life, the three little chicks I looked after, never wondering where they were or what they were doing because they were always waddling behind me, following my lead, mimicking my every step. When I was obsessed with Justin Bieber, they timed themselves to see who could sing the lyrics to "Baby" fastest. When I announced, for a short two months, that I was a vegetarian, they peeled and cut and dressed my vegetables into elaborate salads, arguing with my mother in my defense when she refused to support my newfound life purpose. "For the planet, animals, and ourselves," Jake reminded her at only six years old, his red hair sticking up on the back of his head.

As a child, my great aunt Edith used to call me "Agony and Ecstasy." I was always either miserable, crying hysterically, having hissy fits in the middle of shopping malls, stomping my hands and feet on the floor of high-end restaurants, or endlessly loving, laughing, pleasant, giving away free hugs and juicy kisses. There was never anything in between.

Even when my father worked long hours at Yale and then owned one of the most successful cosmetic surgery clinics in the country, he always made time for my mother in the evenings. They'd lie in front of the fireplace, her long, smooth legs sprawled across his lap on the couch as he sipped his whiskey and read another impossibly dense biography. I admired the fact that their devotion to us was equal to, but never more important than, the time and effort they dedicated to each other.

They had a small group of friends, all Israeli, and every other Saturday night my siblings and I found ourselves stuck in a different basement, playing cards or dress-up with their friends' snotty-nosed kids until the food was ready. The men were all doctors, and aside from my mother, the wives stayed home. They were referred to as housewives, except that all of them had cooks and cleaners and babysitters, so none of them actually did any of the housework. I took in every detail about these women, their stiff Botox-injected smiles, the vintage Alhambra pendants dangling from their necks, their fingers dripping with diamond rings. I noticed it all, including the playful looks they gave to one another's husbands across the table and the footsies played underneath it.

My mother didn't notice, though. While she was a vital part of the crew, she didn't, at the time, invest in her physical appearance as much as the other women did, even though her own husband was a plastic surgeon. She was comfortable with her natural beauty and focused her energy on expertly taking care of the domestic duties. As Arik Einstein played in the background, she passed around the *shakshuka* and *malawach*, which rested on hand-painted plates, discussed the endless problems of Israeli politics and what they were reading at the time, and told stories that always ended in a chorus of laughter. By the end of the evening, even Natalie, Jake, Emma, and I would sit back in our chairs, unbutton our jeans, and, just like the adults, sip on hot water with mint leaves, an Israeli tea that was known to help with digestion.

My mother reminded me of a Yemenite goddess: tall, golden skinned, with sharp features and a noble aura. Gentle and loving and incredibly organized, she studied literature and earned a master's in education, but she spent the hours after teaching emptying the dishwasher and folding laundry. She put herself last, always, and was the epitome of what a mother was supposed to be. She made everyone feel like they were the most special, like the universe circled around them, but the real center of her life was my father, and she, his. He relished her dark eyes, dark hair, dark skin, while she tried to lighten herself, obsessively staying out of the sun and adding highlights to her chocolate curls.

My father, the son of Polish immigrants and Holocaust survivors, with his blonde hair and blue eyes, was her Ken doll. He grew up to follow the only career path suitable for a good Polish son: medicine. "There is only one profession," his father always used to say. My father was my mother's dream partner, a doctor and professor, the man who'd helped her discover the secret to a happy life: knowledge. It was as if he could lead her anywhere she wanted to go, the wise conduit for her endless questions and anything common sense. He spoke four languages fluently, solved organic chemistry equations in his head, and insisted that the best show in the history of television was *Curb Your Enthusiasm*. He once spent an entire afternoon describing the plot of an episode to my mother and me in exquisite detail, in which Larry David slams his hands against the table in the middle of an important business meeting to symbolize to his colleagues that he wanted it to end.

"And you know what?" my father said in his Israeli accent, wiggling his eyebrows.

"What?" my mother said.

"I've applied this tactic to my own meetings, and it actually works! I'm the real-life Larry David." As I rolled my eyes, I looked over at my mother, a teenage smile plastered across her face. She was still just as in love as she was when he ran over to her at the borderline between two places, twenty years before.

All this time, I thought my Prince Charming was in America, because where else would he be? But maybe my Prince Charming wasn't the captain of the hockey team. Maybe he was a half-Moroccan, half-Australian army officer from the North with the fullest lips I'd ever seen and a bubble butt that was shapely even through his uniform. Maybe he was the man I couldn't stop staring at, with a rough demeanor and a soft heart. Maybe, like my parents, Liam and I would fall in love and live happily ever after.

Maybe not.

Chapter 5

Thank you very much, I thought, when I got my first look at Liam the following morning, standing in front of the cafeteria, a gray three-story cement building with no windows. I suddenly had the sensation that I had arrived at a maximum-security prison, until I shuddered at the thought that reality might actually be worse. At least Liam looked like a snack. The more I thought about it, the more it made sense to pursue a relationship with him, at least while I was stuck here. This crush gave me a sense of purpose and motivation and most importantly, that flicker of hope that kept people in the most horrendous situations alive. Buried under a crumbled building after an earthquake? Hope. Sinking on the *Titanic*? Hope. Sitting in a hairdresser's chair after he cut your sideswept bangs a centimeter too short? Hope. Hope is what I needed to survive, and Liam was that hope. While I didn't expect to see him again after our date at the Pineapple Bar, fate brought us back together for a reason. *Right?* Right.

"Soldiers, in formation; welcome to the first day of kitchen duty. Half of you will be washing dishes while the other half eats. Tomorrow, you switch." Liam turned and walked into the cafeteria. I hadn't seen him since the first day of the army, yesterday, which somehow felt like months ago, and as we followed Commander Mia toward the cafeteria, marching past the other trailers, past soldiers guarding each entrance to the base, past another cactus, my eyes were constantly on the lookout for Liam. Finally, there he was, standing in front of me again, this time, I noticed, freshly shaven. Lingering in the cafeteria air was a stench that reminded me of ketchup and dirty rags. I was one to throw up easily— on ski trips in high altitudes, on boats and planes, and especially in cabs after a night of drinking—so the heat and my nerves and being around Liam made me feel like I was a second away from vomiting all over the filthy tiled floor.

By day two, we were already dehydrated, exhausted, and, most of all, clueless. What did kitchen duty mean? What was the schedule for the day? When would we be able to sleep? Shower? God forbid *rest*? And when, most importantly, would Liam and I be able to actually talk? I couldn't think about anything else. I needed to talk to him. I felt like I was on another planet, one that had its own government, its own social contract, its own moral code. Whatever happened in army world stayed in army world.

While the other girls mumbled in confusion, I raced to the front of the line half a foot behind Liam. If the opportunity of talking to Liam wasn't going to present itself on its own, I was going to create it.

"Can we talk for a minute?" I asked. The clinking of plates made it difficult to hear myself. I needed to make my life in the army easier, even if talking to Liam at that moment wasn't exactly the right time. He turned his neck half an inch so he didn't have to look at me but could still see me through his peripheral vision. Was he *ignoring* me? He kept walking to the empty tables at the end of the cafeteria like I wasn't there.

"Are you seriously not answering me?" I said again, this time laughing out of pure embarrassment. Who did he think he was? Two nights ago, he was ordering bottles of Sancerre and asking me about my favorite sex position, and now he was acting like I was air?

"Soldier," Liam yelled at me. He raised his voice loudly enough for the other girls to hear, my embarrassment growing with each second that passed. They fell silent. "To the back of the line."

Shocked, I walked to the end of the line while the other soldiers stared at me. I stood beside Anna, humiliated.

While Liam sent the girls at the beginning of the line to the kitchen, the rest of us sat at one of the long folding tables at the far-right corner of the cafeteria. My thoughts jumped from one to the other. *Wait, so Liam is going to act like he doesn't know me from now until the end of my service?* While I was busy contemplating whether I wanted to date him, the thought of him not being interested in dating *me* hadn't even crossed my mind. How full of myself could I be? If he wasn't going to date me, he wasn't going to give me special treatment, which meant I wasn't going to survive the army. My heartbeat sped up under the sudden heaviness of my uniform.

Liam and Commander Mia sat down first, and only afterward were the soldiers allowed to join them. When they stood to fill their plates with food, we stood, too, but ate only after they took their first bite. There were ranks, and being a boot camp soldier was at the very bottom. I couldn't believe I had to stand and wait for Liam to fill his plate with food, unfold his napkin, and start eating before I could even sit down, when a little over forty-eight hours ago, we were sharing a pizza. We briefly made eye contact, and I swore I could tell by the way he smirked between bites that he was enjoying the situation.

Once we sat down with our food, I stared at my plate. Gray chicken drumsticks with specks of oregano, watery mashed potatoes, and a single hard-boiled egg. Why wasn't I biting into a hot buffalo chicken sandwich with extra pickled jalapenos from Greenwich Deli right now?

"Well, 'Merica, you gonna eat?" Anna said.

"What's your problem? Can you get off my back?" I said.

She shrugged. "Just looking out for you. You know the next time we eat is 9:00 p.m. tonight, right?" It was only 11:00 a.m.

"How do you know?" I asked.

"It's really foggy on Mars, isn't it?" she said when she saw my face. "Let me straighten things out for you. You eat when you can. You sleep when you can. You shower when you can. You listen to whatever your officer says, and most importantly, you stay under the radar. My sister had an easy service because she barely talked. I don't think her officer even knew her last name. That means less kitchen duty and," she leaned closer to me, "practically no *bathroom* duty. The soldiers that stick out are the first ones that come to the officers' minds. The officers can't remember most names off the tops of their heads, so they put down the first name that comes to mind. If you stay under the radar, your name won't come to mind. You get what I'm saying?"

Right. So much for staying under the radar.

"I get it, thanks," I said. "Anna, right?"

"Yup," she said, the mashed potatoes slushing around in her mouth. I still couldn't touch mine.

"Why aren't the officers talking to the soldiers? Who am I supposed to go to if I have a problem?"

"You don't go to anyone about anything. You can go to your direct officer—to Commander Mia, in our case—if you really need to. Other than that, you solve your own problems. You lost your beret? Steal someone else's. You forgot your gun in the bathroom? You go to jail. Nobody here's going to help you, especially not the officers. If you do something really severe, if you get in serious trouble, then you'll be sent to Officer Levine's office." *Light bulb moment.* I telepathed the thought to Julia. "You don't want to find yourself there. Higher-up officers don't want to deal with us. Plus, they're extra tough and keep their distance. Having any kind of personal relationship with an officer is illegal."

"What do you mean, *illegal*?" My heart was pounding.

"My cousin's best friend, Amelia, fell in love with her officer after a year in the army, and when everyone found out, the chief commander immediately threw the officer into the Pit for two months and then expelled him from the army for life, without pension. An officer being with a soldier is just something you don't do. It's kind of like an old guy dating an underage girl. They don't have equal power in the relationship, so it can't actually *be* a relationship. Period. It's unfair, and it's unhealthy. The more distant an officer is with you, the better," she said. "Distance is a form of respect." Anna eyed the chicken on my plate. "You gonna eat that?"

I shook my head, relieved to get the gray chicken out of my face.

"If you happen to serve under a kind officer, one with *neshama*," she said, putting her hand over her heart, "they sometimes break the distance on the last day of your army service. For two whole years, they don't look in your direction, except to give you orders or check your uniform or tell you what a worthless piece of shit you are, and then, on the last day, they'll break the distance. They'll smile and hug you and show you that under all of those layers, they're real people just like us. Look at Officer Levine. What is he, like, twenty-five? He goes out on the weekends, probably drinks, has sex with girls. He might be a normal guy. But here? Here, he's like a god. He controls our everyday lives. Pretty weird to think about, huh?"

"You can say that again," I said.

"Again? Why again?"

I rolled my eyes. "I don't mean literally. It's an expression."

Anna shook her head, her blonde hair grazing the buttons of her uniform. "You Americans with your illogical expressions," she said.

I couldn't eat. I had to come up with a plan. Dating Liam was illegal, which, I figured, was why he was ignoring me. It wasn't that he didn't *want* to fuck my brains out; it was that he *couldn't*. But everyone knows that a man's desire is stronger than his will to stop it. As long as I knew deep down that a part of Liam wanted me, I had something to work with. All I wanted from Liam, at least as a start, was for him to give me a sign, some sort of signal, that I was special and different, that I wasn't like the rest of the girls. I wouldn't be able to survive here if I didn't have him looking out for me.

Making Liam fall in love with me wasn't going to be easy, but it wasn't impossible. After all, I had a secret weapon, the Goddess Rules. They never failed me. I needed time alone with Liam, and if I wanted to talk to him one-on-one, I would have to get in serious trouble. Like my father always said, "There are people who sit around and wait for things to happen, and there are people who go out and make things happen."

I stood up, picked up my plate, walked over to Liam as he ate, and sat down in the empty seat beside him, where only officers were allowed to eat. The other soldiers looked at me like I was crazy.

I thought Liam would tell me to get up and go back to my seat, but instead, he continued to ignore me. Commander Mia was about to say something, but Liam silently raised his left hand as if telling her to hold off. She ground her teeth together. I lifted my gaze to meet Liam's, and while he tried to look away, the second his eyes met mine, something in my stomach dropped. *You're special*, his eyes said. I grabbed the hard-boiled egg sliding around on my plate and took a bite out of it—the white falling apart into little pieces in my mouth—trying to be bold and strong and carefree while he spoke to Commander Mia, still ignoring me. He wasn't going to let me get in trouble today, I realized. I'd have to do something more drastic. Something really crazy. Yet, just as I gave up and stood up to go back to my seat, I felt Liam graze my thigh under the table with his fingertips.

"God," he said to Commander Mia, loudly enough so I could hear, "the things I would do for a bite of pineapple pizza."

Chapter 6

Six months before we moved to Tel Aviv, something terrible happened while I was out running errands with my father.

To him, I was a princess, his crown jewel. All my life, he reminded me that I was his proudest achievement—more than his business investments or successful procedures. I was the beginning of him and the end of him from the moment I was born. When I called while he was at work, he always picked up.

"Is it urgent, sweetie? I'm in a meeting," he'd whisper, in front of his investors.

"No," I'd say, with a sly smile. Before he hung up, I'd wait to hear his apology.

"Sorry about that, guys; it's my daughter, my crown jewel."

If ever I snapped at him for something stupid like opening my bedroom door without knocking or speaking Hebrew in front of my friends, it was only a matter of time until I'd text him to ask if he was mad at me. His answer was always the same.

"Mad? At you? Never."

His love for me was immeasurable and unconditional, and he made me feel like there was nothing more important to him in the world—not his job, not his friends, not even himself.

"You're a princess, Ella," he always said. "Being with you is like winning the lotto. If you wanted to, you could open up any magazine, flip through the pages, and point to whoever you want. The Prince of Monaco would be honored to be with you. Do you hear me? You are a crown jewel. Don't you ever forget that."

———

The day our fate changed, my father was wearing white. A white shirt, white shorts, and a white sweatshirt tied around his waist. We were going to run errands and, as a reward, play tennis. After we had breakfast at his favorite Mediterranean diner, he bought a new wet suit at the store nearby for his morning swims, and then we went to check on the renovations at the beach house my parents had recently bought in Westport. In the car, he told me about his work at the hospital, the last Nabokov novel he had just finished reading, the new museum exhibit he wanted to go to. As we drove from place to place, I sat in the passenger seat looking over at him, proud that he had chosen me as his companion for the day. No matter where we were or what we were doing, I felt worthy in his presence. He treated me like an adult, and I never cared that every time we planned to spend time together, we ended up doing whatever he wanted to do—fishing, swimming, hiking. By the end of our day together, I'd feel empowered, like I had a plan in life, like I had nothing to worry about because the world was going to work itself out as long as he was by my side. There was a real connection between us, as if we were surfing the same wave at the same pace. When I was with him, the rest of the world descended below water.

When we arrived at the beach house, I couldn't wait to take a quick look and then head off to the tennis court. As we parked the car to check on the renovations, he was in the middle of a story about his trip to the Galapagos with his father.

"You wouldn't believe how your grandfather laughed, Ella. It was such a relief for him to actua—" He stopped mid-sentence.

He put the car in park and stepped out, his forehead scrunching curiously as he walked toward the front door of the new house, my own footsteps following behind him. All my life, I walked behind him, desperate to impress, to absorb, to emulate my father's strength, to adopt his unapologetic outlook on life.

He walked slowly and then faster, his steps growing bigger and wider, until he stopped in front of the door. I hadn't noticed yet. I just stood there with him, staring at his face, watching as the shock hit, as he started to understand what had happened. My eyes darted to where his eyes were looking, to the white door, and there I saw an enormous red swastika spray-painted across it. I recognized the symbol immediately, the way the color symbolized blood and murder and death—the way its size showed no doubt of its intention.

And then, silently, my father touched it. He stepped even closer to the door, reached his hand out, and traced the swastika, the paint still wet, staining his hands with every stroke. It seemed so out of place, the red paint against the white door, against the blue sky, against the backdrop of a quiet suburban town, dirtying the white outfit my father wore that day.

It wasn't the swastika that made my gut lurch—it was the realization that my father was hurt, that whoever had dared to commit this hate crime had shattered him.

We drove straight to the Westport police station to file a hate crime report. The police officer, a man in his mid-fifties with fat, red cheeks, sat behind his desk, unfazed.

"Nothing I can do about this," the officer said. We seemed to have interrupted an important game of computer Solitaire. "Fill out this form, and I'll relay it to the big boss," he promised.

My father filled out the paperwork apathetically while I sat next to him, still studying his face, searching for a sign of the stubbornness I had grown up witnessing. Where was the man who didn't take *no* for an answer? I wanted to help him, to be the one he could lean on, to make him feel like I was the right person to be there with him on this day of all days, but instead, I just sat there uselessly. As we drove home in silence, no longer in the mood to play tennis, I wondered how anybody in the neighborhood even knew we were Jewish. Did our last name give us away? Was Davidson that Jewish? We had barely spent any time at the new house, especially since my parents had bought it as an investment to later lease out to future tenants. *And why*, I kept asking no one in particular, *didn't that police officer do anything?*

I thought I was American, that since I had grown up in Connecticut, spoke fluent English, celebrated Thanksgiving, and lived for McDonald's chicken nuggets, I belonged. That since I went to school in America, since all my friends were American, since I learned about the Civil War and read Mark Twain and Toni Morrison, I was as American as a crisp autumn day at the apple orchard. But after this happened, I knew that no matter how hard I tried, I would never feel that way again.

After that, a cold clarity permeated our home. My father's face said it all: It's over. We were immigrants. In the end, after all and above all, we were Jews. And Jews, well, they belonged in Israel. My father's mind was working, though; I could tell from the way he kept biting the space on his hand between his thumb and pointer finger. Something in me already knew our lives were about to change.

Six months later, we were on the plane to Tel Aviv.

Chapter 7

I needed the perfect transgression that would send me to Liam's office. What could I do to be punished? Forgetting a gun in the shower meant two weeks in jail. Not worth it. Hiding my phone in my suitcase after hours would only mean a late-night guarding session and a quick lecture from Commander Mia. I needed to do something drastic enough to be able to talk to Liam but not too drastic to actually have to face the consequence. I needed to be alone with him. The second he and I could talk honestly behind closed doors, Liam would take off his mask. I could look him in the eye the same way I did that night at the bar and figure out my next move from there. I hadn't been hallucinating when I felt his fingertips against my thigh at the cafeteria. There was that hope again. I couldn't let go of the opportunity of personally knowing, and almost kissing, the most powerful person on the base. The more I worried that maybe Liam wasn't interested in me, the more I wanted him.

———

During our fifty-minute evening break, Anna's head popped up at the top of the ladder of our bunk. "Can I join you?" she asked while climbing under the covers next to me. As hot as it was in the desert during the day, it was just as freezing at night.

"Well, you kind of already have," I said. Israeli girls had no boundaries.

Anna slept in the bunk bed beneath mine, and she was always so quiet I barely noticed her. She was a neat, compact young woman, and even through her uniform you could tell she was curvy. She grew up in Even Yehuda, a town east of Netanya, and the officers usually were extra tolerant with her because apparently her mother was a famous singer in Israel. Her mother could have been the Ariana Grande of Israel for all I knew, but if she wasn't prancing around a stage in an oversized sweatshirt and a high ponytail singing "Positions," she wasn't a singer I cared about.

Anna looked over my shoulder as I read the Goddess Rules, the rules I knew by heart but always loved to refresh. I longed for the feeling of control I felt as I read each line, closing my eyes and repeating them in my mind. *Laugh at his jokes, but not too loudly. Be experienced, but not slutty.* The rules were my mantra, and I fell asleep knowing that as long as I followed each one carefully, Liam would eventually be mine.

"What can I do to get into enough trouble that I would have to go to Liam's—I mean, Officer Levine's—office but not enough trouble to go to jail or have to guard?"

Anna looked at me suspiciously. "He's got you, too?"

"What do you mean?"

"You're crushing on Officer Levine? Already? Join the club. He's practically every girl's fantasy, at least here at the base, although I don't see what they see in him. To me, he seems kind of, I don't know, dark."

"Who has a crush on him?"

"Who doesn't? Don't you see the way the girls perk up whenever he's around? He's like the Chris Hemsworth of the unit. The charmer.

The Don Juan. There's no hope for any of the girls, though; he and Commander Mia have been on and off since she joined two years ago. My sister told me."

Commander Mia. That bitch. Of course. That's why she kept giving me those looks when Liam called out my ID number. How could he *not* be with her—she was only the most effortlessly stunning woman I'd ever seen in real life.

"But I heard through my older sister's friend, who's also friends with Commander Mia, that they're not together right now. Apparently, he said he needed space when he found out she went for lunch with her guy friend." Anna knew all the juice.

I shook my head. "Seriously?" I wanted to know every detail of Liam and Commander Mia's conversation, but I didn't know how to ask Anna without giving myself away completely. Plus, by the way her eyes kept reverting to the Goddess Rules, I could tell she was starting to become uninterested in our conversation.

"What are you reading?" she asked.

"This? The Goddess Rules. The rules to finding love. I wrote it with my best friend from home. We haven't really shared it with anyone, but I'll let you peek if you tell me more about Commander Mia," I said, only half-joking.

"Turn that light off," Rebecca, the girl in the bunk bed next to mine, hissed.

"We're reading the Goddess Rules over here," Anna said to her, trying to perfect her English accent when she repeated the title.

"I don't care what you're reading," the girl said. "I want to sleep."

"Rebecca, you'll love this. It's a book about dating. All the rules you have to follow to get the guy you want," Anna said. "All the American secrets to finding love, but since you're so tired, we won't share them with you," she teased.

Rebecca slowly lifted herself up on her elbow and leaned her head on her hand. "I want to hear the American secrets. Israeli guys love American girls. Read it to me, too—I won't share the rules," she said.

So I read the rules aloud as quietly as I could to her and Anna, translating each sentence into Hebrew, and as the minutes passed by, the other girls in the room slowly propped themselves up to listen, too.

> Sit up straight, but don't look like you're trying.
>
> If an opportunity doesn't present itself, create it.
>
> Be yourself, but not overly honest.
>
> Laugh at his jokes, but not too loud.
>
> Discuss your accomplishments, but never before he does.
>
> Look youthful, but not childlike.
>
> Be experienced, but not slutty.
>
> Don't complain, but say what's on your mind.

"How can you look youthful without looking childlike?" Rebecca asked.

"Yeah," Anna chimed in. "And I don't get how you can say what's on your mind without ever complaining."

What do they not get?

"You can look youthful by doing your hair. If you crimp it with a crimper, for example, it looks young, like you didn't do anything to your hair, but you actually did. It doesn't look childlike, though, because each hair is in its place. Or you can do your makeup, but not heavily," I explained. "Wear mascara but not eyeliner, put a little extra blush on your cheekbones to make it look like you're sunburned, but skip the lip liner. That's looking put together and youthful without looking like a child. Children don't wear mascara, you know?"

"This girl thinks she knows it all," Rebecca said.

They may not have agreed with the Goddess Rules, but they were all interested, which was enough for me.

"These rules are as intriguing as they are dumb," Rebecca said. "But keep reading to us, America." We all started laughing, and as I continued to explain the first few rules, we passed around the bag of Cheetos I brought for emergencies only, licking our orange-stained fingertips until the Cheetos were all gone. I had become the army dating guru of the unit overnight, with the secret answers I shared only with the girls in my room. My girls. As I turned off the light and pulled the pink satin sheet over me, I felt like maybe, just maybe, I was starting to fit in.

———————

It was another Sunday morning at the base. *Shvizut yom alef*, Anna said it was called, which is synonymous to that dreadful Monday morning feeling as you think about the long week to come. In Israel, there was only one day of the weekend, Saturday. Sunday marked the first day of the week, which seemed absurd to me. Not only did I have to start my life from scratch in a new country, but this country also took half of my weekend away. I had barely seen Liam since sitting with him at the cafeteria two weeks earlier, but I was relieved to feel like I had something to look forward to.

Imagine not having Liam to think about. My morning would have revolved around the garbage juice that spilled down the leg of my uniform when Commander Mia forced me of all soldiers to take out the trash in each of the girls' rooms. The clock hit 10:45 a.m., which, since we had breakfast before the sun came up, meant that lunch was right around the corner, and still no sign of Liam. I had come up with a plan to secure at least a few minutes with Liam alone, but I couldn't go through with it—I couldn't *create the opportunity*—if Liam wasn't going to be there to watch me.

Anna and I walked alongside each other toward the cafeteria, which was bustling with soldiers from all over the base, officers and top-ranking commanders, and cooks in their aprons stained with dirty handprints. The white tile floors were barely visible, covered as they were by the black army boot prints everywhere.

And then, finally. There he was. Liam sat with his back hunched over his plate, taking large bites of a schnitzel and hummus sandwich. He chewed with his mouth closed, but I could tell by the size and frequency of each bite that he was hungry. There was something about grown men eating that immediately transformed them into little boys at the kitchen counter picking food off of their plastic plates. My heart melted. He looked like a vulnerable child, his gaze off somewhere in the distance, probably thinking about home.

As Anna and I took a seat at the long plastic table, I looked down at my own plate: white rice with little specks of black pepper and fried chicken swimming in oil. Anna was already halfway done with her meal when I forced myself to eat. Just as I took the first bite, I felt a sudden, unfamiliar crunch. At first I thought it was an undercooked piece of rice, until I spit out my mouthful—and right there before my eyes, I saw it.

A fucking cockroach head. I couldn't believe it at first, but when I saw those dark, compound eyes staring back at mine, I squealed and elbowed Anna, whose face turned white.

On a regular occasion, I would have spit the insect out and run to the bathroom to throw up. But *this*—this was it. My opportunity. This was my chance to cause a scene. It was all or nothing.

In the midst of my panic, I strapped my gun over my shoulder and stepped up onto the table. Anna moved the other soldiers' plates to the side so I had room to stand.

"Attention, everyone!" I yelled. At first, the bustling continued.

"Attention! Attention!" I yelled again, my gun swinging against my hip. I imagined what Julia would have thought in that moment, watching me stand on the table, my heart beating hard. She probably would have gotten up on the table with me. I heard the clinking of forks against plates, until the cafeteria fell silent. My eyes darted to Liam. He stopped chewing mid-bite. The cafeteria looked bigger from up on the table. My bird's-eye view gave me a heightened sense of dominance, and I yelled louder than before.

"Stop eating immediately! There is a cockroach in the rice! I repeat, there is a cockroach in the rice! I just bit into its head, which means there is a body and legs and antennae floating around somewhere in there, which you are probably eating as we speak. This is dangerous! Highly contamin—" I could have gone on for minutes, the adrenaline throwing me into the words, but I felt the tug of my sleeve and looked down to see Liam, his face white with rage. I knew this was an embarrassment to him, to have one of his own soldiers step out of line in front of the entire base, but he was the one who wouldn't talk to me under normal circumstances, so I had to do what I had to do.

"Come with me," Liam said when he forced me to step down from the table. *Bingo.* The cafeteria returned to its status quo as if nothing had happened, except for Commander Mia, who seemed to have lost her appetite. Her cheeks were flushed, and she sat stiffly in her chair, not once taking her eyes off Liam. I followed him as we walked out of the building toward his office.

We walked in silence, one step after the other, and I couldn't help but notice how gorgeous Liam was. *Does he do dumbbell squats? How is his butt so firm?* I needed Liam to see me as the girl he met that night on the beach, not the clueless army soldier who was like every other girl at the base. It drove me crazy to imagine that Liam could completely forget about the night we had and ignore me without a bit of empathy.

Was this human nature? Wanting what you can't have? Wanting the first guy who ever ignored you? I had never felt so inadequate before, and I didn't like it, but it challenged me to work harder and be seen. I wanted to prove to Liam that I was worth seeing. He didn't see me at the beach when he ran by either, I remembered. I was my father's crown jewel, but to Liam, I barely existed. That, I promised the universe, was about to change.

As we inched closer to Liam's office, he walked past it. I stopped in front of the office building, thinking Liam was too wrapped up in his thoughts to notice we missed it.

"Lia—Officer Levine," I said, but he kept walking like he didn't hear me. I followed behind him. We walked down a long hallway until we reached a door on the left equipped with an electronic screen. Liam punched in a four-digit code, opened the door slowly, and closed it behind us. We were alone in a lounge with a sign above the miniature refrigerator that read "Officers Only." Real coffee mugs, not paper cups, lined the kitchen counter, and the Nespresso machine at the far-left corner near the sink was more appealing than a sparkling new Dyson Airwrap.

Liam plopped down on one of the couches, swinging his M16 off his shoulder and resting it beside him. I thought I would be nervous to be alone with him, but as soon as he closed the door behind us, I felt his demeanor change. He patted the seat next to him, and when he looked up at me, I saw the same vulnerable twenty-five-year-old I'd seen a month ago at the beach. I sat down beside him, aware of my every move. Was this my good side? It was my good side.

"Listen, we really need to talk," he said. He was relaxed, and all at once, I felt an anger bubble up inside me. How could he drag this out for almost four weeks before finding the time to talk to me? I smiled at him, disguising my irritation.

"I know we need to talk," I said.

"I'm not going to waste time talking about what you just did, standing up on the table like a lunatic," he said. "I know why you did it, and, admittedly, I respect your courage. You have balls. I want to hear what you have to say." A wave of relief washed over me. He was speaking to me at eye level. In this magical lounge, Liam and I were equals.

"I can't believe you're my officer," I said.

He laughed. "Make this stop. Please, Ella."

Now that I could get a closer look at him, I could see that he looked exhausted. He had a few days' worth of stubble on his face, not enough for an army guard to notice, but enough for me to notice, and his hair was messy, the same way it looked that night after the beach when I ran my hands through it.

"Do you have any idea how hard this is on me?" he said, covering his face with both hands. "If I would have known . . . if only I would have known you were going to be my soldier, God damnit, my soldier! I can't believe this. Why didn't you tell me? You could have said something."

"I had no idea you were even an officer! How was I supposed to know? This isn't my fault. You realize that, right?"

"So whose fault is it? Mine? You could have told me the truth, maybe? Instead of making up bullshit stories."

My cheeks were red now. "You didn't say anything about being an army officer. Not a single mention of any of this." I waved my arms around the lounge.

"You cut me off! Maybe if you hadn't spent the night talking about yourself, you would have had time to listen to me," he said.

I was losing it. I took a deep breath and remembered the Goddess Rules. *Be yourself, but not overly honest. Be smart, not right.* What was the point of arguing with him? It would only complicate things.

"You're right," I said. "I should have said something. But now we're here, right? So let's figure out what the next step is. I can see how stressed out you've been over the past two weeks." I looked into his eyes. "I don't want to be a burden on you or your job or your life," I said. *Ha! A burden on his life?* These were by far the worst four weeks of my almost twenty years of living, and he had the power to turn that around. Easily. Liam pushed his lips together and offered an appreciative smile. Call me Wendy the Wind-Up Doll. I could recite everything he wanted to hear with one turn of a key.

"Listen," he said, waving his forefinger from me to him and back again, "this has got to end. This has got to be the last time we talk informally in the army or outside of it. When we walk out of here, my name isn't Liam anymore. Capeesh? It's Officer Levine. And your insane behavior is making me look bad. I have to keep my soldiers under control. Do you understand? This job is my life. It's my only form of steady income."

"Okay, I get it," I said, but when I wanted something, I went after it.

"That night at the beach was a one-night thing, for God's sake. We didn't even kiss. But whatever happened, happened, and I never want to think about it again. It's more than that. You know what this is really about? Morals. There are rules and regulations in life, and following the moral code is the least I can do as a responsible officer. So promise me, Ella, you won't say a word to any of the soldiers. I could lose my job. I could lose my entire career. I pay my mother's rent from this money. I don't have a degree; this is all I have. Do you understand me?" he said. "I'm not an American princess who has everything served to her on a silver platter. I don't have money for expensive clothes and penthouses in Tel Aviv."

Good God, couldn't he explain himself without putting me down? I bit my tongue. "You have nothing to worry about. I'm not going to say anything to anyone. If you want us to ignore each other, if that's really what you want, I'm fine with that. I understand where you're coming from, Officer Levine," I said.

Liam calmed down as soon as he understood I wasn't going to rat him out. When I got up to leave, his demeanor changed.

"Not yet," he said with a smile. "I said I'm Officer Levine once we *leave* this room. Give me a few more minutes."

There it was again. That sprinkle of hope. Two rules in one conversation, and I could already read right through him. Liam wanted me; he just didn't *want* to want me. The tingling I felt between my legs when I shook his hand at the beach crept up on me again. I leaned into him subtly so he could get a whiff of my Marc Jacobs Daisy perfume.

"God, you smell so good," he said.

Easy as pie.

"What do you want?" he asked me.

I wanted to date him. I wasn't going to fall in love with him—I could only see myself marrying an American guy, not an Israeli. But still, I wanted to sneak out in the middle of the night and let him fuck me against the army bathroom sink. That sort of thing. I wanted to know that my guarding duty was nonexistent, that I wouldn't ever have to clean a bathroom in the two years of hell at this place. That I had someone to trust. But more than anything, I wanted his familiarity. I wanted to feel at home. Of course, if I told him that, I would have no chance of ever being with him. Honesty in the beginning of an illegal relationship? Please. Liam was used to girls falling at his feet, and while I wasn't challenging him in an obvious sense, I knew exactly how I was going to.

"I want what you want. To pretend none of this ever happened. It makes my army life harder hoping for an interaction with you. I'd rather just know that whatever happened or didn't happen between us won't . . . ever . . . happen . . . again." I said the last three words slowly, staring deep into Liam's eyes while resting my hand against his knee.

"You're killing me, cowgirl," he said as he cradled my neck in one of his hands and pulled me into him. He let his lips linger along the space between my earlobe and my neck, before I pulled away. If Liam wanted to play this game with me, I would play it better.

Just as I put my finger on Liam's lips, we heard the dial of the electric code and watched as the doorknob turned. Liam was only a few inches from me, my hand creeping up along his thigh.

As the door creaked open, I saw the long, lanky arm and silky hair I could recognize from miles away.

"Commander Mia, hi," Liam said, standing up immediately, covering himself with both of his hands. He turned to me, speaking quickly as he walked toward the door. "That's all for now, soldier. Get organized and meet the rest of the unit back at the cafeteria."

Commander Mia didn't even try to hide the look of surprise on her face as she stood in the doorway. I noticed how Liam brushed up against her as he stepped out of the lounge.

"Your weapon, Officer?" she said.

Liam lost his breath. An officer forgetting a weapon, a loaded M16 gun, meant at least two weeks of jail time, unless, of course, Commander Mia wouldn't say anything. Unless I didn't say anything. Liam raced to the couch to retrieve his weapon without looking at me. I was back to being his soldier again, only now more knowledgeable about the situation. I knew what Liam was thinking. With a few solid rules and a little bit of patience, my plan had to work.

As I gathered my own things—the flask, the stupid hat, my gun—I stepped toward the door hurriedly. The last thing I was in the mood for was a "you're a very bad girl" conversation with Commander Mia.

But right as I was about to step out of the lounge, she flashed a pitiful smile, exposing her pearly white teeth.

"Oh, Ella, you have no idea what you've just gotten yourself into."

Chapter 8

"Officer Levine has been pissed all week, thanks to you, 'Merica," Rebecca said.

"Shut up, Becca," Anna said. "She was trying to protect us from eating cockroaches."

"Well, who asked her to? I would rather not have known there were cockroaches in my food in the first place. I haven't eaten anything since."

"He's had a sour look on his face every day this week," Rebecca continued as she undid her ponytail and scratched her scalp. "He and Commander Mia are cooking up something for you; I'd be careful."

She had no idea what it was, and neither did I.

———

"Get up, get up, get up!"

I woke up in the middle of the Israeli desert at 3:00 a.m. in a dirty bunk bed to Liam's voice screaming an inch away from my ear. This was not how I imagined his voice before I fell asleep that night. Before he stormed into our room, I had been sleeping—sleeping in the army sense of the word, of course. Nothing like the Saturday afternoon naps

I was used to taking, when I'd lather my skin in La Mer grapefruit-scented body cream while listening to relaxing rainforest sounds on my speakers. I was "army sleeping," which meant I wasn't fully asleep but half-asleep, wearing a uniform and black combat boots under the covers, with an M16 under my pillow, the bulge of the firing pin digging into my temple, reminding me to prepare for the worst.

"What's happening?" I yelled to Anna.

"We're under attack!" she said.

I didn't even have time to react before she burst out laughing.

"Relax, 'Merica, it's just a drill," Becca said, barely able to contain her own laughter.

What a surprise, I thought as I realized what we were going to be doing. Liam and Commander Mia had woken us up to run around the base and crawl in the mud.

Still groggy, we stood in uniform in a line outside of our room, one soldier behind the other, our teeth chattering from the cold.

"On the count of three," Commander Mia called, "you will drop down to your knees and crawl to that can over there." She pointed to a trash bin that was barely visible in the dark. I had a Mean Girls moment, imagining myself tackling her to the ground.

Liam set up an electric army lamp so we could see. Desert critters crawled into the sand when the light turned on, and I couldn't believe I would have to crawl on top of them.

"Whoever crawls there and back in under one minute," she said, "will be free to shower and go back to her room. Whoever doesn't will continue to crawl until she crawls fast enough to meet the expected time. We'll stand here for hours if we have to. Understood?"

We all nodded.

Is this even legal?

With the blow of Commander Mia's whistle, we dropped down to the muddy desert sand and crawled on our knees and elbows toward the trash bin. I followed behind Anna, the taste of morning breath still lingering in my mouth. A few minutes went by.

"Nice work, Soldier Anna; you're free to go," Liam said.

"Rebecca, forty-two seconds!" Commander Mia said.

As the minutes passed, each soldier crawled back and forth in under a minute.

Except for me.

"Keep going," Commander Mia said when I looked over at her, my face and uniform dirtied with mud. I was the only soldier left. Liam stood next to her and said nothing at all.

That's it, I thought. *I'm not showing her any weakness. I'm going to crawl as fast as I possibly can, and there's no way it will take me more than a minute.*

I counted the seconds in my head as I reached the garbage can. Forty-five, forty-six, forty-seven. Done.

"Nope," Commander Mia said. "Do it again, soldier."

This bitch. From the floor, I looked up at Liam and tried to make eye contact with him, but he and Commander Mia were laughing so hard their faces turned red.

I crawled back and forth again and again and again. I held back the tears, which came after I realized Liam was laughing at me. Commander Mia was as cruel as she was beautiful, I realized that night, but Liam? His laughter exposed a side of him I didn't know. I wasn't going to give either of them the satisfaction of seeing me break down. If they wanted to play this game with me, I could play it. And I would win.

"All right, come on," I heard Liam say to Commander Mia after what felt like an eternity. "Let her go," he said and nudged her with his elbow.

"Barely under a minute, but I'll take it," Commander Mia said when I reached the trash bin for the last time. "I'm getting sick of standing here, to be honest."

When the drill was over, a few of the other girls and I lingered in the shared shower space. I took off my muddy uniform and folded it beside one of the rusty sinks, my naked body on display, removed from myself.

There were naked women of every type, yet our humanity was so minimized that it felt like we were all the same: bodies with breasts and hair and bones and skin. Emotions and embarrassment were luxuries. We didn't have the time or energy for that. My eyes hollow like a zombie's, I stepped out of the shower and dried off. Shaking from the cold, I put my dirty uniform back on, dragged my feet to the room, slipped into the bunk bed, and wept until the discordant voices in my mind faded and I finally fell asleep. We were up again for breakfast at 5:00 a.m. sharp.

Our guns had to be held in front of us, never behind or on the side of our bodies so we were in full control of the weapon at any given moment. I didn't think I would ever hold a gun, let alone carry it with me for weeks, shower next to it, sleep with it, and wake up with it. The army just pushed it into my arms on the very first day after they gave me my uniform, and that was that. I despised that gun for everything it represented—misery, cruelty, violence—and for the deep purple bruises it left against my hipbone that took weeks to fade.

We stood outside of the cafeteria again while Liam and Commander Mia scanned our every move, looking to find something wrong so they could punish us. Was your shirt hanging out of your pants? Two hours of guarding duty. Was your boot lace untied? Three hours. Was your gun hanging over your back instead of across your hip? Weekend base duty. We weren't allowed to speak, eat, shower, touch our faces, or smile without asking. Every action of mine needed approval from Liam.

That night, Commander Mia went over the following day's schedule. "You're on bathroom duty tomorrow. Girls' bathroom again," she said to me, trying to hide her smile. The last time Anna and I had girls' bathroom duty together, we had to scrape dried period blood from one of the toilets, each of us trying not to gag while our foreheads dripped with sweat.

When I was around Commander Mia, I tried to make myself as quiet and small and unimportant as I could to avoid standing out, but it was already too late. Every opportunity she had to stick a knife in my back, she did and then twisted it.

As soon as she finished reading through the schedule, Liam made an announcement. "Actually," he said as he looked over at Commander Mia, "bathroom duty is canceled for today." I felt the hair on my arms stand up. Liam had canceled my bathroom duty today, but he'd degraded me as I crawled in mud yesterday. One minute it felt like he was stepping on my neck; the next minute I was higher than a kite.

I couldn't stand to have our phones taken away, and I waited for the one hour in the evening I could get lost on Instagram and TikTok and forget what my life had become. That evening during *shaat tash*, I sent a selfie to the Davidson Family group chat, sitting slouched on my bunk bed, DAVIDSON engraved into my uniform, my eyes black pools from lack of sleep, cheeks pale from lack of food. Sorry, roaches weren't my taste. I sent the picture in hopes of stirring up feelings of pity in my parents so they would feel a minuscule particle of the inexplicable suffering I was enduring and find a way to rescue me.

———

A few days later, when the commanders woke us in the middle of the night for the *masa kumta*, I was prepared. This was an army tradition in which soldiers walked in the desert sand for hours until the sun came up, eventually earning their *kumtas*, or army berets. I felt the way the Jews probably felt, aimlessly wandering the desert for forty years, punished by a ruthless God. I didn't know if I would survive walking through the desert all night long, marching under the open sky.

For the first three hours, I used the hovering technique, breathing in and out until we stopped for water. The backs of my feet felt like they were on fire, and I knew the skin alongside them was rubbing off with each step. Yet, each time I looked at Commander Mia, her eyes switching from the soldiers to Liam and back, I felt a determination bubble up inside of me that I didn't recognize. I wanted to prove to the other girls that I wasn't as soft as the Victoria's Secret pajamas I wore on the weekends. If I thought I was going to quit when we started, I decided I wasn't going to give quitting another thought. As I hiked, I thought about the way life took you on its path. Then I thought that, actually, life took only losers on its path. Winners *chose* their paths; they didn't let life control their destiny.

I marched faster and faster, looking down at my feet at first and then looking straight ahead at the endless desert surrounding us. This wasn't easy for the other girls sweating beside me either, their faces red and wet, their cheeks burnt from the scorching sun. *If they can do this, so can I*, I thought furiously. None of these girls were stronger or smarter or tougher than I was. *No one is stronger than me*, I kept telling myself, without believing it for a second. This was my new mantra—when I took off my army boots and patches of flesh peeled off the backs of my heels with my socks, when I lay alone in my bunk bed listening to the deep breaths of the other soldiers in the tent with me, when I woke up in the middle of the night holding a mini flashlight between my teeth to show Commander Mia that, yes, I could reassemble my gun in less than forty-five seconds. I asked myself, sometimes out loud and sometimes under my breath: "Who is stronger than me?"

And the answer? It was always the same. Even when I was 100

percent sure that it was 0 percent true, I said it anyway, over and over again: "No one."

As the sun came up and we continued walking, the terrain shifted from desert to mountains and back to desert again. We hiked past trees every few hours, taking turns relishing their minimal shade. I missed lying outside on the hammock at my parents' house, the fruity scent of petunias lingering in my nostrils. I thought of how my father used to sit at the table drinking a beer and telling me stories about his life in the army, and I suddenly felt his presence so intensely that for a second I almost thought he was there with me.

There were smells in the desert, too, mainly the smell of vomit when the girls couldn't hold it any longer. The officers acted like this behavior was normal, but I caught a glimpse of Commander Mia gagging whenever a soldier threw up. Liam was in the front of the line, ahead of the rest of us, leading the way like he always did.

On that day, the day that changed my entire perspective of the army, I saw my first rattlesnake, though technically I *heard* my first rattlesnake and only saw it afterward. It sounded like a maraca, an unmistakable shaking that stopped me in my tracks. Commander Mia, so engrossed in the hike, didn't notice the snake, and was a second away from stepping on it.

"*Snake!*" I yelled, pushing her out of the way. She fell to the ground beside me, and I was sure she was going to punish me for pushing her, but when her eyes met mine, there was an enormous amount of gratitude in them. I held out my hand to help her up, and she took it.

"Thank you, Ella," she said, calling me by my name for the first time since that night in the officers' lounge.

The rest of the march was slow and steady, my heart beating unusually fast because of the incredible physical exertion I was under and the deadly creatures I was presented with. From the snake incident on, instead of walking with my chin up like the officers had taught us in boot camp practice, I scanned the ground obsessively with each step, while simultaneously repeating my mantra. *Who is stronger than me? No one.*

When we arrived at our "destination," which was just another patch of sand, I looked around at the other soldiers beside me and began to feel a sense of accomplishment. We had walked before sunrise and past sunset, and although the journey was hard and, frankly, pointless, I couldn't help but feel like I had done . . . something. My gun, as bulky as it was, almost felt like an imaginary friend. Who could ever have imagined that I would travel the Southern Israeli desert carrying a weapon across my shoulders? I could do the impossible. I was stronger than I thought. These thoughts, whether muddled by the heat or not, were real.

For the first time since joining the army, my complex life felt simple, and it stunned me. I focused on my physical dread and forgot about how complicated my life felt emotionally. This was how the army was going to be. Don't think too much; just take orders from officers. Someone else would do the thinking for me. Was that really so bad?

I dreamed of the weekend, when we were allowed to go home—dreamed of taking a bite of my mother's crispy chicken schnitzel, of sinking into the ocean of cotton sheets in my queen-size bed, of taking a shower in hot water, but more than anything, I couldn't wait to text Liam. Outside of the base, there was a chance he would be himself. During the week, he could control me, but on the weekend, I had my agency back.

If we were physically out of the army base on the weekend, Liam had to answer me, didn't he?

———————

My mother picked me up from the base, waiting outside with her car headlights on and music blaring. I had never been so happy to see her. As soon as we drove toward home, the army base disappearing behind me, I texted Liam.

> ELLA: Hey . . . can we talk?
> LIAM: Hi, soldier. Is everything okay? Is there a problem?
> ELLA: Liam, will you stop for a second? Seriously. Please.
> LIAM: Officer Levine.

"Ella, honey," my mom said.

"What is it?" I said without looking up from my phone.

"Well, how was your week? I'm your mother, not your chauffeur. What's going on with you? You aren't yourself," she said.

"Obviously not, Mom. I was supposed to be popping Adderalls and studying for finals right now," I said, "not counting down the minutes until I have to go back to an army base."

"I know, but open your mind. You have the entire weekend ahead of you. Plus, there's always something good lurking around the corner if you're smart enough to see it. Dad and I met in the army, you know. Have I ever told you that story?" she joked. "But really, honey, good things will come. Give it time. Maybe you'll even fall in love."

Chapter 9

The weekend went by in what felt like a split second, and I was already in the car with my mother on the way back to the base.

"When you look good, you feel good," she said. Another Goddess Rule, this one my mother's favorite.

The only problem was that looking good in the army was practically impossible.

The uniform pants hung low, making it look like we were wearing adult diapers, and the shirts were loose and baggy, unflattering on even the most sculpted body.

If I wanted to snag Liam, I needed to look the part. I knew that looks shouldn't matter, that brains and personality were supposed to be more important, but let's face it, this was reality, and looks came first. Commander Mia was undoubtedly more beautiful than I was, but I could tell by the way Liam dismissed most of what she said that he wasn't in love with her, that he'd had her enough times.

I had an idea. "Mom, you know my extra uniform? The one you washed? Can you take it to the tailor? Ask her to make the pants tighter, and make sure they hug the butt really tight in the back," I said. Although it was illegal to alter the uniform in any way, how could they prove it?

A few days later when I was back at the base, my mom sent the uniform to me in a taxi, and when I received special permission from Liam to pick it up, I found my straightener and a bag of Sour Patch Kids hidden inside the bag sitting on the back seat. I was so overwhelmed with joy that I started crying right then, wishing I could jump into the cab and ride home to my mother, snacking on Sour Patch Kids the whole way back.

I spent the rest of the day sneaking into the bathroom to straighten my hair at lightning speed and change into my new and improved army uniform. I dabbed on a little bit of cheek and lip blush and stepped into the cafeteria, pretending to be confident. How pathetic was it that I had to lean solely on my physical appearance to get Liam to notice me? I knew physical attraction shouldn't have carried that much weight, but for me, it did. As soon as Liam spotted me, he smiled at me, and I watched as his Adam's apple bobbed up and then down. His eyes gave him away. I had grown obsessed with gaining Liam's attention, with wanting something I couldn't have. I let a few soft pieces of hair hang around my face and ears, and although I was still stomping around in black combat boots, for that moment, I felt like a princess.

As I walked past Liam, I tilted my head forward so my beret accidentally fell to the ground. I picked it up slowly, right in front of him, my newly fitted uniform pants accentuating the curves I barely had. I was obviously acting ridiculous, but desperate times called for desperate measures, right? When I stood back up and looked at Liam, he shook his head, his eyes closed, an adorable soft smile forming on his face.

Guess so.

After dinner, Liam and Commander Mia led us to an open shooting range to teach us how to shoot an M16. In the dark.

"Don't ever point a loaded weapon at anything except the target," Liam said, pointing at the balloons tied to the targets twenty-five yards from where we were, each target lit up with a small flashlight in the ground. "You each will get four bullets and four chances to hit the balloons. Whoever pops their target balloons will receive a *chupar*, a prize," he said with a smile, "and will be pleasantly surprised."

"I know I said he was kind of an asshole, but I have to admit, he looks really hot today," Anna whispered to me.

"Tell me about it." I took a deep breath.

Liam continued, "When I finish explaining, stand in a single-file line pointing your weapons toward the targets. Your weapons are not loaded. Wait for me to double-check that they are not loaded. I'm going to slide this metal rod into the gun"—he held up a metal rod about two feet long—"to make sure the weapon is clean and ready for shooting."

We each stood five feet away from one another and waited for Liam to check the guns. When he reached me, I took a step backward so I was closer to him. I could feel the warmth of his breath against the back of my neck. He slid the rod into my gun swiftly and pulled it out, making a swooshing sound.

"You can stick your rod into my gun anytime," I whispered. I lowered the weapon to the floor like he told us to and lifted my gaze to meet his. Liam's face turned red, and I could see little specks of sweat against his forehead, but he wasn't angry. He was insanely turned on.

There were three balloons on each target, and we each had four bullets—four chances—to hit them. If it weren't for Liam, I'd probably pretend to feel sick and sit out this whole shooting shit show, but I kept feeling like I had to prove myself to him. I had to show him I was more than just the American girl he thought I was, and if firing at these stupid targets was the way to do it, I was in. I loaded my gun and shot one bullet. *Pop*. The pink balloon was gone. Another bullet. *Pop*. The blue balloon, gone. I had one balloon left, black, and two bullets to hit it. I shot again. *Pop*. The black balloon, gone. I hit all three targets with only three bullets, the fourth sitting in my gun, left over. Beginner's luck.

As Liam walked by me, I felt him graze the back of my thigh. I turned quickly and caught his gaze, and although his face was completely still, his piercing eyes said it all.

When target practice was over, Liam announced that I had won the *chupar*. "Soldier, come with me," he said after the other soldiers applauded. Only Commander Mia looked down at the floor.

We walked toward the officer building in the dark, this time on our way to Liam's office, while the rest of the soldiers followed Commander Mia to their rooms. Liam walked swiftly ahead of me, and each time I caught up to him, he increased his pace. To an observer, it must have looked like I was chasing him.

We walked into the enormous cement building, the desert stars above our heads. Liam nodded at the guards to assure them I was allowed to enter and then unlocked the door to his office. "Officer Liam Levine," the sign read. I followed behind him. Liam put his gun on the desk in front of me and walked toward the door again. He stuck his head out and looked to the right and then to the left, making sure no one was watching us, before he closed the door and locked it.

I sat there, staring at him, wondering how it was humanly possible to get exponentially hotter with each minute that passed.

He glanced around the office wearing his ridiculously hot uniform, and I imagined for a second what would happen if I had the nerve to get up and unbuckle his belt, right then and there.

Liam walked over to his desk and sat in the chair behind it, the glare of his computer reflecting against his skin. On his desk were a mountain of paperwork seconds from toppling over and a clear glass cup filled almost to the brim with old Turkish coffee.

"Have a seat, soldier," he said. The way he referred to me as his soldier made me furious, but it also turned me on in a way I had never experienced before. It was as if I were in some sort of soft porn movie, where the sexy officer was in charge of his soldier, telling her exactly what to do and when, both of them fully consenting. It was simply protocol, but whenever he expressed his authority, I fantasized about him unbuttoning my uniform and taking me on his desk. Still, I couldn't ignore the images flashing through my mind of Liam's eyes going dark. He had two sides to him.

"Sit," he said. I rolled my eyes and sat in the chair in front of him.

Liam stood up and put his hands on his hips. He seemed on edge, but I wasn't sure if he was annoyed with me or with himself.

"Why did you say what you said?" he asked.

"What did I say, Officer Levine?" I asked innocently. If he was going to play the officer role, I could play the submissive soldier.

"Don't play dumb with me."

My heart fell down to my stomach for a second, but I quickly regained my composure. If he wanted to play this game, he picked the wrong opponent.

Out of nowhere, Liam lifted his chin toward the ceiling and let out a yell. It was a grunt mixed with a deep, frustrated scream, and it was so loud and out of place that I jumped in my chair.

"What is wrong with you?" I yelled back.

He looked into my eyes. "These next two years—they're the most important two years of my army career. I have worked for eight years to make it to this point, and I'm not going to let you ruin it, Ella. I graduated from officer school. I deferred my acceptance to business school." He started talking with his hands as he paced the office frantically. "But since you've gotten here, I haven't been able to think about anything else. I see you out of the corner of my eye everywhere I go. The way you strut around the base with that cute little clueless look on your face, the way your eyes glisten in the morning when the sun comes out, the way your lips curve at the top like a rose petal. I can't stop thinking about you. Here at the base, even at home. And, well, it's got to end. It's got to stop. And you know what? I've come up with a plan. I know how to make it stop."

My teeth started digging into my lip as I looked at him, and I swallowed hard. He looked like such a snack, pacing around, losing control. I saw myself in the reflection of the window, the army beret resting effortlessly on my head. Thank you, Goddess Rules. God, they worked every time.

"You've been ignoring me, and I know I told you to forget anything between us ever happened, but it seems like we need closure. Okay?"

"Okay," I said.

"Let me fuck you once," he said.

I felt the muscles in my body tighten. My nerves jumped with excitement. With Liam, I had begun to realize, life was a roller coaster. There was no stability, no steadiness, just a chaotic array of twists and turns, of ups and downs, until the ride ended and my heart galloped, beating a thousand times a minute.

"Every time I've fucked a girl, I've gotten over her. Even my last girlfriend. I stayed with her because it was comfortable, but as soon as I fucked her for the first time, the minute I came, I'm telling you, my mind was on to the next one. I'm fucked up. I have a problem. But for this situation, it's the solution."

I laughed. "Wait, did you seriously bring me to your office to ask me to have sex with you? After your whole speech in the lounge about ending this? About, what was it? *Morals?* Is this a joke?"

For a few seconds, Liam didn't say anything. He looked around the room as if something in it was going to save him. He walked toward the window, turned around, and then walked to the door and unlocked it. Then, as soon as he reached his desk again, he picked up the glass coffee cup and hurled it at the door, missing my shoulder by a few inches. I gasped at the proximity of his throw and his sudden loss of control.

"What the fuck?" I held on to the chair's armrests, feeling like this situation could spiral out of control.

Liam knelt down beside my chair as if he were about to propose.

"Look at me," he said, still on his knees. "I will take you places you have never been before."

This was a side to Liam I hadn't seen before, and deep within me, I couldn't deny that I felt uncomfortable. It reminded me of the way I had felt when I looked up at Liam from the filthy mud and saw him laughing at me with Commander Mia. Could this be turning into more than a silly game? Liam was serious and strong, and the way he threw that coffee cup, the rage in his usually serene face—could he hurt me if I made the wrong move?

"Why did you laugh at me when I was the last one left crawling on the floor? I was at my lowest, literally, and instead of stopping Commander Mia from torturing me, you stood beside her and laughed," I said.

"When?" Liam asked.

"When we were crawling in the mud during that ridiculous drill," I said.

"Laughed at you? Are you kidding me? You must have been hallucinating. I would never laugh at you. I felt so bad for you in that moment, I had to use every muscle in my body to stop myself from slapping the shit out of Mia and picking you up, telling you everything was going to be okay. But laugh at you? Are you crazy? You're insane. I would never." He sounded so sure of himself.

Maybe I was overreacting. It was really dark; maybe I could have imagined it. No way. What does he think I am? Stupid?

Liam interrupted my thoughts. "What do you say? Will you give me a chance? Just once. I can't live my life without knowing what it's like to feel you," he said, both of his hands in fists so tight that the skin around his knuckles had turned white.

"I'll think about it," I said, although even with the doubt that flickered in my mind, my body already knew the answer.

When I stood up to leave, Liam pulled me back down onto the chair. "I haven't released you yet, soldier," he said. He leaned in and kissed me, the smoothness of his tongue and the smell of Burberry cologne even crisper than I had imagined all those nights in my bunk bed. *Finally.* I slipped my tongue into his mouth and kissed him back, both of us aware of the unlocked door, addicted to the thrill of knowing that anybody could walk in.

That's when I saw it.

Behind Liam's desk was a framed picture of the back of a woman's head, her long brown hair gliding down the back of her sundress, against a backdrop of an evening bar, a bar packed with people, a bar decorated with pineapples.

I recognized the shape of my own body, the color of my own hair.

The picture he took of me at the Pineapple Bar that first night we met.

He had it printed and framed and hung up right there in his office. I put my hand against my forehead.

"That?" Liam said when he noticed what I was looking at. "I had it printed out the next day. I don't think you understand what I've been feeling," he said.

Chapter 10

A few weeks after we arrived in Tel Aviv, before I enlisted in the army, my mother asked me to stop by the supermarket to buy milk and eggs for breakfast. Where was my medium unsweetened hazelnut Dunkin Donuts coffee that tasted slightly of dishwater? Where were my weekends in the city at Ralph's Coffee sipping my flat white and smearing French butter and strawberry jam on a freshly baked scone? I missed America and was growing allergic to Tel Aviv, with its humidity, its ruthless sun, and the people walking the streets, always on their way *somewhere*, looking tan and effortless and stopping to greet friends they saw on the way with two kisses on each cheek. I felt like I were strolling around some miniature town equipped with an invisible gate stopping people with ambition from crossing it.

In line at the supermarket, as I waited for the cashier to scan my items, my phone lit up. Julia. She wanted, *needed*, advice about a guy she had just met. I nodded while I listened, the sound of her voice taking me back to the sweet car rides waiting in the Starbucks drive-through line for our vanilla almond milk lattes. Yet, as I started giving her advice—*don't call him; don't text back so quickly*—the grandma standing in line behind me butted into our conversation.

"Listen to me, honey—forget those rules! Tell her to make him dinner!" she said to me in Hebrew. Suddenly, she grabbed the phone from my hand. "The best way to a man's heart is through his stomach!" she yelled into the speaker.

I stared at her in disbelief, shocked by the rudeness of this Israeli grandmother, who, in essence, embodied the blunt vulgarity of all Israelis everywhere. I couldn't see that she had only wanted to help, that she had felt the same comfort with me that she probably felt with her own granddaughter. That was the thing about Israel—there was a sense of community, of family, among the people—and the more I tried to push that connection away, the closer it kept creeping up on me.

On the morning of cafeteria duty at the base, Anna and I pulled on our latex gloves and stood at the enormous sink, washing dishes. Plate on top of plate, thousands of forks dirtied with specks of green and brown, and a stench that smelled worse than a carcass.

"This is disgusting," Anna said, wiping her cheek with her forearm.

"No, *that's* disgusting," I said, tilting my head toward the chef I had been watching for a while. The *tabach* was a soldier who specialized in cooking the food for the units. There was the head *tabach* and a few other *tabachim*, but in the army world, these soldiers were known to be troubled. They had a week on and a week off in the army, which meant that each week, the chefs alternated. This week was Mattie's shift, a chef from Northern Israel who went home each week to work his second job as a pool cleaner.

When I looked over at him, he had just finished cutting the tomatoes and cucumbers for the huge salad the entire base shared. The bowl was so enormous it couldn't really be considered a bowl. It was more of a massive bucket, three feet long by three feet wide, and to mix the tomatoes and cucumbers together, Mattie leaned down into the vegetables until his elbows were buried in the bowl. He mixed as he squatted, and after a few good mixes, he stood up, stuck his arms out above the bowl, and with his right hand, he squeezed the leftover vegetable juice from his hairy forearms and let it drip into the bowl. Then, with his left hand, he did the same—squeezed the leftover vegetable juice into the salad, the hair on his arms wet, sticking to his skin.

"The salad is the only thing I used to eat," Anna said.

"Not anymore," I said.

As we washed and dried, I couldn't help but smile as soon as we made eye contact.

"What is it?" she asked. "How are you?"

"I'm fine," I said and looked around the kitchen to make sure nobody was listening. "I have to tell you something, but you have to promise not to tell anyone."

"I promise, I promise," she said.

"I'm sort of dating Liam. Yes, Officer Levine. I need your advice. His behavior . . . he's erratic. He threw a coffee cup at the wall, and now he wants us to have sex," I said.

Anna put her latex-gloved hand over her mouth.

"You're dating Officer Liam Levine? He wants to have sex with you? I can't believe this. I can't. How did it start? When? I swear to you, I had a feeling."

"*Shhh*, we're not *dating* dating. I don't know what to call it. But don't make it so obvious. I promised him I wouldn't tell a soul. You won't believe it, but the night before the army started, I met him randomly at the beach, and we spent the entire evening getting drunk at a bar together. I almost fainted when I realized he was our officer when we got here the next day. I don't really know what to do, though, Anna. I don't just want to have sex with him; I want to be with him, you know? My first instinct says not to have sex with him right away so he'll want me more, but I also kind of can't get him out of my mind."

Our final task was to clean out the baba ghanoush machine, the eggplant and mayonnaise dripping from it all the way down to the floor. Everyone knew that cleaning the baba ghanoush machine was the worst job on kitchen duty. Still overwhelmed by the fact that I was illegally making out with our head officer, Anna couldn't stop asking me questions.

"Have you kissed?"

I didn't answer.

"Have you seen him naked?"

"God, Anna."

"Is it big?"

"No! I mean, probably, but I don't know!"

Mattie the *tabach* came over to see why we hadn't yet gotten to work on the machine, the gooey mayonnaise starting to crust on the edges.

"Officer, we're not touching that," I said to him.

"Yeah," Anna added for support.

Mattie laughed.

Then we cleaned it.

"I still can't believe this. I just can't," Anna said again. "You have to tell me every detail. You know the rules you've been reading to us at night? *Never call him, don't text first, make him wait*, all of that? If you want Officer Levine for real, there's an Israeli rule you have to know. See, I can teach you something, too. It's called the Umbrella Approach," Anna said as we scrubbed.

"What's the Umbrella Approach?" I asked.

"My grandma always told me that the best way to find a husband is through the Umbrella Approach. Just like these American rules, you don't show him who you really are, at least not in the beginning, right? You show him exactly who he wants you to be: feminine, cheerful all the time, motherly. Only later, once he falls in love, do you show him your true self. Metaphorically speaking, you stick the umbrella up his ass while the umbrella is closed, slowly pushing it and pushing it in so subtly he doesn't even feel it, and then, once he's already yours, once that umbrella is deep in there, when he least expects it, *boom!* You open the umbrella and show him who you really are."

I stared at her, shocked, until we both started laughing uncontrollably, our hands and our minds full of baba ghanoush.

That night, Anna and I sat outside during *shaat tash*, sipping Turkish coffee before bed. We were so tired that the caffeine had no effect on us. Before heading back to the room, Anna pulled out a pack of cigarettes from the breast pocket of her uniform.

"Want one?" she asked. I took the cigarette from her hand. She lit it for me.

She took a drag of her cigarette, and I tried to copy her, inhaling the smoke into my lungs.

"You know, growing up, my parents were so in love," she said. "My mother is a singer, and I remember waiting backstage with my father for her after every show and watching her walk down the stage steps in her neon platform heels. I used to love to look at her up close, to count the sparkles scattered across her cheeks. She wore bright blue mascara, and sometimes, when she was sweating, it ran, making it look like she'd been crying." She took another drag. "It made her look sad. Her eyes looked sad, you know? My father—he's a Tunisian Israeli—he would take her face into his hands and wipe the mascara clean from under her eyes with his thumb, then pull her close to him and inhale her, without kissing her. He used to get so close to her lips that they would almost touch, until she'd beg him to just kiss her already, but after the shows, he never did." Anna looked at me, reading my expression. She flicked the ashes from her cigarette.

"My dad, he only wore black. He never let my mother bring a housekeeper into our home, no matter how much money we had. It was my mother's job to take care of the home, he said, because when a mother cooks and cleans it isn't the same as when a stranger does it. What do you think about that?"

"Is that how Israeli men are?" I asked.

"Some of them. Maybe he had a point, you know? Whenever he walked into the house, my mother's whole demeanor changed. She became tense, and her face fell. It literally fell. The edges of her smile swooped down into a frown, and I just waited for him to focus on someone else, on something else, to take a shower or lose himself in some basketball game. My mother watched him like a hawk as he slipped off his sneakers and left them right there in the middle of the living room. He used to sit on the couch and give her orders—*bring me this, bring me that*—until he stopped doing anything for anyone, including himself.

"'Do me a favor, honey,' he said to her one scorching summer morning when he'd just come home from the gym. 'Come take off my socks for me.' And she would! Can you imagine? When they fought, he'd punish my mother by cooking inedible foods like teriyaki chicken omelets mixed with mint toothpaste and dog food."

I grimaced at the thought.

"When she refused to eat," Anna went on, "he gave her the silent treatment for days. Once, when my mother was on a diet, she asked him to grab her a peach from the fruit bowl. He made her a huge bowl of ice cream overflowing with whipped cream and then cut up half a peach into tiny cubes and sprinkled it on the top. Once, he became so angry with her for raising her voice that he decided he wasn't going to flush the toilet anymore. For months, my mother spent days after coming home from the recording studio scrubbing the house clean and flushing his literal shit and urine down the toilet while he sat around, depressed that he'd lost his job as a cab driver." Anna paused. "Love? I don't believe in love."

"Anna, that's fucked up," I said. "And what's even more fucked up is that you had to see that as a kid. But love is real. Love exists. Don't let your parents' story dictate your outlook on love. You'll see, you'll fall in love with a guy, and he'll even flush his own toilet." I took a drag of the cigarette, getting used to the burn. "You'll find your Prince Charming one day. We both will."

Chapter 11

From the moment Liam's lips touched mine, everything between us changed. We walked around the base carrying a secret. I knew he loved the way I smelled and fantasized about me in the shower. He whispered it while we stood in line at the cafeteria, texted it after the sun went down, my hair wet in a hair clip, smiling to myself in the army bunk bed with the pink satin sheets encompassing me. He left desert flowers underneath my pillow with a tiny note that read, *Just because.*

Everyone thought I was the clueless new girl in the army, the girl who didn't like hummus and cited *Legally Blonde* during random scenarios, the girl who had a twelve-step skin-care routine in the morning and read the Goddess Rules at night, but none of them knew I was winning. I had snagged the most sought-after officer on the army base, and I was driving him crazy, causing him to risk his entire career for a chance to have sex with me, all with the help of a few measly dating rules.

When Liam told me to sneak my phone into the cafeteria during lunch, I did. While I was eating cornflakes with chocolate milk, my phone vibrated in my pocket.

LIAM: You look cute today.
LIAM: Hello?
LIAM: Ella.

I pretended to tie my army boot and tried to type under the table.

ELLA: Where r u?

Less than five seconds later, my phone buzzed with another text.

LIAM: That's it? I just complimented you, and I don't even get a thank you?
ELLA: Thnx.
LIAM: I'm in the bathroom thinking about how hard I'm going to fuck you tonight.

Tonight? Didn't I say I was going to think about it? When did he decide I had already made up my mind? I wanted to make Liam wait a little bit longer. I loved the power I suddenly gained, knowing he was waiting to fuck my brains out. The newbie soldier wasn't so helpless after all, was she? Plus, life in the army was already improving, although insanely slowly: Liam canceled my bathroom duty, switched my weekend guarding with a new soldier who just joined the unit, and didn't even think twice before making it clear to Commander Mia she needed to take it easy on me from now on.

"What are you doing under the table?" Anna asked me.

"*Shhh*, I'm texting him," I mouthed. She went back to eating silently with the rest of the soldiers.

"Relax," Anna said.

"If any other soldier or officers find out, Liam could lose his job," I said.

"I know, I know. Don't worry," she said.

A few minutes later, Liam walked into the cafeteria, his army uniform making him look ten times more attractive than he actually was. The girls at the table followed him with their eyes, and as he got closer to our table, they fixed themselves up, lifting their chins, pushing their shoulders back the way employees in an office do when their boss walks in.

> LIAM: Meet me behind the weaponry studio tonight at mid-
> night. I'm locking up, so I'll wait for you there, and we'll
> go somewhere else.
> ELLA: Is this your version of date night?
> LIAM: For now. But I'll make it up to you.

When Anna and the rest of the girls fell asleep after *shaat tash*, I kept myself awake until midnight thinking of what a future with Liam would look like. I let my mind wander, imagining cooking dinner for the two of us in a cozy apartment in New York City, after having been accepted to Columbia University for premed. Yet the image of us was blurry. Would Liam be happy in a country he had never stepped foot in, exposed to a culture he didn't know? Could our relationship even work outside of the army? Were our worlds too different to possibly integrate? When did our relationship go from a game we both played to something that suddenly seemed . . . real?

I felt like Cinderella, staring at the long hand of the clock above the army room door until it hit midnight. Crawling out of the top bunk bed, I slipped on one of the steps and fell on the floor, waking Rebecca up.

"Where the hell are you going?" she asked groggily.

"To pee," I lied.

She rolled over, unimpressed, and went back to sleep.

I snuck out of the room, clutching my gun against my chest and marching toward the weaponry. Tonight I was finally going to know what it felt like for Liam to run his hands through my hair, to lift me up against the wall and thrust into me. *If a guard stops me before I arrive,* I thought, *I'll say that my gun is broken and has to be fixed immediately, that going to sleep with a defective weapon is a danger to my own safety, and that I need to fix it before the weaponry closes. I had no idea I wasn't allowed to be out of the room after* shaat tash. I'd bat my eyelashes and lie. As I walked step after step through the desert sand, looking around at the pitch black that surrounded me, I began to feel a sort of courage I'd never felt before. Who was this girl, sneaking out in the middle of the night to sleep with her officer illegally, all while carrying a loaded weapon? In Connecticut, the most dangerous game I played was inhaling a can of Dust-Off in the high school parking lot with Julia before a football game until we were so dizzy we could barely walk. Back home, I was always surrounded by other people, by lights, by cars, by the subtle hum of the radio playing in the background. But here, there were moments when I was truly alone.

When I reached the weaponry, Liam had already turned off the lights and locked up. Where was he? I walked to the back of the building, peeking my head between two garbage bins. Could he have changed his mind? Suddenly, I felt a gravitational force scoop me up and sling me into the air. My stomach fell hard into Liam's shoulder.

"Liam!" I yelled, gripping his neck, worried he was going to drop me. "Put me down!"

"*Shhh!* Shut up!" he whisper-yelled. "Someone's going to hear us. Stop fighting it; you're not going anywhere, soldier."

I pressed my face against Liam's back as he carried me to his office building only a few feet from the weaponry. I smelled his scent and felt safe. I felt like I was home. While the rest of the soldiers and officers in the unit were fast asleep, our night was only beginning.

Once we reached Liam's office, he lowered my feet to the floor and shut the door behind us. I immediately started yelling at him, trying to push him out of the way so I could pretend to try to escape, but he leaned in closer to me and shoved me against the wall, grabbing both of my wrists with full force, pressing them hard above my head.

"Ella?" he said, looking at me with an intensity that made my heart beat erratically. I heard the click of the door lock as Liam pressed his chest against mine, the warm pressure of his mouth against my lips.

Despite the aggression behind his kiss, his tongue was soft and warm against mine, its texture like silk. I let myself drift off into his world, a universe I had no control over. Liam was the officer of our unit, the master of this relationship, the boss. And me? I was his weakness. A weakness so strong that it gave me the power to be in control.

Liam's lips made their way down to my neck when he suddenly released his grip on my wrist to slip his calloused hands under my uniform. He squeezed each breast desperately and then slowly unbuttoned my uniform shirt, exposing me. I looked down as his fingers traced each nipple and watched as he brought his tongue closer and closer to them. I was shocked at the moan that rushed through me when I felt his lips sucking each nipple slowly and then harder and faster until I grasped at his hair and pulled him closer to me, feeling the tug of his teeth against my breasts. Still attached to me, Liam pulled us both down to the floor of his office, my back rubbing against the cream Moroccan-style rug. Like our first handshake that night on the beach, I felt Liam's kiss in my entire body, and we both knew by the moans and the gasps escaping us that our bodies wanted more than our mouths could deliver. I felt Liam's grip against my thighs as he swung me on top of him. The way he stared into my eyes like some sort of wild animal gave me a feeling of power I had grown addicted to. The army degraded my sense of worth, of control, of agency, but no matter how hard it tried to take everything away from me, it could never take away my sexual power. I slipped my tongue deeper into Liam's mouth and led his fingers to my underwear, letting him feel the wetness seeping through.

"Don't move," Liam said.

"I love being bossed around by you," I answered. "Part of me is like, yes, please just tell me what to do so I don't have to think."

He started laughing, kissing my cheeks and my neck, touching the inside of my underwear with his fingers.

"I just feel safe and relaxed," I said, "knowing you can decide what I do and when. It's a relief, in a way. It makes me feel like I don't have to worry, like you're in control of everything and wouldn't ever let anything bad happen to me, you know?"

Liam stopped to really look at me. His face grew serious. "I love that kind of thing. I love the idea of taking care of you, of you needing my help. I think I have a thing about protecting or being a protector. It's in my blood. Like, if you asked me to lift a heavy piece of furniture or open a pickle jar for you, I'd probably fall in love with you."

"Fall in love with me? Already?" I smiled coyly.

"Don't look at me like that," he said, slipping his fingers into me. "I love when you look helpless like that; I just want to tell you what a good girl you've been."

"What if I'm not such a good girl?" I said. "Then what are you going to do?"

"Well, I'll have to put you over my knee and punish you." He gripped my hair hard, pulling me in for a kiss.

"I'll do whatever I'm told," I said. "I'll be whatever you want me to be."

"Don't be anything," he said. "Just be yourself."

He spread my knees wider on either side of him, and I didn't resist.

"Good girl," he murmured. "You're really being very good today."

"I'm very obedient when I want to be," I said. "Do whatever you want."

All of a sudden, Liam lifted me up, turned me over, and slammed me down against the rug, causing my head to hit the floor.

"Ouch!" I yelled, stroking the back of my head to calm the pulse racing through it.

Liam's expression turned from desperation to concern. "Oh my God, I'm so sorry—I didn't mean to!" He lifted me to a sitting position and rubbed the back of my head before starting to kiss it profusely. "You're so fragile . . . I was so excited . . . I'm sorry, Ella. I'm such an idiot—are you okay?"

"I'm fine," I said. "Except that you might have ruined our steamy moment, considering I feel like I'm going to have a bump the size of Mount Everest on my head by tomorrow."

I didn't think anything of the fact that Liam accidentally hit my head against the floor. Things happened during acts of sexual aggression, right? It wasn't like we were about to make love. This was a test for the both of us—well, for Liam, really, to see if after having a taste of me, he'd be "cured" of his desire for good.

"I don't know why I ever thought sleeping with you once would make me forget about you forever," Liam said. "I'm already addicted to your smell, and I haven't even entered you yet."

Wow.

He continued. "I have to tell you something else. That night you crawled in the mud while Commander Mia laughed? My heart broke. I couldn't sleep all night knowing I could have protected you from her and didn't. Nobody in my life has ever lived rent-free in my mind and refused to leave for a second the way you have. Since the moment I met you, five minutes haven't gone by without me thinking about you, about your smile, your ass, your boobs, your hair. But your mind . . . God. You're so much more than you think you are. I am so proud of you for being here, really, really proud of you for coming all the way from America and dealing with the army. I want to kiss you all the time. All the time. If I kissed you every time I had the urge to, you wouldn't be able to breathe. I'd smother you. This isn't easy for me. I'm worried, too."

In my most immaculate fantasies, I couldn't have imagined a speech like this one. I thought Liam was interested in exploring our options, but I didn't know he was already falling for me. His honesty only opened my heart to him more, and I slowly felt the pain on my head subsiding.

"Why are you worried? What is there to worry about? We don't have to tell anyone anything," I said.

Liam leaned in closer to me, his forehead against mine. "Because I don't recognize myself when I'm around you. You make me want to change. You make me want to be a better person. Different than what I am now. But what if I'm not enough for you? What if I can't change to become what you deserve? This whole thing is new to me. I can't remember the last time I've felt this way about anybody, and I just want to prove to you that I'm worthy of you. That I can do this."

Liam's eyes grew glossy around the rims, and I relished his vulnerability. I wanted to believe him, but since the day we met, he'd been adamant in making it clear that he didn't want anything serious, that he wasn't "the girlfriend type." What if I gave in to him only to find that after a week or a month or two he'd walk away and make my life in the army even worse?

"I don't know," I said, although inside I knew I wasn't going to let this chance slip away.

"What do you need me to do, Ella? How can I show you I'm serious about this? About us?"

"Don't fuck me," I said.

His eyes filled with disappointment that quickly turned to determination. "Okay, I'm okay with that. I can wait. I'll do whatever it takes," he said, standing up.

"Don't fuck me," I said again as I started to unbuckle his belt. Liam leaned his head back and let out a deep moan. "Don't fuck me," I said, looking up at him. "Make love to me."

"Stand up," Liam said as he helped me up. "Take off your clothes." I did. He stepped back and took a good look at me, even at my goosebumps visible in the harsh fluorescent office light. Even though we were already talking dirty to each other, my first instinct was to cover myself, but the smile that sprawled across Liam's face as he eyed me from my head to my toes made me feel like I didn't have to. "You're the most beautiful thing I've ever seen," he said, his boxers cradling his ankles, his abs even more defined in the light. Of course this light complemented him. How could it not? Liam stepped closer to me and put both hands on my shoulders to turn me around. He pressed his thumbs into my back and rotated them upward and then down. I felt the wetness between my legs slide down the side of my thigh. Liam continued to massage my neck and my back until I felt him grab my hair and hold it in a ponytail with one hand.

Liam turned me back around and led us to his office chair, where he sat down. I climbed on top of him, and he put both of his hands against my hips. I sat on him slowly and felt him glide inside of me, a surge of heat erupting in my body. With a newfound sense of energy, Liam lifted me up and down on top of him slowly, pushing me down hard with each thrust while sucking on each of my nipples. It felt like the first time a man had ever touched me. Ethan was a boy. But Liam— Liam was confident and sexual, intimate and mature. His hands were stable, his lips purposeful, his intention clear. In one final thrust I felt his neediness, kissing me everywhere, doing nothing but succumbing to my body unapologetically.

"Liam," I whispered. "My God, Liam."

"Ella," he moaned.

"Liam!"

I bit down against his neck to muffle the sounds that escaped my body after that, my entire being feeling the release of what we had been waiting for. For a second, I felt like I was going to faint, and suddenly the pulse on the back of my head sped up again. At the same time, Liam's body trembled as he pulled me down onto him one last time, groaning. His body jerked with his release as I felt him fill up inside me, breathing heavily into my ear.

"God damn it, Ella." Liam let out a deep breath and lifted me up off him, the cum spilling out and down my leg.

I began cleaning myself off with the tissues on his desk, and he did the same. After a few minutes, I said, "You never asked me if I was on birth control."

"Who cares? I'd make a baby with you," he joked.

I laughed. "First, falling in love and now baby talk already? It was that good?"

"I'm kidding," he said.

"Obviously," I said, "I can't go to med school at Columbia with a baby, can I?"

"You could; it would just be harder. Although I'd follow you there regardless," he said.

Whoa.

A few minutes after we were dressed, Liam walked me back to my room in silence. The energy between us said it all. Just as I was about to open the door, Liam whispered something in my ear, but I didn't hear it clearly.

"What?" I asked.

"You just might be the best thing that's ever happened to me," he said.

I fell asleep replaying the night over and over again. How could Anna be so cynical? How could someone not believe in love? Love was in the palm of my hand. Love was real.

At 5:20 a.m., the sky began to lighten, and I watched the sun peek through the army room window, casting a slanted shadow against the bunk beds. A soldier outside emptied the garbage bins. The sound of combat boots marched back from their midnight guarding session.

Another day.

Chapter 12

Two weeks before our flight to Tel Aviv, we took a family trip from Connecticut to Manhattan—my mother, my father, Natalie, Jake, Emma, and I took the train into Grand Central Station. I tried to ignore the tension, the feeling that something terrible was going to happen, that something would irrevocably bust open, leaving our family wounded until the end of time. I had an intense craving for a cigarette since smoking in the car with Julia each morning before school, but instead I stood in line with my mother at Starbucks, ready to burst.

"What do you want?" she asked me.

"Whatever you're having."

"A skinny vanilla latte is what I'm having," she said.

"So, a skinny vanilla latte."

I took a sip of that vanilla latte, and it came back up like the warm apple vodka I used to drink with Julia before parties, like the pills Ethan used to slip into my hand when we sat squished at the corner of the dirty couch at his older friend's frat house, Ethan's teeth biting his bottom lip as he looked at me.

It was hot in the city, and the white T-shirt I wore clung to my body from the heat. I wanted to get back early that day to make it to Julia's birthday party, which she was throwing while her parents were away walking along the Maldivian shore—and which would end up being raided by the police before the majority of people even arrived.

I wanted to throw up as we walked out of Grand Central to a waiting cab. My father opened the door for us and told the driver to take us to the Met, and while I sat there, the milk in my latte moved in lapping waves, and my father put his hand on mine. I loved the way it felt to have him on my side, to see him smile at me no matter what I did. We spent the morning strolling through the museum, my father teaching my mother about each painting, my mother nodding while he spoke, and me carrying a load of unexplainable anxiety on my shoulders and a sour look on my face.

We stood in front of Gustave Courbet's painting *Woman with a Parrot*, while Natalie, Jake, and Emma bickered with one another, the audio recording filling my ears like beer foam overflowing the glass. In that moment, I felt like the woman in that horrific painting. I was enraptured by it, the woman lying naked and helpless on her back against a white satin sheet, her hair disheveled, her face begging to escape this life.

"I don't want to go," I blurted out to my father—it just spilled out of me. "I'll kill myself if you take me to Israel."

And that's when my mother grabbed my wrist and pulled me in one swift motion toward her, and even though I was almost as tall as she was, I felt so small in that moment. Tiny, like the child I used to be when I'd slip into her bed in the middle of the night and nudge closer and closer to her until I was practically breathing her hair into my nostrils.

"*Ma yesh lach!* Don't you ever talk like that again! I never want to hear those words come out of your mouth again, do you hear me?" She took my shirt and bundled the fabric up into a ball in her fist. And I never mentioned it again.

I never mentioned to anyone that on late nights in the army after everyone was asleep, I'd walk to the shared bathrooms and turn the lights on, stare into the mirror and trace the dimensions of my cheeks, turn to one side and then the other, and ask myself, *Really, what am I doing here? What is the point? Where do I belong?* I was desperate to find out who I was, to reach down into the deepest parts of my soul and pull out the girl I used to know.

At this point in my life, the lowest point in my life, when the army had broken me down and turned me into nothing, there was Liam's strength, his tall body, his unexpected bursts of goodness, a discreet smile, a long, tight hug in the privacy of his office. In his arms, I felt like I belonged. Like I was home. I would do anything to preserve that feeling, to keep it safe. Anything.

It was a feeling I was addicted to. That was it. It wasn't just that I was falling in love with Liam, that I loved the way he smelled, the way he tasted, the complexity of his brain, the way he was in control; it was that he had chosen me. Out of all the girls in the unit—hell, all the girls in Tel Aviv, because he really could just walk alongside Rothschild, point to any girl, and choose one—he wanted *me*.

I felt like I was above average, like I was better than the other girls. I felt the way I felt back home. The other soldiers thought I was an American brat, but I had one-upped them all. On late nights when they talked about how sexy Liam was, how handsome he looked in his social media pictures, I sat around with them and smiled in my heart. *Mine. All mine.*

"Look, he has a little heart tattoo on his neck," Rebecca said, zooming in on the birthmark I had grazed my fingers against. While they fantasized about him, I got to live that fantasy.

"It's a birthmark," I said under my breath.

Chapter 13

Almost every morning, I'd wake up before dawn, the wind awakening me repeatedly throughout the night, smacking against the curtain door in loud bursts. I'd sometimes start crying, my teeth chattering, hoping one of the girls would lift her head from her pillow and ask me what was wrong, but they all slept so deeply or at least pretended to, and I was left alone with the silence.

Most days, I lingered in bed, my eyes heavy, and waited for my alarm to go off. I set it to Taylor Swift's "Our Song," a song that reminded me of summertime sunshine, but I had grown allergic to it, each note leading me closer to the day to come. The clock hit 5:20 a.m., and I watched as the other girls wriggled in their beds, looks of disdain already on their faces.

Up until pursuing a relationship with Liam, everything about my life in the army seemed like it was from a horror movie. I used to fantasize about running out of the trailer, calling my mom to pick me up, and hopping on a plane back to the city, back to normalcy. How could it be that life had the ability to spiral out of control so quickly?

But today . . . today was different. Today, I was no longer alone. I had him.

"Ella, your bed smells like flowers, and it's giving me a headache. Stop spraying your perfume all over the place," Anna said, snapping me out of my haze.

"It's not perfume; it's Diptyque room mist," I said.

"What is that?" Anna asked.

I read from the back of the spray bottle: "'A berry-tainted room spray that makes any room a livelier and more vibrant place.' And this room could use some liveliness, don't you think?" I laughed.

"Someone woke up on the right side of the bed this morning," Anna said to Rebecca, gesturing her head toward me.

Suddenly Commander Mia barged in, parting the curtain door. "Up, up, up, ladies!" She motioned her hand up and down. "Seven minutes on the clock to mop these floors."

I hopped off the bunk bed and slipped into my newly fitted uniform. Anna threw a stick at me, one that looked like a broom with a window cleaner at the bottom of it. I looked at her blankly.

"So what's up with you?" Anna said as we mopped. "What's with the smile? Did anything happen last night?"

"What?" I said, blushing.

Anna looked at me suspiciously. "You're humming Taylor Swift songs, and you haven't even had your coffee yet. Very weird." Anna's eyed widened. "Did you guys do it?" she whispered. Light bulb moment.

I side-eyed her mischievously. "That, my love, is none of your business."

Anna watched as I mopped the floors, the water slapping against the ceramic tiles. "For someone who's never done this before, you're not half bad," she said.

When you're falling in love, nothing seems all that bad. Not even mopping floors.

That evening, as I stood in line at the cafeteria for lukewarm chicken soup, Liam crept up behind me. Before I even heard him, I knew he was there just by his smell—Burberry cologne mixed with smoky oak again.

"I can't stop thinking about last night. Meet me at the guard post at 2:00 a.m. I know it's late; I'm sorry," he said, his face stone-cold, in case anybody was looking at us. "We need to talk."

"Are you sure it's safe?" I asked him, thrilled.

"I'm sure. And it's not a request, soldier. It's an order," Liam said and walked away.

———

When the clock hit midnight, it was officially my twentieth birthday, not that anyone had a clue. The other girls were asleep. I zipped up my army coat and checked the alarm—1:32 a.m. I hadn't slept a minute since getting into bed, even though my eyes were so tired they burned. I tossed and turned, imagining what I was going to say to Liam. The Goddess Rules told me to play hard to get, to let him chase me, but what if I tried being honest? My feelings for Liam were maximizing by the minute. *I want to be with you. Let's try to make this work. I won't tell anyone if you don't.*

I sneaked out of bed, the bunk ladder creaking between each step. If anyone saw me, I would say that I had a medical problem: sleepwalking. It happened at home, I'd tell any officer who stopped me. I had practiced a zombie stare in front of the mirror before going to sleep that evening.

I stepped out of the trailer, the wind hitting my cheek, and walked in the darkness toward the guard post. The stars were bright against the blackness of the sky.

When I arrived at the guard post, I had to climb something like thirty steps to reach the top. Liam stood facing me, gripping the handle of his gun. I couldn't see his face yet; my eyes hadn't fully adjusted to the darkness, but the outline of his broad shoulders was unmistakable. My gift from God, the man sent to protect me.

"Hey," I said.

His eyes lit up. We were finally alone, looking down on everybody through the watchtower.

"Come here," he said, motioning me closer. "I know I said having sex with you was going to cure me of wanting you, but it's only made everything worse. I want more of you, every day, all day, Ella."

We sat down together, talking, snacking on a bag of Bamba, while the muffled sounds of the radio were like a relaxing white noise behind us. There was something soothing about being so high above ground, as though we were on a different level than everybody else.

Liam cleared his throat. "I love it out here, you know? It reminds me of the nights I used to go out with my friends up North. We'd walk home drunk, looking up at the sky. I used to count the shooting stars. I did that here, too, while I waited for you. I counted five in the past half hour."

"I've never seen a shooting star."

"Come here," Liam said again, patting his lap. I sat on him, trying to push against my heels so my weight wouldn't be uncomfortable for him.

We looked out of the guard post up at the sky, watching the stars, as Liam inhaled the space between my ear and my neck. He'd brought a portable speaker with him and now played John Legend's song "All of Me."

"I love this song," I said.

"It's one of my favorites," he said. "Whenever I come out here in the middle of the night to guard, I play music and think about my mother. I picture her sitting in her hospital bed looking out the window at the stars, the beeping of the machines the only sound keeping her company. Since I'm not there, we're both looking at the same stars from different places. At least I'm protecting her in another way, you know?"

"How does the Alzheimer's affect her? Does she remember you?" I asked, careful not to offend him.

"Sometimes. Usually she'll look at me with a blank stare until I try with every cell in my body to remind her that I'm her son. I tell her bad jokes and show her videos of us on my phone. She's had Alzheimer's bad for almost seven years now. The doctors say she's an anomaly. They don't know how she hasn't lost her memory completely. I know it's harsh, but that's what they say. For now, it's like a chronic illness she carries. It's funny, though, because she used to be so bright and happy. She would dance and sing and carry my little brother on her hip and take videos of him. But a few years before my parents divorced, she got sick, and while I know I can't blame anyone, I still do. I blame my father."

I looked into Liam's eyes, the specks of yellow visible even in the dimness. I wanted to let him lean on me, too, to give him a break.

"For years he would treat her like shit, telling her she was a good-for-nothing dumb bitch whenever he was mad. That had to have some sort of effect on her brain. Then he would apologize after throwing plates and slamming doors and terrorizing our home. He'd come out to the kitchen while my mom cleaned up the mess, and he would start helping her clean up, too. I didn't think anything of it, though. I was used to it, you know? But whenever they fought, the spark in her eyes dimmed. Sometimes it even turned off. Even back then, I promised myself I would never be like him."

"Yeah, I used to think my parents had a flawless love, too, until I got older and realized that there was no such thing."

"You think they've dealt with deep shit, too?"

"I do. Not like your family, but still. Each family deals with their own shit. I know my mother puts up with too much, and it pisses me off. At the same time, though, I admire that about her. I admire the way she puts herself last. I don't know how she does it."

"That's what mothers do. That's what wives are supposed to do. My mother is the same way now, but she didn't used to be like that. She learned to park her car outside and leave the parking spot in the garage for my dad when he got home from work."

"I don't know if that's what mothers and wives are supposed to do. They should be able to put themselves first sometimes. Don't you think?"

"She did. Trust me. She was a stubborn one, and she knew how to drive my dad crazy. She always wanted us to have Friday night dinners together, and one time, my dad was watching soccer. I think it was Real Madrid against Barca, something good, and she kept asking him to turn it off and come eat before the food got cold, but he was so into the game he just ignored her. She got so mad she marched into the living room and turned off the TV.

"I thought my father would laugh it off or whine or tell her to turn it back on, but instead he grabbed the remote from her hand. There was this darkness that enveloped the house—I was used to it already, to the feeling of my stomach dropping like that," he drooped low and back up again, "and right there in front of me and my brother and sister, he backhanded her and knocked her to the floor. He took the remote and started hitting her with it. I thought it was playful for a second because I hoped it was, and when she lifted her arm to protect her face, he hit her so hard with the remote that I heard the bone crack, and I knew her arm was broken. I heard it, Ella, and I didn't sleep that night because the sound of that crack played over and over again in my mind."

"Oh my God, no. What did you do? You just sat there watching him?"

"No, I got up off of the couch and tried to help her, but she didn't want me to see her like that. She just said, 'I'm fine, I'm fine. It's just a stupid fight; go to your room,' but I didn't. My father was going to kick her even afterward—I knew him—but my brother and I rushed over to help her, and he dropped the remote, went to the bedroom, and slammed the door. Her arm was deformed, and I could see the redness in her cheek where he hit her. My brother and I took her to the hospital, and my dad showed up the next day with a bouquet of red roses—his way of saying sorry.

"For a month after that, he was the best dad in the world, winning the fucking number-one dad award. He took us all out for dinner, bought my mom flowers. We played cards in the living room and watched movies. It was the best month of my life. And then it happened again. Want to know the worst part? I was happy it happened again. Can you believe how sick that is? I was happy because it meant that my father would be nice after that, and we would be a family again. It meant he would spoil us all, especially her. I think somewhere inside my mother, she was happy when it happened again, too."

"Yeah," I said. "That's fucked up."

"I never open up like this. I don't know what it is about you, Ella, but I know it's trouble."

Liam lit a cigarette. I took a drag from it to show my solidarity. But when I went to give it back to him, he told me to keep it and lit a new one.

We sat there without talking for a few minutes; the silence was comfortable.

"Oh, look at that." Liam pointed to a shooting star. "Your first one. Make a wish."

Please let him fall in love with me.

Liam reached into his pocket and pulled out a small box.

"Happy birthday," he said.

How did he know? I didn't tell anybody. "What? How—"

"I have all your records from the polygraph test. I know that the first time you ever smoked weed was in ninth grade during a lifeguarding shift with Julia. I know you live in Tel Aviv, that you moved here from Connecticut, that you drive a red Mini Cooper. The week after you enlist, they release all your information to the officers. I have all of it, the documents, the videos, everything. I'm your officer, remember? You can't hide shit from me," he said, laughing.

I was simultaneously impressed and a little creeped out.

I opened the box, and inside was a double heart-shaped pendant on a thin gold chain. The hearts were intertwined, the two becoming one. Liam moved my hair and clasped the necklace around my neck. We weren't allowed to wear jewelry in the army, but I had a feeling my officer wouldn't mind.

I leaned into Liam, my face nestled into his neck. "Thank you," I whispered.

We sat there quietly together, and I decided in that moment he was the one. This was the man I wanted to spend the rest of my life with. *The love of my life is right here, at the Mifrasit Army Base, and he's been waiting for me this whole time.*

"I want to meet your mother one day," he said after a few minutes of silence. "Your father, too."

"What about this weekend? There's a big family dinner at our house."

Liam's demeanor softened, and he said, "They'll never accept some poor guy from the North. But we can give it a shot," he said.

My heart dropped when I looked into Liam's eyes. All this time, he never failed to show me his strength, and with one sentence, his walls broke down, and I could see how insecure he was.

"Are you kidding me?" I said. "You don't know my parents. They'll love you."

I was officially twenty—an age that had always held a special and slightly terrifying resonance for me. It sounded like a number that would take forever to reach, like a castle in the clouds.

But here I am, twenty years old, really and truly grown up, I thought. *Am I the right kind of twenty-year-old? Have I reached the necessary milestones to make me a successful girl in my twenties?*

As I walked back to my trailer, I realized I was lucky and not just for obvious reasons. I was lucky to wake up and pour instant coffee under my tongue, the taste so bitter I had to stop myself from gagging. I was lucky to be able to call my mom from the base, crying a little extra to feel her sympathy. I was lucky to have my entire life ahead of me, to make mistakes, to reach my goals. I was lucky for all of that, because it meant that I was alive, and being alive meant that I was officially and absolutely falling in love.

Chapter 14

The day Liam met my parents, he showed up with my father's favorite twenty-one-year-aged whiskey and a white orchid for my mother.

"You're sure she like orchids?" Liam had asked for the hundredth time.

"What are you so worried about? They're going to be obsessed with you."

Liam walked through the door, my heart beating as we waited for my mother to greet us. She held her arms out to hug him, and I relaxed as soon as his charisma lit up the living room. Liam's laughter was contagious, and while my father had a tough demeanor, he smiled whenever I smiled, and I knew he could get used to the idea of me dating Liam.

Liam was awed by our apartment—the three balconies, the maids, the pool table, the hot tub—and as the night drifted by, Liam's subtle bursts of affection became more frequent. He held my hand under the table and squeezed my butt when no one was looking. As shallow as it was, coming from a well-off family gave me a sense of confidence around Liam, and I felt like he had fallen in love not only with who I was but also with his potential future. We snuck into the kitchen to take a shot of the whiskey, and right before he threw it back, he put his arm around my waist.

"You look so good," he said. "Skinny and small. My Tiny."

Liam even had a new nickname for me: Tiny.

Outside of the army, Liam was different. He was no longer worried anyone would catch us. He let himself fall into the relationship we were building and made me feel like I was the most precious gift he'd ever owned.

———

"I just want to see you happy. That's all I care about," my father said as we stood outside on the balcony that night at dinner. He poured me a glass of Miraval. My father always chilled the wine glasses for a few minutes in the freezer before opening a fresh bottle of rosé, and I was falling in love with a guy who didn't know the difference between dry wine or semi-sweet. Liam was inside complimenting my mother on her *maamoul* cookies, her eyes lighting up as she looked up at him. I *was* happy. When I was with Liam, it didn't matter if I was in Israel or in the United States. In his arms, I was home.

Time moved in fast bursts; weeks in the army sped by, weekends even more quickly. Our relationship, which may have started off slowly, skyrocketed after Liam met my parents, and it was as if army life and real life had no correlation. Liam introduced me to his mother and siblings, talked endlessly about moving in together, and gave me a key to his Tel Aviv apartment the army paid for. On Friday nights when Liam was stuck at the base, I visited his mother at the hospital alone, looking through old photo albums on her hospital bed of Liam as a baby.

"He's tough on the outside—always has been," she'd say. "But I can see that he loves you. He's chosen you. Don't take it lightly. He hasn't brought a girl home in years. You must be pretty special, young lady." After a brief silence, she looked at me and said, "He's such a good man. Nothing like his father."

———————

It took six months for Liam to introduce me to his father, the father who beat his mother when they were young, the primitive Moroccan I had already made preemptive judgments about. I had no interest in building a relationship with him. According to Liam, I hadn't yet had the chance to meet his father because he was away on business in Bucharest selling handmade jewelry, but Liam's mother insisted that her ex-husband was "screwing whores and gambling his savings away."

Yet when Liam merely mentioned him, his entire demeanor changed to one of intense respect, and I knew that Liam's father was his father, and Liam loved him no matter what.

"My dad's landing from Romania at 3:00 a.m. today, Tiny. I have a unit meeting tomorrow morning, so I have to be at the base by 7:00. I'll be dead tired. You go, okay? That way you can meet him for the first time, bond during the ride, whatever. Don't worry about coming in late—I'll say I gave you permission to go to a doctor's appointment."

"Wait—I don't even know him. Pick him up from where? At 3:00 a.m.? And then drop him off where?"

"Drop him off at his house. What's the big deal? It's practically on the way to the base," Liam said, propping himself up on the headboard of my bed. "What? You don't want to? You know I have a problem asking for help. I finally feel comfortable enough with you to ask for something, to take some of this weight off of my shoulders, and you give me that look?"

"You can take a spoiled princess out of America . . . ," I tried to joke, but Liam's face had transformed to darkness again. It was a stone-cold front I couldn't break through, no matter how hard I tried to melt it away with warmth.

I calculated the time I'd have to spend picking his father up. First, drive to the airport, which was half an hour away, at 2:30 a.m., and then drive the old geezer to his house, which was another hour and a half away from the airport. From there, I'd have to drive all the way back to the base and start the week tired and spent. It was something like a four-hour ride. There is a special place in hell for people who insist on being picked up from the airport.

"Baby, listen," I said, my voice as gentle as I could make it. "Couldn't he just take a cab? I'd be happy to meet him like a normal person when we come home for the weekend. Not alone in a car in the middle of the night like his freaking chauffeur."

"This is important to me," Liam said. "If you want to be a selfish bitch about it, I'll ask my brother to pick him up. If you want to help me the way I've been helping you for the past almost, what, year, I'd appreciate it," he said, getting out of bed, his Hugo Boss boxer briefs hugging his bubble butt. Liam stepped into the bathroom and closed the door, the sound of the shower water muffling my thoughts.

Whoa. Selfish bitch? My heart fell to the floor, and I felt like Liam had smacked me across the face. Then, another thought. *Maybe I am being a little bit selfish. If this is that important to Liam, I'll do it. Relationships are about compromise, aren't they?* I didn't have the energy to argue with him; we had the entire week to spend together at the base. *Be smart, not right.*

The shower water stopped splashing against the ceramic floors abruptly. I knocked on the door. "Babe, it's fine. Of course I'll pick him up; all good."

Liam didn't answer, but when he walked out of the bathroom, the steam rushing out from behind him, I noticed his face soften and felt a wave of relief wash over me.

That night, or technically that morning, my alarm woke me up at 2:00 a.m., and I looked over at Liam, his mouth half-open, drooling beside me. After getting dressed, I made myself a cup of instant coffee and poured it into a to-go cup, surprised to find my father sitting at the edge of the couch in the living room. As soon as we closed the door behind us, Liam and I were so wrapped up in our own world that I sometimes forgot I was still living with my parents.

"Where are you going, sweetie?" he asked when he saw me walking down the stairs. He was wearing his United Polaris Business pajamas, the free set all business passengers receive on the plane. He looked spent, but aware, like he was desperate to fall asleep but couldn't.

"I'm going to pick Liam's father up from the airport," I said, rolling my eyes.

"It's much too late for that," he said. "You're a princess. You should be sleeping. How can he ask you to do something like that for him?" He looked at the clock. "Now?"

I nodded.

"I can pick his father up for you. You want me to? Go back to sleep, my love. I can't sleep anyway."

"No, it's okay, Aba. I have to pick him up and meet him for the first time, or whatever, and straight from there I'm going to the army," I explained.

"That's an all-nighter. When do you intend to sleep? What is this? You're acting like a wet rag, letting this guy drain and step on you. I don't like it."

I had no interest in listening to another one of my father's lectures. If I listened to my father's advice, I'd be single forever.

"Daddy, it's fine; I want to," I lied, closing the front door behind me.

In the car, my eyelids drooped; I almost missed the exit and had to swerve to make it. When I drove into the terminal, I waited in the arrival parking area, looking for Liam's father. From afar, an overweight, bald man waved at me. I waved back, until the look on his face turned to aggravation.

Oh, I'm such an idiot. He isn't waving to say hi; he's waving me over to him.

I drove to where he was standing with his single, maroon-colored suitcase and stepped out of the car to greet him. *Fuck my life*, I thought as I plastered a fake smile on my face. When I went in to hug him, he didn't even squeeze me back.

"I have a bad back—can you lift this into the trunk?" he asked without even saying hello.

Um, hi? I turned away to hide the surprise on my face. I was used to people helping me with my luggage, not the other way around.

Liam's father plopped into the passenger seat as I lifted his suitcase into the back of my red Mini Cooper, pushing and turning it to fit, the chilly after-midnight air encompassing me. In the car, he asked for a bottle of water, which I didn't have, considering I wasn't a professional Uber driver.

"You don't think someone wants to drink something after a long flight from Europe?" he asked me, completely serious. I didn't answer.

After a bit of small talk, he fell asleep in the passenger seat, his mouth slightly open while his tongue bobbed up and down with each breath. He looked just like Liam did that morning when I looked over at him in bed beside me.

I had already planned topics of conversation for the car ride— his father's work trip, his favorite breakfast food, Liam's army accomplishments—but his father barely looked at me, as if I actually were a taxi driver and not his son's girlfriend. I was secretly relieved.

When I dropped him off at his house, the sun was already starting to come up, and I didn't get out of the car to help him with his luggage. *Fuck this guy.* I looked down at my nails and examined them closely. I needed a new manicure, but more than that, I needed the feeling of quiet, sitting in front of the manicurist and listening to her gossip about me to her coworker in her native language. Liam's father didn't even wave goodbye before unlocking his front door and closing it behind him.

I drove to the army base, which took a little under two hours, checking my phone for a text from Liam to make sure I made it across half of the country in the middle of the night alive. Nothing. With just enough time to shower and no time to sleep in between, I met Liam and the rest of the soldiers at the cafeteria for lunch, my hair still wet. I tried to make eye contact with Liam, to look for the subtle smile he usually gifted me with, but he didn't look at me.

During lunch, I snuck up behind him in line at the cafeteria.

"Hi?" I said.

"My dad said you were a fucking snob," he whispered.

I started laughing. "I picked him up in the middle of the night, dropped him off in the middle of nowhere, and he tells you I'm a snob? He was asleep the entire ride!" I whisper-yelled. "I don't think he looked me in the eye once! I was his chauffeur."

"I'm just telling you what he told me. Sorry that you aren't used to doing any favors for anybody else. That's what a favor is. It's doing something you don't necessarily want to do. But you wouldn't know that because you don't do favors; people do them for you," he said, plopping mashed potatoes on his paper plate. "Isn't that right, soldier?"

"Oh, please, Liam," I said, half-sarcastically, half-pleading. Tears filled my eyes within milliseconds. I was already exhausted at the mere thought of arguing with him.

"It isn't sexy when you cry," he said.

Lately, whenever I'd react with emotion, Liam loved to point out how unappealing it was to him. I wanted everything to be okay, for my life to feel balanced and steady. Since when did my own happiness rely solely on whether or not Liam was angry with me?

————

During my junior year at Greenwich High School, we had Career Fair Day. Students would walk along the front lawn of the school, strolling from booth to booth and contemplating what career path to take. The teachers didn't actually expect us to choose our careers right then and there, but for some reason I felt like I had to. I chose medicine. Part of the reason was probably because my father was a doctor, another because I could solve complicated calculus equations in my head, and the other part must have had something to do with the fact that the doctor booth was flooded with a group of fresh-faced young doctors in green scrubs. As I made a beeline for them, I noticed that there was only one female doctor among the handful of men. While I cared that there probably weren't enough female doctors in the field of medicine, and I knew that if I became a doctor, I could help change that, I also especially cared that choosing this career path would mean that I would be surrounded, at least most of the time, by men. So I decided that I wanted to be a doctor.

Or maybe I just wanted to date a doctor.

My father insisted I get a taste of the medical life before committing to pursuing it, so I spent the summer between junior and senior year volunteering in the oncology wing at Yale New Haven Children's Hospital, reading to sick children in the playroom and shading inside the lines of their coloring books as they stood behind me braiding my hair and peeking over my shoulder only to tell me what colored pencil to use next. Whenever I'd bump into a young doctor on my way to the bathroom, I'd eye his left hand stealthily, searching for a wedding band that was almost always there. While I didn't have any luck finding a doctor boyfriend that summer, spending my days in a hospital and tending to other people had opened my eyes to what actually mattered in life, *whatever that meant*. I stopped fighting with my little brother over the remote control, and I let my sisters use my straightener whenever they wanted without asking.

On tough days at the hospital, it was sometimes too overwhelming. It was too much for me to watch the mothers grow grayer as their children became sicker with each week that passed, and I used to spend lunch breaks in the bathroom hyperventilating with selfish anxiety that this monstrous disease would, God forbid, creep up on me. But the reward of coming home and plopping on the couch with my father as he cracked open a beer, eager to hear about my day, made me feel like we shared a secret language my siblings and mother didn't understand. As a physician, my father knew what it felt like to be exhausted, surrounded by the cold, minty smell of the hospital rooms, and to simultaneously long for the power that came with wearing scrubs, of being on the other side, of catching the desperate gazes of the patients and their families and realizing that in their eyes, you, and maybe God, are their only hope. Even though I was light years away from being a doctor, that summer, I had grown one step closer to my father, and no matter how difficult the career path I had chosen was going to be, it was all worth the way he'd squeeze my arm and lean into me to whisper, "My crown jewel."

My plan was to graduate high school, complete four years of premed at Columbia University, take the MCAT exam, and become a doctor.

There's a Hebrew proverb my mother always said whenever somebody talked about future plans: *Ha-adam metachnen tochniot,*

Elohim mzachkek tchokioit—"People make plans while God sits back and laughs."

————

It took a few days of the silent treatment, but Liam finally forgave me after I had apologized for what felt like the hundredth time for treating his father with "disrespect." Life in the army passed by, divided by weekends at home that I longed for like the first sip of coffee in the morning.

One day, I was guarding at the base with another soldier, and Liam was the officer on duty. Every few hours, he'd show up at the base and check each trailer office while the soldiers were upstairs sitting in a booth and watching the cameras. My shift was from midnight to four in the morning, and as I sat there watching Liam make his rounds, I imagined him busting into my booth, ripping off my clothes, and giving it all to me right then and there. In the middle of my daydream, the door creaked open, and there he was, a mischievous smirk on his face.

He didn't say anything. He just held my head in his big, calloused hands and kissed me, his tongue slipping into my mouth like it had always belonged there.

All the Goddess Rules I put into play before actually snagging the bachelor of the unit had worked. Every conversation we had circled around him; I never called him first—or even called him back when I missed his calls; I was always busy unless he asked me out days in advance, and I made him jealous by being extra friendly with his guy friends. Even though Liam didn't have a lot of money, he took me out on weekends to the sushi restaurant near his house where his best friend worked, and since we were far away from my Tel Aviv apartment, we didn't have to worry that anyone would see us. For months, we spent every minute out of the army together. I read Hemingway out loud to him in English, and he taught me how to change a tire.

That weekend, when we were both home, Liam called. "Come over—I want your help with something. Now." Liam was in one of his dangerous moods—excited but mysterious, and based on his risky text messages, I thought I knew exactly what he wanted. *I woke up so hard this morning. I can't stop thinking about you.* I showed up at his house an hour later wearing nothing but a black lace thong under a gray trench coat. When I walked in, I saw his roommate playing video games on the couch to my left.

"Let me take your coat," Liam said.

"I'm good," I said. I held the collar tightly so he wouldn't pull it off me. "Let's go to your room."

"Oh, okay. I like that." Liam rested his hand on my lower back. I hopped on his bed with the coat still on, waiting for him to close the door.

"I missed you," I said.

"I had a dream you were here, tied up and sitting in that chair"— Liam pointed to his desk chair in the corner—"waiting for me to wake up and fuck you."

"Well, what else happened in that dream?"

Liam's tone stirred something in me I didn't recognize. I flung open my coat for him to see what was underneath. Within seconds, I was looking down at Liam, his face buried between my legs. Unlike Ethan, he actually knew what he was doing, and as I slid into another universe, I remembered looking up at the ceiling and wondering what kind of unenlightened life I used to live before this.

When we were done, Liam crawled on top of me, kissing my neck until I pushed him away.

"Stop it," I said, even though I never wanted him to stop.

"Promise me something," he said.

"Okay." I would have promised him anything in that moment.

"Promise me you'll never touch yourself when I'm not around. I can't live without this body," he said as he traced my nipple. "I want to be the only one touching it."

In the car on the way home, waves of nausea engulfed me. I wanted to go home and clean myself up, to wash away the feeling of worthlessness that overwhelmed me.

I unlocked the door to our apartment, relieved to see I was alone. My parents were probably taking a walk on the beach; my siblings were still at school. I put my keys on the kitchen counter and opened the drawer underneath the dishwasher. The hidden drawer, I used to call it, where I hid a pack of Marlboros in the way back. I pulled out a cigarette, made myself a cup of instant coffee, and went to sit outside on the balcony. Below me, mothers pushed strollers alongside each other, stopping every so often to pick up the toys the babies threw on the ground. Cars honked, the sun cast shadows on bicyclists racing by, and life went on. So why did I feel like mine had stopped? I was alive, but inside I didn't recognize what my life had become. When I was finished, I went to the bathroom to brush my teeth and wash my face to get rid of the cigarette stench. My mouth was minty, but in my trachea and down into my lungs the cigarette's poison had infected me. Like the dirtiness I suddenly felt after being with Liam, taking a shower would clean me off externally, but inside, the smoke remained.

———

The following weekend, Liam and I decided to go for a picnic in a secluded corner of the park. Hidden from view, we could lean into each other freely without worrying about running into someone from the unit. After applying waterproof mascara and picking out my favorite white ruffled shirt with pink flowers, I couldn't wait to be alone with him.

Pick up sushi and we'll meet there? he texted. *I'll bring the Sancerre.*

I spent 340 shekels, almost one hundred dollars, on a few salmon avocado rolls, two miso soups, and a tataki tuna appetizer. As I walked from the restaurant to the Tel Aviv HaYarkon Park, my phone lit up with a text.

Actually, can you grab the wine on your way?

When I arrived at the park, my arms full of sushi and wine, Liam, shirtless, was lying on the blanket sunbathing. He spotted me and waved from far away.

"Well, look at you," I said as I stepped closer. "Prince Charming waiting for his servant to arrive, are we?" I joked, but surely he could feel the pang of annoyance in my voice. His smile disappeared.

For the next hour, I tried to make conversation while Liam sat next to me, his sunglasses on top of his head, the trademark trait of a true Israeli army officer, barely sipping the wine.

"You aren't eating?" I asked.

He shook his head silently, his lips pressed against each other, the sashimi already crusting on the edges from being in the sun.

"Did you put on sunscreen? The sun's really hot out here," I said after a few slow minutes passed while he sat with his back half-turned to me, looking away.

The afternoon crept by, but Liam kept quiet. He answered me with one-word sentences, never looking me in the eye. I wanted to grab his face and scream, but I didn't have the energy to argue. I hoped he would decide to get over it without making a big deal. I kept waiting for Liam to put his hand on my thigh, to notice that I regretted what I had said about him being a Prince Charming. At a certain point, I wondered what time it was, but the sluggish descent of the sun told me we had already wasted the day.

I observed the people passing us by, mothers picnicking with their children, turning their babies over for tummy time, fathers tilting their heads from their phones every so often to check on their kids. Along the boardwalk, teenage boys bicycled around, yelling cuss words over the loud yells of children playing. To the left of us was a couple lying on a blue plaid blanket, eating watermelon with Bulgarit cheese, leaning against each other without a care in the world.

Liam coughed into his fist, and I was transported back to the reality of our afternoon. This had started happening to me more and more often with Liam. I'd catch a glimpse of someone else's world, even just for a few minutes, before being jarred back into ours. I sat paralyzed, waiting for him to decide when we were going to leave. Since the first day of the army, my life had become a waiting game. I waited for kitchen duty to start, waited for *shaat tash*, waited for Liam to talk to me, waited for the week to fly by, waited for my army service to end.

"You are the most inconsiderate person I've ever fucking met in my life," Liam said so quietly I barely heard him.

My heart hurled against my chest.

"Do you know where I was before this? Do you really want to know?" he asked.

"I . . . I don't know." My heartbeat accelerated as the words jumbled between my tongue. I felt like I was constantly on edge, continually under investigation.

"At the hospital! At Assuta with my mother, holding her hand during her chemo." He lifted his wrist to show me the hospital bracelet. "And you come here like an entitled little bitch cracking jokes? What do I need this for? Who taught you how to act? You should be ashamed of yourself."

Stunned, I started apologizing profusely, as if it were partly because of me that his mother was going through chemotherapy in the first place. I put my hand on his forearm, his veins protruding. "No, no, I'm sorry. I—I had no idea."

"Yeah, well, that's because you don't give a shit about anybody except yourself. You're so wrapped up in your own life, in your sushi and rich people shit, that you forget about the problems in the real world. This right here," he said, gesturing toward us, "this is real life. Things aren't always easy; they're not always pleasant. People scream and fight and go through chemo. You're too young to know that, but life isn't all roses and butterflies. When we first met, I didn't want you, because I knew how much work I'd have to put in to make you better. I didn't know it would be this hard, though, Tiny."

I felt relief wash over me as he called me by my nickname, the last sentence laced with a hint of empathy. "I know . . . I could never imagine what you must be going through." I wanted the conversation to end before it took a wrong turn.

"Over time, you're going to learn that the world won't serve you on a silver platter," he said as he brushed his hands through his hair the way he did that first day on the beach. "You have to work for happiness. It doesn't just come. But you know what? That's why I know our relationship is going to survive. Because you're willing to put in the work, and so am I. There's nobody else I can trust the way I trust you. No one else I can be completely myself with. All I need is to fix you up a bit." He elbowed me jokingly in the ribs.

"And it starts with that shirt," he continued. "It makes you look cheap." He took a swig of the wine and leaned in to kiss me, the acidity of the grapes making me sick. Or maybe it was something else.

Liam snaked his hand up under my shirt, my favorite shirt, and circled my nipples slowly. He licked the side of my neck until he reached my earlobe and sucked gently, a familiar sense of want bubbling between my thighs. The fight was over, thank God, and although I was worried someone would see us, I felt relaxed that he didn't want to fight anymore. Liam slipped his tongue in my mouth with a confidence only he had, like he could control what would happen with my body. I longed for his authority, for the sweet relief of letting go. Suddenly, he pulled away and looked me in the eyes, his thumb in front of my ear, the rest of his hand gripping the back of my neck.

"These cheeks," he said, "these chubby little cheeks—I could just eat them." He pretended to snack on my cheeks, nibbling on them playfully and then sucking them, suctioning the skin between his lips so hard it hurt.

"Ouch!" I said, pushing him away. I put my hand to my cheek.

"Oh, come on, don't overreact, Tiny. It's just a cheek hickey. I'm sorry. You're so damn cute I got ahead of myself."

I pulled away. I opened the camera on my phone. On my cheek was a round, perfectly circular, dark purple bruise, the outline of Liam's lips visible on my soft skin. What was I feeling lately? I was so confused. On the one hand, I wanted Liam, and I wanted him to want me. I looked for his approval and wouldn't rest until I found it. On the other hand, a sense of anxiety followed me whenever I was around him, and I wanted nothing more than to escape it. I lived in a constant state of uncertainty.

"I want to go home," I said.

When Liam dropped me off, I hoped my parents were out. For the first time in a long time, I was afraid to see them. I wanted to lie in bed and watch *90 Day Fiancé* by myself, to turn my brain off and let it rest. Liam was only playing around, right? He didn't mean to hurt me. On the contrary, his love was so immense, so childish, that he could barely control himself. He accidentally kissed my cheek too hard. Big deal. He didn't know my skin was so sensitive, and he didn't know the strength in his kiss. Like a pit bull too strong for his own good, Liam had hurt me but not on purpose. Right? Why did I feel like he could have been more careful, like maybe it wasn't an accident?

I opened the front door and walked into the kitchen, where my mother was frying chicken schnitzels, her hair tucked into a shower cap so that the smell of frying oil wouldn't stick to it. My father sat on the couch reading the newspaper, and when he looked up to greet me, I smiled, put my hand over my cheek, and turned away.

"I'm so tired," I said and raced up the stairs. From my room I heard my parents talking.

"What's gotten into her, Maya?" my father asked.

"She's tired. She's still adjusting to the army. It isn't easy moving an American high school girl to this country. This isn't a normal situation."

"No, no, it's something else. She's been turned off. Even when she smiles, her eyes aren't smiling. They're turned off. I'm telling you. I know my daughter."

"She's fine, Ben."

The bedroom door creaked as I closed it, and without taking off my shoes, I fell on the bed. I nestled my head into the pillow, feeling the pulse in my cheek. Louie scratched and meowed against the door, sensing my pain, wanting to come in. I wanted him near me, too, to feel his purr against my heart, but I was too tired to get up.

I covered the bite with Chanel concealer, the thick one I used only for going out at night. I answered Liam's calls that weekend, since he'd freak out if I didn't, but I kept the conversations short. The energy I used to have, cracking jokes, working out, helping Emma with her math homework, had drained from me completely. All I wanted was to be alone. I kept a safe distance from my parents, never getting too close for them to notice my cheek. For the entire week at the army and even before bed, I applied layer after layer of the concealer so that nobody noticed.

But on Friday evening, during Shabbat dinner after two glasses of Chablis, I was eating chocolate Nutella babka with my father in the living room when he caught a glimpse of my cheek in the light. I looked down at the cake, the chocolate spilling over the edges. He lifted my chin toward him.

"Look at me," he said. "What is this?" He grazed his finger over the mark.

"It's nothing, Daddy. Liam was playing around and accidentally bit my cheek. I have really sensitive skin, though, like Mom. I can't even get a manicure, just a polish change most of the time. I bleed as soon as they cut my cuticles." I tried to make a joke of it, but as soon as my father realized Liam had done this to me, I could see in his eyes that he was no longer listening. His mind was working, and his face, like mine, was suddenly turned off. He tapped his fingers against the table, his eyebrows almost touching each other. His mouth frowned naturally, the edges of his mouth turning downward.

"Wake up! You have a purple bruise on your cheek! You have a bruise on your face. Wake up. Wake up," he said, again and again, like he was telling it to himself. He brought his hand to his mouth and, like always, started biting the space between his forefinger and his thumb.

"Stop that," I said, pulling his hand away from his mouth. "I'm fine; it was an accident! It's no big deal. Don't worry."

"I don't like that at all, sweetheart. No. I don't like that," he said. "Look at yourself."

When I went to sleep that night, I kept thinking about what Liam said about growing up with a silver spoon in my mouth. *Not everything in life is roses and butterflies.* I thought that accidents happened, especially something as minor as a cheek hickey. My father was overreacting, and I resented his constant need to shelter me from what he believed to be danger. Liam insisted that I needed to toughen up, and maybe he was right. Unlike him, I didn't know what it was like to pay my parents' rent, to live without checking the price tag.

My last day in the army ended as abruptly as it began. The commanders didn't organize a special ceremony; fireworks didn't explode in the sky; pink confetti didn't decorate my army room. Liam was busy commanding a new group of soldiers, while Commander Mia decided not to break the distance with us, so I was never exposed to her true face. Liam didn't break the distance with any of the other soldiers, although it was safe to say he and I had broken our distance long beforehand.

When I stood looking clueless, Commander Mia told me to drop off my uniform and gun at the main office and take a bus home.

"Good luck," she said, shaking my hand for the last time.

I couldn't believe it was actually over. The days felt long, but the two years I spent in the desert, crawling through mud, learning to shoot a gun, my body wrapped in Liam's arms, suddenly seemed like they had gone by in the blink of an eye. I didn't think I'd meet the man I'd fall in love with six thousand miles away from Connecticut, but whenever we were together, I felt safe. Protected. Loved to the bone. The army had broken me down and molded me into a soldier, and while being there was the hardest thing I'd ever gone through, for Liam, I would have done it all again.

Chapter 15

"You're gonna wear *that*?" Liam looked at me in the bathroom mirror. I ignored him, hoping he would change the subject. We were getting ready to celebrate my release from the army, but Liam had asked me not to invite Anna or Rebecca, as he still didn't feel comfortable being out with his former soldiers. This was, he insisted, a perfect opportunity for me to spend some time with *his* friends. I traced my fingers alongside my collarbone, my bare chest visible above the black Reformation sweetheart neckline top I was wearing.

We'd just had shower sex and were getting ready at Liam's apartment, when the green mold in the corners of the bathroom triggered a dry cough that I tried to subdue.

"What's wrong?" Liam asked. "Are you sick?"

"I'm fine; I think it's a reaction from the mold," I said, relieved.

"Oh, the mold is bothering you, Queen Elizabeth? I'm sorry this isn't Buckingham Palace."

I could handle a little mold, couldn't I? So what if there were barely any power outlets to plug in my Dyson Airwrap, which meant I had to blow dry my hair blindly on the kitchen floor. I hadn't expected Liam's apartment to be this dirty either; the visible centimeter of dust lining the windowsills was worlds away from Liam's spotless army office. The apartment was as unkempt as a typical bachelor pad, just without a hint of luxury. I'd spent the previous few hours cleaning the place, and Liam admired my willingness to roll up my sleeves and get to work, but it was more than admiration—it was expectation. If I was going to be his girlfriend, I needed to keep the house kept: *Cook and fold and clean until the house is spotless, but don't be a housewife.*

When I was around Liam, he made me feel like he was living life on a deeper level, with his bus card and worn-out Birkenstocks, and I wanted to reach those depths, too. I'd mop the floors the way the girls at the army had taught me, fold his laundry, revive the house with homemade cooking and scents of basil and oregano creeping down the hallways, and throw around sentences like "Put a sweatshirt on; it's cold in here," all while goosebumps lined my own arms.

"You're gonna wear *that*?" Liam said again.

"What's wrong with what I'm wearing?" I asked, my heart dropping. I slipped into a black lace thong and high-waisted bootleg jeans.

"You look like a whore," he said.

"Don't call me a whore," I said.

"I didn't call you a whore; I said that shirt makes you look like one," he said.

"What do you want?"

"It's the first time you're meeting my friends—don't you think you could be a little bit classier? Put a sweater on, for God's sake."

"I didn't bring a sweater with me."

He walked out of the bathroom for a minute and then returned.

"Here you go," he said, handing me a pastel pink-and-purple-striped turtleneck sweater.

"Seriously? It's not even cold out."

Liam ignored me, looking at his phone. "Shit, I don't have any battery. Can you grab the car charger on our way out?"

Ten minutes later we were out the door, and I spent the car ride to the bar scratching my chest from the cheap, prickly wool.

Liam held my hand as we walked into the Teder, an outdoor hipster bar in downtown Tel Aviv that served pizza and beer. The place was buzzing with young couples smoking hand-rolled cigarettes and gaggles of recently discharged army soldiers enjoying their newfound freedom. Two handsome young men sitting at the table to the right of the bar waved us over, their faces familiar to me. Where had I seen them before?

"Tomer, Danny, this is Ella," Liam said.

I put my hand out for them to shake, but they both went in for a hug. "So great to meet you; we've heard wonderful things," Tomer said, his beard grazing my cheek.

Liam ordered beers for the table, and I spent the majority of the evening listening to stories of how they used to sneak around their kibbutz, steal motorcycles in the middle of the night, and hide them in sand dunes for fun. Liam held my hand under the table and asked me every few minutes if I wanted anything else. I still felt, sometimes, like I had to pinch myself. Was I really Liam's *girlfriend* now? *The* Liam Levine? From the outside, we looked like the perfect couple. I was feminine and cheerful, he was strong and powerful, and he would protect me for life. With him, I hoped, nothing could ever hurt me.

Toward the end of the night, after a few drinks, the conversation shifted. We tilted our heads back in laughter at the story of how I found a cockroach's head in the rice at the army. I glanced at Liam for reassurance, but he gave me a pinched smile, the kind most Americans give a stranger when passing them on the street.

"Liam, you said she was pretty, but you forgot to say also smart, funny, charismatic," Tomer said, taking another swig of his beer.

"Oh, stop," I said, touching Tomer's shoulder. Liam didn't laugh.

"Must have been nice having big, strong Liam to protect you in the army, huh? Huh?" He nudged Liam with his elbow. I laughed.

"What are you laughing at?" Liam barked at me.

"Wait, wait," Tomer said, slurring his words a little bit now. "I gotta know. Did you guys fuck at the base?"

"I swear to God, Tomer, one more word, and I'll knock your teeth out," Liam said.

———

The energy in the car on the way back to Liam's apartment was as dark as a public library after midnight, haunted and still. I sat silently in the passenger seat of my Mini Cooper, glancing at Liam through the corner of my eye only to catch him staring straight ahead, his jaw clenched.

"What's wrong?" I asked.

He still didn't look at me. "You embarrassed me."

"How?"

"Laughing at all of Tomer's inappropriate questions? Touching his shoulder as if I'm not sitting right there? What were you trying to do? Flirt with him in front of me? I took you to meet my friends, not give them hope for a gang bang."

"I was just trying to be nice."

He laughed a wicked laugh. "Nice. Always trying to be nice. You might have put that sweater on, but you're still an American whore underneath it."

I sat there silently, the car jolting us forward. *Who the hell does he think he is?*

"Stop the car. I'm getting out," I said.

He pressed on the gas. "You know," he said after a few minutes of driving too fast, "I said you embarrassed me tonight, but really, you embarrassed yourself."

"Okay, Liam."

"Okay, Liam," he mocked.

"Can you stop the car already? I want to get out," I said calmly, my breathing speeding up.

"Can you plug in the car charger?" he asked, ignoring me.

I scrambled to find it. "Oh shit. I forgot it on the counter," I said.

Liam glared at me, his nostrils flaring. "Oh, come on, Tiny! Damn it!" he yelled as he smacked the steering wheel.

"It's not a big deal, Liam. Stop the car; I want to get out!" I yelled.

"I don't care what you want," he yelled, the echo of his voice lingering in the car. "You don't know the difference between a fuckin' phone bill and an electricity bill," he said. "You think you can tell me what's important?"

My hands were shaking. "Listen to what I'm telling you to do. Stop the car!"

I felt the car accelerate as the weight of Liam's foot pushed on the gas pedal again. He took his eyes off of the empty, pitch-black road and looked me in the eye. "Don't you *ever*," Liam enunciated each word clearly, "tell me what to do."

"I—"

And then, like an explosion, he screamed, "Do you hear me?" He slammed on the brakes at the red light.

"Liam! What the hell are you doing?" I yelled back as my seat belt stiffened against my chest with the abrupt stop.

"You said stop the car, didn't you?" he said, his voice suddenly quiet and steady. I heard the click of Liam's seat belt as he put the car in park, opened his door, got out, and slammed it.

My reflection in the window was that of a woman. It was as though I had aged ten years since meeting Liam. I felt again like the woman in Courbet's painting at the Met, *Woman with a Parrot*. Except I was not just the woman—I was the parrot, too. Liam's parrot. I wasn't the girl

I was used to staring at in the mirror. It was as if this night had already scraped off a few good years of my life, and the anxiety creeping up into my chest was beginning to plant deep roots, endless roots, spiraling around and around the coronary arteries supplying blood to my heart. Was this the life I wanted for myself?

Liam's image shrank as he walked farther and farther away from the car in the dead of night, and I sat there feeling, all of a sudden, like I had done something terribly wrong. And then I started feeling bad. Really bad. *Maybe I was too harsh with him. I must have been if he just up and left like that. How could I have forgotten that stupid charger? If only I was a little less forgetful, this whole fight could have been prevented. Why did I put my hand on Tomer's shoulder? What was I thinking?*

The more I thought about it, the worse I felt. I called Liam. He didn't answer. I called again. He didn't answer. Instead of jumping into the driver's seat of my own car, driving home, and leaving him to walk all the way to his apartment by himself, I started to cry. I didn't understand why I was crying; I just knew that an unbearable feeling had come over me. I would do anything to make things right.

I didn't want to end the night like this. I knew I wouldn't be able to fall asleep. The anger that bubbled up within me wasn't directed at Liam; it was directed at myself. How could I have been so stupid? I wasn't a fighter. Even in high school, I preferred to apologize first and prevent a fight than to stand my ground and deal with one, and Julia fought for me most of the time. Finally, as I sat glued to the passenger seat, dialing Liam's number over and over again, he answered.

"What?" he said quietly.

"Liam, where are you? I'll pick you up. Come on, let's . . . let's just be done with this stupid fight. Let's go to sleep."

"I need time to think."

I refused to get off the line, and after ten minutes of persuasion, Liam agreed to get back into the car.

He didn't speak a single word. He was giving me the silent treatment. I had grown up in a house where the air was clear; it never crackled with the unsaid. If something—anything—was wrong, my family and I addressed and resolved it. I tried to get a word out of Liam, but he refused to even look in my direction.

When we arrived at Liam's apartment, we brushed our teeth in silence. I heard the running water splash against the sink and the bristles of Liam's toothbrush scrubbing aggressively against his teeth. *Spit. Brush. Spit. Brush. Spit.* I waited for him in bed.

"Liam, you're scaring me," I said.

He looked at me, and I didn't recognize his expression. I was confused by what happened from the beginning of the night until now, but still, I wanted to fix things. Fix him. Fix us.

Liam crawled into bed and picked up my phone, which I had placed on the nightstand beside him. "Funny thing," he said, "and all this time, I'm thinking, Ella's loyal; she's not one of those sneaky bitches I'm used to dating. She's too innocent for that. She doesn't hide things from me."

He unlocked the code to my phone, although I'd never explicitly told him what it was, and opened Instagram.

"You've been friends with Tomer this entire time. You knew exactly who he was and what he looked like, but you made me look like an idiot when we walked into the bar, looking for him and Danny as if you didn't already recognize Tomer's face, as if you haven't probably, I don't know, fucking masturbated to his pictures," he said.

"You're nuts," I said and turned my back to Liam. A vague memory drifted back into my mind. "You know what, I think Tomer stopped to ask for my number on the boardwalk weeks ago when I went for a run.

I gave him my name, and he added me on Instagram. He probably tried his luck with fifteen other girls that afternoon." The atmosphere in the room shifted to ice, and two thoughts went through my mind.

He's done with me.

Or he's going to hurt me.

I felt Liam throw the blanket off and get up out of bed. He walked toward the door.

He's leaving?

How stupid was I? Why did I accept Tomer's friend request to begin with?

I jumped out of bed and stood at the entrance of Liam's bedroom door, but he pushed me aside and raced down the hallway to the front door of the apartment.

"I have to go," he said, "before I do something stupid. Let me go, Ella."

He ran down the stairs, practically galloping, skipping steps, but I ran after him, my Victoria's Secret black silk pajamas swaying with each step.

"Wait, Liam, please, wait a second," I said as I caught up to him on the landing of the third floor. I pulled his shirt with everything in me and shoved myself in front of him. He grabbed both of my shoulders and pushed me out of the way.

———

"Don't move," Liam said. I felt the coldness of a wet hand towel dabbing the top of my cheekbone. "I'm almost done."

We were back in Liam's apartment, and his touch felt soothing in contrast to the sting I felt on my face and elbow. I tried sitting up, but Liam pushed me back down gently. "Tiny, please, you fell. Let me help you," he said.

"Help me with what?" I stared up at the ceiling, the harsh light too bright. *Where was I? What the hell just happened?* My lips were pounding, and as I brushed my tongue against them, I tasted something metallic. Blood.

"You really hurt yourself," Liam said. Our eyes met. His were filled with concern and a hint of lingering anger.

I closed my eyes again. *Why is he angry?*

Tomer.

The charger.

The friend request.

The stairwell.

The shove.

You really hurt yourself.

But I didn't hurt myself.

He hurt me.

He pushed me.

"You hurt me," I said, and suddenly, saying it out loud made it all feel real. My body hurt, but it was nothing in comparison to what I felt inside.

He started pacing the bedroom, nervous. "You're okay, Tiny," he said. "We'll be fine."

"You hurt me," I said again, the thought repeating itself in my mind.

How did I end up bloodied on the floor of Liam's apartment?

How could this happen to me?

What the hell is happening?

"You hurt me," I said.

"You fell down the stairs," he said quietly. "Go ahead and call your daddy to help you. I'm sure he doesn't know what a liar his little princess is."

When we got into bed, Liam turned his back to me, and I fell asleep with my pillow soaked in tears.

I woke up the next morning to a deep pulsing sensation in my cheek and Liam's hand groping my ass. I had barely opened my eyes when he started kissing my neck and cheeks. He turned me toward him and looked at me lovingly.

Is this a dream? A nightmare? Had I imagined the whole thing?

I looked at him. "No, like, seriously, what the fuck, Liam?"

"What?" he said.

"Something horrible happened last night. Don't you understand? I can't . . . we can't," I said, crying for myself, for our relationship. "Now you're just acting like everything is okay?"

"Oh, come on, Tiny, don't be so dramatic. You fell. It's all going to be okay," he said, kissing my cheek gently, running his hand along my hair. "What's in the past is in the past." He slowly slipped off my pajamas and lifted himself on top of me as I sat there lifelessly, tears rolling down my cheeks. He didn't stop, and something in me didn't want him to.

"I love you," he said for the first time. "I love you; I love you," he said over and over again as he thrust deeper inside of me.

I hugged him closer to me and sobbed silently on his shoulder, but this time, his voice didn't penetrate through my soul like it always did. It felt like he was stabbing me, the sharpness of his words coming at me like a million paper cuts.

This will be the last time I let him fuck me, I thought to myself. I waited for him to tremble with pleasure, but it took him more time than usual. I felt wetness on the pillow next to my head, and I realized that Liam was crying, too. He knew that what he had done couldn't be fixed. That I couldn't allow myself to be in this situation, to be *one of those girls*. His public acts of humiliation, his subtle manipulation, his controlling behavior, the gaslighting, that could all be swept under the rug, right? Because it couldn't be seen. But now this—I couldn't forget what happened last night, and I couldn't hide the bruise on my face.

When he was done, I pushed him off of me.

"I'm sorry," he said so quietly I could barely hear him. "I'm sorry, sorry . . . I'm so sorry . . . I'm sorry." His words were full of panic, and I realized that he, too, knew what he had done.

When I got out of bed, I felt the muscles in my body tense up, but the freedom of no longer being physically under him triggered an unexpected sob. I slapped my hand over my mouth as I got dressed without showering, grabbed the keys to the car and my phone from the nightstand, and left his apartment for the last time, his whispered apologies fading away behind me.

The car ride to my parents' house was a blur. *Who am I? Who have I let myself become?*

———

When I stepped into their apartment, my mother was sitting at the kitchen table, dipping a sugar-free cookie into her coffee. When she saw my face, she stood up immediately, touching my cheek.

"What happened?"

"I fell, Mom," I said. "I fell down the stairs last night at Liam's. We fought, and I don't know what happened—I just tripped over my own two feet and fell," I said to her, trying to convince myself that this was the truth.

My mother's face turned white. "Sit down," she said. "Let me make you coffee."

Then she said to herself, "You fell."

"Promise me you won't tell Dad," I said, looking at her earnestly.

She said what she always said, a long and skeptical "Okaay," her face scrunched in suspicion. I had heard this "okaay" all my life. It meant something along the lines of *Keep going, I'll listen, and when you're done,*

I'll take your side. This elongated "okay" bought my mother the time she needed to read my reaction—my face, my mood, my opinion—and then agree with it. She was my comforting cheerleader, the balance to my father's intensity.

"I love you," she said. "I love you on your best days, and I love you on your worst days. This is one of your worst. Take a moment to yourself. Think."

A week went by without a single call from Liam. I checked my phone every few minutes and still, nothing. I hated him for what he had done, but how could it be that I hated myself even more for hoping he'd talk to me? I woke up in the middle of the night, sometimes at 2:00 or 3:00 a.m., the reflection of the moon peeking through the blinds, and sobbed, losing myself in a TV show and waking up from the trance only when a commercial came on.

After thirteen days of silence, he texted me.

"I love you. I'm sorry. I don't deserve you."

Although I had waited for what seemed like an eternity to hear from Liam, I didn't answer. That night, an enormous bouquet of balloons was waiting at my doorstep. The note read what it always read, "Just because." But this time, it wasn't "just because."

The next morning, Liam called while I was taking a walk on the beach, the same beach where we first met. I answered on the fourth ring. "Hear me out. I know you need time, and I want to give that time to you," he said.

"I'm done," I said, my lungs filling with fresh air. "Don't call me. Don't text me. Don't show up at my house. It's over."

"I respect that," he said. His voice was composed, but I could picture the veins in his neck bulging out. "You're the best thing that's ever happened to me, Tiny. I'll give you all the time you need. But I won't be able to live with myself if I let you go for good."

"Goodbye, Liam," I said, the tears streaming down my cheeks.

I hung up the phone, and for the first time since meeting him, I felt like I had finally done something right.

————

For the next three months, I found the time to work on myself. I applied, panic-filled, to Columbia and NYU for premed, anxious to leave Tel Aviv and Liam and the army behind forever. I worked out in the mornings, smoked cigarettes with Anna on her balcony while sipping our favorite Flam Classico red wine in the evenings, and felt, for the first time in a long time, like the lingering anxiety that had infected my daily life was creeping away.

The nights were still hard, so much so that I'd sneak into my parents' room, quietly wake up my mother, and ask her to come to my bed. I spent those nights falling asleep as she stroked my hair, the heartbreak so deep it ached in my bones. I fell in love with a man who hurt me. Me, of all people. But wasn't it always like that? Didn't you always think something like this could never happen to you? That you're smarter than those girls who stayed? That you wouldn't let yourself get to that point, no matter how much you loved him? There were many times I'd seen these women in movies, women I thought were weak and pathetic, and I couldn't wrap my mind around what was going on in their heads. I used to think women who kept coming back were stupid, but what if the reason was because they were simply in love? As I lay beside my mother, wrestling with my feelings, I realized leaving Liam was like losing the one person in my life I loved most. It felt like he had died—like my person had died. The grief I felt, no matter how much he hurt me, was enormous because throughout my time in the army, Liam had become the center of my world. I had lost my lover, my protector, my best friend.

Chapter 16

The morning before I left for New York, I posted an Instagram story of my pink suitcase overflowing with clothes. *Columbia University, here I come*, I wrote, secretly hoping Liam would see. As I brushed my teeth and got ready for bed, my phone lit up with a text from him.

"Can I call?"

My heart raced. Four months had passed since the last time we spoke, and I wasn't going to ruin that now. On the other hand, I was officially leaving Israel and starting school at Columbia, so I didn't have anything to lose. In the midst of my contemplation, he called.

"I had to talk to you, Ella. I can't stop thinking about you. I'm sorry about the way I acted. About everything. About my anger issues, about hurting you, about us breaking up. I know the list is long. You have no idea what I've been going through. I can't believe you're leaving tomorrow. I'm really happy for you. Didn't you say you were going to stop worrying about getting an education, though?"

His voice was sad, and I felt a pang in my heart for him.

"Stop? I never said I was going to stop. Who said I was going to stop? You know I always planned to go to Columbia to study in the greatest city in the world," I told him.

"What?"

"You knew I wanted to move back to New York after all of this was over."

"After what was over?"

"The army, this whole Israel interruption. You and me. I'm ready, Liam. Ready to get back on track and start my life right where it left off," I said.

"How long have you known this?"

As if I owed him an explanation. I liked the way his voice shook, the way he feared losing me for good.

"That's it. We can go our separate ways," I said.

"So what if you're going to New York? What does that have to do with separate ways? Deep down, I wanted to take a break, too, but I didn't know you were leaving."

"You can't have your cake and eat it too," I said.

"You want to leave us behind for good to go get some stuck-up fancy education nobody's going to give a shit about?" he asked. His voice had turned cold.

"Don't degrade my education," I said.

"I'm sorry. I didn't mean to. I'm saying desperate things. How are you feeling? Are you ready?"

"I'm scared," I said. "My flight's tomorrow morning, and I'm going to be alone in New York for the week, and then orientation starts. I'm excited, though. You know I've been waiting for this for a long time."

"I didn't even know you applied to schools. I didn't know you got in. I wish you were still a part of my life. But there's something I need you to know, and this is why I called," he said.

I waited to hear what he had to say, but he fell silent.

"Well, what is it?" I said.

"No matter where you are in the world, I will be there to protect you if you need me. I'm a phone call away. If you are ever afraid, or you feel alone, know that you aren't. You're never alone. I'll drop anything I'm doing, I'll swim across the ocean if I have to, to wherever you are, and I'll make sure you're okay. I will always protect you, Ella. I will always make sure you are safe."

The doorbell rang, interrupting our conversation.

"Wait, someone's at the door . . . one second," I said. I opened the front door to a delivery man holding an assortment of colorful balloons.

"Congratulations on getting into your dream school," Liam said, his voice soft on the other end of the line.

I sat on the porch steps turning up the volume on my phone so I could hear every word Liam had to say, so I could replay this conversation for the twelve-hour flight ahead of me, my hand gripping the assortment of balloon strings so they wouldn't fly away into the moonlight. I told Liam about how hard the last few months had been for me, about how nervous I was to start over alone, about what I thought were real problems. He told me that his mother was getting sicker and nobody in the world could help her. He said he finally understood what was important in life.

"I'm tired, Tiny," he whispered into the phone, exhausted.

"Me, too," I said. I closed my eyes and imagined his scent, a smell I was addicted to.

"Let me know when you're back. I'll be here. Waiting," he promised.

II

The Prince

New York City

Chapter 17

When I arrived in New York City, it was August, and I was twenty-one years old. I stepped out of Newark Liberty International Airport wearing a flowered Reformation dress, which seemed like a mistake in the air-conditioning of the plane but suddenly felt right as I stood there waiting for my Uber Black. The warm air smelled like lavender and garbage, but I breathed it deep into my lungs anyway. It didn't matter that I had been to New York countless times with my family. This was the first time. The first real time I was there, alone, not as a tourist from Connecticut, not as an army soldier, not as Liam's girlfriend, not as my parents' daughter, but as an official New Yorker. I didn't know the names of the bridges, I couldn't tell the difference between the East River or the Hudson, but I felt like I was leaving behind the girl I used to be and on my way to finding somebody new, somebody better. In front of me was a blank slate, a fresh start, and remarkably, against all contrary evidence of life, I really believed everything was going to be okay.

I stepped into the Uber. The driver tipped his Yankee baseball cap toward me with a smile and put my luggage in the trunk.

That's more like it, I thought, remembering that after-midnight drive with Liam's father.

The driver offered me a bottle of water, and I rolled down the window as we drove toward the Lincoln Tunnel. I felt the freshness of the cold water in my throat and watched for the skyline. After half an hour of bottleneck traffic, I saw it. With the hope and resourcefulness of a twenty-one-year-old, I thought to myself: *This is it. I'm actually doing it. A new chapter.*

When I arrived at my parents' fully furnished apartment on 80th and 1st Avenue, a bouquet of flowers waited for me with the doorman in the lobby.

"Who is it from?" I asked, looking for a note. He didn't know.

For two weeks, I organized the apartment, turning it into what I hoped would feel like home. I got rid of the modern glass dining room table and switched it with one made of mid-century oak. I ordered a bookshelf from West Elm and filled it with novels and candles and framed pictures of my family and of Julia and me. I cleaned what I could of the apartment, since my parents had leased it up until now to an elderly couple, and called five different housekeepers I found online until one of them was free the following day.

It had been almost half a year since I officially broke it off with Liam and two weeks since moving to the city, and besides that single slipup after the Instagram story I posted, my plan to cut him out of my life seemed to work. Nobody had to know that I brought one of his old hoodies with me across the globe or that I would fall asleep sniffing it. I hated myself for missing him.

I seemed to hate myself a lot lately.

————

I met Andrew Garnier within the first five minutes of orientation at Columbia. He had taken a few gap years to work for his father's law firm in Monaco until finally deciding to earn a degree, and I felt comfortable being around someone my age as opposed to the typical eighteen-year-old freshmen I was surrounded by. We were standing outside of Butler Library when he walked up to me in his navy suit jacket and stylish glasses while the professor was explaining the schedule for the day and, in a French accent, said, "You might be the most beautiful American girl I have ever seen."

"So you're saying non-American women are more beautiful than I am?" I whispered.

He shrugged. "Maybe some, but most of them, no." He locked his eyes with mine.

After a weeklong flirtation, he held my hand as we sipped dirty martinis at Bemelmans Bar on the Upper East Side where he introduced me to his city friends. That's where I met Chloe, a Norwegian model who was also starting premed at Columbia but had missed orientation since she was in Paris on a job for Valentino.

"I like this girl," she said to Andrew when I asked for another round of martinis. *These*, I thought, *are my people.* They read Machiavelli, smoked thin cigarettes, and had intellectual conversations about masterpieces at hidden art galleries in the city. They lifted me up, made me feel like I had more to learn, and were interested in what I had to say. Andrew asked me questions about the army and begged me to show him pictures in uniform. He sat quietly when I spoke, and when I finished a sentence, he waited to hear more. His attention felt worlds away from Liam's scrutinizing stares, or worse, the way he'd ignore me or look away or talk over me when I spoke.

Andrew and I sat there at the bar while Earl Rose played the piano, and I thought about how my life was falling back into place. We talked about the last books we had read. I was rereading Joan Didion's *Play It as It Lays*; he was reading Francisco Goldman's *Monkey Boy*. We argued over the best sushi spots in the city, and I realized there were other people in the world besides Liam. Other guys. I looked around. New York made me feel like I was a speck in an enormous universe and my life wasn't as grand and important and overwhelming as it felt. New York reminded me that I was small and my problems were smaller, and I loved that feeling.

That night, when Andrew and I stepped out to smoke a cigarette, he drunkenly leaned in to kiss me, and when I tasted his lips against mine, I felt young and beautiful and powerful. There were moments in life you didn't appreciate while they happened, but this one I savored. His eyes were light brown, and I noticed that his lips were slightly parted. He was shorter than I was, but I didn't care. When he slipped his hand under my loose beige silk dress, I pulled him closer and felt his body against me, against a body that for a long time didn't really feel like my own. A body that felt like it was in Liam's control. For that moment I felt good, like this was where I needed to be . . . until suddenly he grabbed me more tightly, and I felt like I couldn't breathe.

What was this? Guilt for kissing somebody else? Or was something about Andrew aggressive? I pulled away and walked back inside with him to grab my purse. I told him I was going to the bathroom, but instead I called a cab and left, my head spinning from the martinis. Andrew called me twice that night, but I didn't answer, even after I listened to his sincerely worried voice message: "Please, *mon amour*, let me know you are safe."

I wasn't ready to start something new; Liam's face flashed through my mind with each kiss. Two years with him had affected me more deeply than I had imagined. It was more than that, though. This wasn't about Liam; it was about me. I couldn't even look in the lobby mirror while I waited for the Uber. I had lost weight since the breakup with Liam, and while I was a vision on the outside, the silk dress hanging on me like clothes on a hanger, inside was total destruction. I had an anxiety attack for the first time that night, waking up clutching my beating chest, the bedsheets soaked with sweat.

I called Andrew the following afternoon and apologized for leaving him at the bar. "I never said I wanted anything serious, did I? I only lied and said some non-American women were more beautiful than you," he joked.

I laughed. "Okay, fine," I said, sipping the foam off the top of my cappuccino at Ralph's. "I shouldn't have assumed."

"No, no, you are right to assume. I never said I wanted anything serious with you, but, for the record, I would not reject the idea. Where are you? I hear cars."

"Ralph's on Madison."

"May I join you?"

We started with another coffee and then walked to Sant Ambroeus for a glass of wine, talking and learning more about each other until the sky dimmed.

We sat next to the window, our knees touching under the table, Andrew's tousled chestnut hair bouncing with each bellied laugh. He told me about his life in Monaco, about how his mother, Linda, used to drive to Italy to bring him the freshest cherry tomatoes and mozzarella cheese, about his father's business, his latest trip to Bali. I listened; my mind relaxed for what felt like the first time in forever.

I had thought, for the two years I spent with Liam, that love hurt, that love was work, that love was a constant battle to fix what was unrepairable and damaged. But as I sat back and sipped that crisp New Zealand sauvignon blanc with Andrew, it was like the old me was still in there. I raised my glass.

"Cheers to what?" Andrew asked.

"To the past being in the past," I said.

Before we left, I stood up to use the restroom, and, like a real Prince Charming, Andrew pulled my chair out. I felt a wave of tenderness wash over me.

"What? It's the French way," he said when he noticed the look on my face.

———

After Sant Ambroeus, Andrew walked me home, and I asked him if he wanted to come up. We had electrifying sex, and he stayed the night. We spent every day together after that for three weeks. We studied in the library, sipping the coffee Andrew snuck in under his sweatshirt. I'd finally met someone who was charming and smart and rich. Could I ask for anything more?

Over time, I started feeling confident and worthy in his presence. My bed was our shelter from the universe, our very own cocoon. After sex, Andrew would cook for me, sometimes French food his mother taught him to cook, like beef bourguignon and Croque Madame, but before he cooked, he'd always open the window and light a cigarette in bed. *The French way.* We'd curl into each other on the couch and talk for hours, our conversations stretching time. *Tu es mignonne*, he'd kiss my cheek and say.

After three weeks, I called Julia to tell her I had fallen in love. It was a Friday night. Andrew was out with his cousin, but we had planned to go upstate for the weekend. "He's amazing, Julia. And he makes me forget about Liam," I told her. "Like, I remember Liam, but I forget that I loved him, you know? Andrew and I are building something real."

"You deserve to be happy," Julia said. My forever cheerleader.

As if the universe were making fun of me, Andrew didn't call that night. Or the following night. My mini suitcase was packed for the trip, but I hadn't heard from Andrew all weekend and started to worry. I wasn't going to call; I still had to play hard to get. But maybe he was dead? On Sunday, in the middle of the night after tossing and turning and checking my phone every few minutes, I texted him to ask if he was alive.

"I'm alive!" he replied the next afternoon, after twelve hours. "Off to the Hamptons. Back in class on Wednesday and will call you then. I remember you said something about craving sushi. Kapo Masa when I get back? Let me take you out. I'm sorry I've been MIA, *mon amour*; this week has been crazy."

Andrew's text was supposed to fill me with sweet relief, but my gut feeling screamed *No*. Was I crazy to hope he missed me as much as I missed him? I had grown used to being with Andrew and couldn't stand the thought of spending this time in New York City alone. Since being with Liam, I felt like I couldn't handle being alone.

When Andrew came back from the Hamptons, he took me to Kapo Masa where we ate caviar and truffle beef tartare and my favorite creamy miso roll, and I laughed like I hadn't laughed since the last time we were together. He apologized for being so bad at texting, and neither of us mentioned the trip upstate that never was. After dinner, we took a cab down to the West Village, and along the cobblestone streets and Federal-style townhouses, he kissed me until the pain I had felt while he was gone seemed melodramatic and far, far away.

September came and went, and Andrew disappeared again. One day he stopped showing up to class, and when I asked Chloe where he was, she said he switched to the Business Economics major instead of premed.

"Don't take it personally; he's kind of a player," Chloe warned. We were sipping coffee at the Columbia Business School library, where Chloe insisted the hottest guys studied. If I thought I studied hard,

Chloe studied three times more than I did. She earned a full ride to Columbia—her parents couldn't afford to send her to a ridiculously expensive Ivy League school—and she paid her own rent through weekend modeling gigs. She didn't wait for a guy to sweep in and save her.

When I threw the Goddess Rules out the window and texted Andrew about missing him, he sent me a heartfelt voice message. A week later, he came back, this time showing up outside the calculus building at 7:30 a.m. with a warm butter croissant just for me. And so continued our on-and-off cycle for two months after that. If I had been smarter, I would have ended things with him sooner, but being with Andrew made me feel like I could open my heart again. Liam hadn't won. He hadn't shut me off to the world.

"I think you and I have something special," he'd say. "We can work on this. You are still the most beautiful American girl I have ever seen."

Meanwhile, school was more manageable than I had expected it to be. Calculus was so easy it started to bore me, and I felt like I could analyze functions with my eyes closed. After two years of being the clueless American soldier in the Israeli army, I was back in my element.

Even though she studied nonstop, Chloe had trouble keeping up in class, and she was in awe when I presented her with the basic rules of derivatives without looking at my notebook.

"You genius bitch!" she said in her accent, smacking my knee.

Chemistry and physics challenged me not because of topics like molecular spectroscopy or organic synthesis—those my father drilled into my mind at the kitchen table growing up—but because my mind wandered to Andrew and sometimes, on nights when I felt truly alone amid a jungle of skyscrapers, back to Liam.

Still, I dropped Andrew's name to people who asked about my love life every chance I had. He was the kind of guy, at least among my Columbia friends, who everyone loved. Ambitious even though he didn't need to be, cool and funny and generous. When we went out as a group, he'd sometimes whip out his American Express Black Card and pay for the table without looking at the bill, with only a slight nod to the waiter.

During weeks when I didn't hear from him, I'd work out and get my nails done and spray tan until I looked ridiculous, stepping faster and harder on the StairMaster while listening to Taylor Swift songs and convincing myself that our tumultuous love meant that there was passion between us. *The French way.*

Yet if I stopped to think, to really think, alone in my bed after drinking one too many glasses of wine, I knew in my heart that what Andrew offered me wasn't enough, and I couldn't help but compare him to Liam. Andrew gave me my space; Liam checked up on me constantly. Andrew made me feel independent; Liam made me feel needed. Andrew liked me sometimes; Liam loved me always. The more I seemed to step back and give Andrew his space, the more of it he took. As the nights went by, my loneliness grew, and for the first time, I knew what Joan Didion meant when she wrote about the loneliness of New York.

Chapter 18

Whenever I saw Chloe in class, I was fixated on her. She looked more innocent sitting at the table across from me than she did vaping at lounge bars or laughing at Andrew's jokes, and I liked both versions of her.

Chloe had soft, white-blonde hair cut shoulder-length and a slim, proportional face. The physical opposite to my brown hair, brown eyes, and tan skin, Chloe didn't just look like a Norwegian model—she actually was one. I liked her so much, based on nothing more than our night out at the bar, that just the sight of her made me feel like maybe things would work out for me here after all.

After class one day, Chloe and I headed for the lawn outside the philosophy building, where there were beverages and free Krispy Kreme doughnuts for the students. Chloe didn't waste a minute and walked right up to me.

"Hey, I have Pilates in an hour and wanted to know if you feel like grabbing a coffee until then?"

I couldn't believe she wanted to continue our friendship. A guy I dated once told me I had a forgettable face but in a good way (whatever that meant), and it had stuck with me ever since. I felt like a regular girl, nothing special. By the time I met Chloe on that lawn, I was having a full-scale identity crisis, confronting the possibility that I was in the wrong place on the wrong career path, wearing ripped jeans, a loose T-shirt, and a pink neck scarf—my idea of looking like a cool college girl who wasn't trying. Chloe was classy and confident, her aura gentle, fairylike, and melodic. It was impossible to overlook her.

We walked to Joe's coffee on campus, ordered two cappuccinos and a muffin to share—of course, she wanted to share; she didn't eat a single bite—and sat in the corner at a small square table, facing the room. Chloe brushed her hair behind her ear and asked me what I was majoring in, where I was from, where I lived, and with whom. She was so interested in my life that I almost looked around to make sure it was me she was talking to. When we spoke, she rested her hand on my leg for a moment or brushed a crumb of the muffin she didn't even taste off my shirt. I had never felt a connection like this one, which bordered on a full-scale crush.

Once our cups were empty, Chloe leaned into me and whispered, "You're the best thing I'm going to get out of this school."

I smiled at how unapologetic she was and wished I could blink and become her. "No, *you* are," I replied.

And in that hour, our attention fixed solely on each other, our heads bent together, laughing as if we had been best friends for years, I put my hand to my chest and physically felt the hole in my heart shrink just the tiniest bit. That day after class, with just one glance and a shy smile, a silent promise was made between us: *Let's stick together.*

Afterward, I walked to my core philosophy class. My father said that if you weren't early, you're late, so I built a habit of arriving everywhere much too early, at least half an hour before the scheduled time. As I waited on the bench in the hallway outside the locked, empty classroom, I skimmed through the philosophy course description on my laptop. The professor made it very clear that we were going to read and analyze a book every week. When he arrived fifteen minutes before class began, I smiled at the slim bald man in his late fifties wearing a suit and tie. He smiled back.

"Come on in," he said as he unlocked the heavy university door. I followed him nervously into the small room. Fifteen chairs surrounded one long table, as if each class discussion would turn into some sort of dinner party. I sat down as Professor Douglass set up his PowerPoint presentation. Everything about him was organized. The way he took off his jacket and placed it on the chair behind him, the bookcases lining the room, the coffee thermos on his desk, and the perfectly placed picture of the eastern Sierra Nevada Mountains on the wall. Professor Douglass had an aura of certainty around him, which made me feel stable and relaxed, as though there were no surprises lurking around the corner. The room smelled clean and cozy, like an old living room whose fireplace had just been put out. I would grow to love this smell; I would escape my apartment and run to it.

"Hi, I'm Ray." He offered his hand for me to shake, his blue eyes piercing and kind.

I stuttered my name and felt a pang of anxiety. I didn't know what it was—maybe that Ray was so inviting and humane that I worried I'd trail off and start crying right then and there and confess how lonely I had been lately, my eyes becoming red-rimmed and puffy. Maybe it was because, in the simplest way, he reminded me of my father, a highly educated, kind man with a welcoming smile. For those first few months alone in the city, I felt constantly on edge, like any single glance, whether pitiful or harsh, could throw me off balance.

Ray presented the class syllabus: Kant, Smith, Aristotle, Plato, Locke, the Qur'an, Gandhi, Fanon, Hobbes, Machiavelli, Rousseau. We were going to study self-love, utility, passion, and politics. *These* were topics I didn't know I loved even more than macromolecules and functional groups. *This* was what I was willing to wake up at 7:15 a.m. and walk in the brutal New York City cold for.

At first, when Ray led discussions on readings, I wanted to impress him. I dug through my mind in search of the most logical answers, trying to come up with what he would probably want to hear. I was so used to telling people what they wanted to hear that I had no idea what I really thought or felt or believed. Yet whenever a glimpse of truth peeked out, Ray recognized it and stopped to grab it. He would ask me another question, prying the answers out of me, until I spoke my truth.

Ray's class began with a PowerPoint presentation on Machiavelli's *The Prince*, a sixteenth-century political rule book on how to acquire and maintain power.

"Has anyone heard of the term *Machiavellianism*?" Ray asked as he stood in front of the class.

Ray clicked the next slide.

> Machiavellianism: the personality trait in which a person is
> so focused on their own interests that they will manipulate,
> deceive, and exploit others to achieve their goals.

For the entire class, we discussed the use of language, romance and power, love and deceit. We analyzed Machiavelli quotes and expressed our opinions instead of sitting silently and clicking away on a calculator or waiting to see some acid solution start bubbling up.

"Machiavelli says, 'It is better to be feared than loved, if we cannot be both.' What do you think?" Ray said.

For the first time that week, I raised my hand. "I think it's better to be loved, definitely. Because when you fear someone, you want to get away from them, but when you love them, you want to be close. And isn't that the Prince's main goal? To be close to the people he is ruling in order to maintain power?"

A handsome Asian student with slicked black hair and a button-down shirt raised his hand. "Sorry, but we're discussing politics here, not romance. If people fear their leader, they'll more likely follow his instruction, will they not? The Prince specifically points this out. I quote: 'Love endures by a bond which men, being scoundrels, may break whenever it serves their advantage to do so; but fear is supported by the dread of pain, which is ever present,'" he said.

I immediately retreated into myself, deflated by this student's proof of my inaccuracy, until suddenly, I heard Ray's voice.

"That's true, Mark. Machiavelli does point out that love is breakable, while fear is more secure, yet his approach to politics may be too authoritative, wouldn't you say?" He listened for another minute, nodding, and then turned to me. "Ella, what do you think about what Mark said?"

My eyes widened, and I wanted nothing more than to hide under the table and forget I ever raised my hand. I didn't understand why Ray was putting me on the spot like that, and it was especially frustrating that he didn't take his eyes off of me or help me out. I took a deep breath and fingered the pink scarf around my neck. Mark stared at me, his hands crossed, his chin raised, waiting for an answer.

What a showoff, I thought.

"Well, um, the Prince's theory is in direct opposition to a moralistic theory of politics, which is what all rulers should strive to achieve, right? And still, while fear may keep people close for some time, human nature ultimately rebels against leaders they fear," I said.

Mark fell quiet. I looked up at Ray, and before he spoke, he leaned back in his chair, clasped his hands behind his head, and smiled. He looked me in the eye and nodded, satisfied.

"Exactly. Write that down, people; it'll be on the midterm."

Though I hadn't heard of Machiavelli before that class, I found myself so absorbed in it that when I went home that night, I finished the pages Ray had assigned and stayed up until 2:00 a.m. reading more. As I snuggled in bed, highlighting in bright yellow marker the quotes that touched me, my reading light glowing on the pages, I felt like an archeologist slowly uncovering the artifacts I had been looking for. I was finally in the right place, on the right cultural landscape. It was as if I were nudging my brain cells awake with each page I turned.

As the weeks passed and I fell asleep alone in my apartment (waking up in the middle of the night to check again that the front door was locked), the thought of seeing Ray's face on Monday and Wednesday mornings gave me something to look forward to. Whenever I spoke, no matter what I had to say, Ray nodded his head, asked me questions, and replied, with deep thought, to mine. He made me feel that, even with his PhD, he was still learning from me. When I walked through the doors of his classroom, I seemed to put myself in his care.

I had Ray's class to look forward to two mornings a week and studying with Chloe, eating celery and hummus and brewing a fresh cup of coffee on the hour, almost every evening. Once we finished studying for the day, we'd make her signature Norwegian honey garlic salmon and eat it while sitting in front of the TV and laughing at silly reality TV shows. It was nice to turn off my brain and relax with Chloe, and every time I'd close the door behind her and remember that I was alone again, I wished she would stay longer.

Finally, though, it seemed that I was adapting to my new life in New York.

Chapter 19

Toward the end of October, Andrew and his friends invited Chloe and her friends to join them in Martha's Vineyard. He didn't reach out to me, but during class, Chloe showed me countless daily text messages from him. Andrew's friends, identical twins Omar and Josef, who had an uncanny resemblance to former One Direction member Zayn Malik, had a mansion there with a heated pool and jacuzzi, a private chef, and an army of maids. All that was missing were the young models, so, naturally, they wanted Andrew to bring Chloe and her crew.

"He's dating my friend Kamila now, you know," Chloe said nonchalantly while we listened to the organic chemistry lecture. After stalking her on Instagram, I learned that Kamila was a French girl with natural boobs so perky they looked fake (they probably were fake), and a porcelain-doll face. I promised Chloe right then that I was done with Andrew for good, not that she cared. But when Saturday morning came around and a Ralph's coffee delivery and fresh butter scone showed up at my front door, I knew things were taking a turn.

"*Mon amour,*" the green and white note read. "I miss you. Come join me in Martha's Vineyard this weekend? Give me a chance. I'll make it up to you."

Obviously it was another tactic Andrew was using to sleep with me or play with my mind or stroke his own ego, but at that moment, reading his words was like opening the blinds on a warm Sunday morning and letting the sun's rays soak in.

When I arrived at the house the following Friday afternoon, Andrew practically ignored everybody there except me. He held my hand, stroked my hair, came up behind me while I washed my hands and kissed my neck in front of his friends, in front of the French model. When night fell and he said he didn't feel like going out, there was nothing I wanted more than to stay home with him. We had sex and talked for hours afterward, just like the old days.

The following day was cold and windy, but Andrew had reserved an afternoon of wine tasting for us at his favorite wine bar. He looked gorgeous swishing the wine in his mouth, teaching us the difference between full- and medium-bodied wines as if the entire group hadn't grown up in obnoxiously arrogant families. He kept ordering more and more bottles, and I could tell by the time we arrived back at the house that he was drunk.

Andrew, Omar, and Josef were playing cards while the Sunday night football game played in the background. Chloe and the models sat outside in the cold, drinking hot tea.

"I'm going upstairs to shower," I said to Chloe.

She nodded. "I'll be here if you need anything," she said before going back to the conversation she was having about a new anti-wrinkle cream she saw on TikTok.

As I lathered the shampoo into my hair, I heard a knock at the door.

"*Mon amour*, are you in there? Can I join you?"

Adrenaline rushed through me. I stepped out of the shower onto the ceramic floor soaking wet and without opening the door, turned the knob and unlocked it. I jumped back into the shower, smiling to myself, washing away the shampoo, and waiting for Andrew to step in. When he peeked through the curtain, he was already naked, his tan, ripped body ready for me. *He's still a little short, but his penis totally makes up for it.* He started kissing me sloppily, the water raining down on both of us, and I could smell the alcohol on his breath.

"Okay, okay," I said. "Take it easy, mister."

He turned me around and pushed me up against the shower wall, this time harder than before.

"Hey, stop it, Andrew," I said, turning to him. He put his hand around my waist and pulled me into him. "What are you doing?"

That's when I heard the click of the bathroom door lock and stopped dead in my tracks. I peeked out from the curtain, covering my wet body with my hands. Omar and Josef stood in front of us, Omar leaning on the bathroom counter as if to steady himself, and Josef looking into my eyes with silent contempt.

"What the hell are you guys doing in here? Get out!" I screamed.

"*Shhh,*" Andrew said, the water hot against my skin. He muffled my mouth with his hand.

"Get out!" Omar mocked, laughing to himself. "Come on already, Garnier, show us what she can do."

"I told you—you can only watch if you shut up. Didn't your mother teach you respect?" Andrew said to them, his French accent suddenly making me sick.

Andrew pulled the curtains back so they could see, like we were starring in some theatre show, his hand still covering my mouth. He pushed my face against the shower wall again before thrusting into me.

"No! Stop! Get off of me!" I said through his fingers against my mouth, but he didn't stop. Omar and Josef stood there, watching, the steam rising up, up, up, and although I couldn't see either of them, I could only feel the tears running down my eyes, I could only feel the water running down my back, I could only taste the snot running down my nose, I could only wish I could run fast and far away. I knew they were there.

When Andrew was done, I pushed him off of me, my push so weak it was pathetic. I fell to the shower floor, and Omar and Josef chuckled uncomfortably.

"Whoa, Ella, relax; we've fucked a million times," Andrew said. "You're the best I've ever had." He dried himself off with the towel I brought for myself. "I just wanted to show you off a little bit—can you blame me?"

"What the fuck, man," Josef said. "Let's get out of here."

"You're sick," I said to no one in particular, and as soon as the three of them were out of the bathroom, I ran to lock the door. I sat there on the floor without a towel, my eyes brimming with fresh tears, never-ending tears that, when they finally stopped pouring out of my eyes, switched direction and poured inside of me until I felt like my soul was drowning.

Nobody but Julia knew what happened that evening.

Back at school, Chloe texted me to say she heard part of the story from Andrew, although I'm sure he didn't tell her what really happened. But I couldn't let it go. Each day in the city was worse than the day that came before it, and that trip to Martha's Vineyard changed my outlook of living alone in New York. If I was once the optimistic heroine chuckling to herself while passing two arguing cab drivers, I suddenly turned into a quiet young woman screening calls from my parents and rejecting all offers to go out, even from Chloe. If I once breathed in the crisp, cold air of Central Park, today, the cold seemed to penetrate my fragile bones. It was as if I'd walked through a revolving door feeling eager and alive and walked out a zombie on her way to the grave. The gloom encompassed me, and the lonelier I became, the more I missed Liam.

Chapter 20

The two years I spent in the army were constantly overshadowed by the big dreams I had: to become a doctor, publish the Goddess Rules as a best-selling dating advice book, move back to the United States, feel like I had control over my own life. It was because I was being held back by my circumstances that I wasn't fulfilling myself, I kept telling myself. But now, here I was in New York City, with endless opportunities at my fingertips, and instead of making the most of it, I was wasting each day skipping class and lying around. Everyone said New York was the best city in the world, but now, when I stepped outside on the balcony and looked out at the rippling water of the East River, surrounded by enormous buildings, I didn't feel inspired—I felt pathetic. If I was living here, why wasn't I happy? Why wasn't I succeeding? All the people behind the windows in the buildings across from me were chasing their dreams, so why wasn't I?

My circumstances weren't holding me back. I was. How could it be that now I didn't belong in America? I missed my family, but I didn't want to speak to them. I missed the warm waters of Tel Aviv's sunny beaches, but I didn't want to swim in them. I missed Friday night dinners, but I didn't want to be surrounded by clattering plates and

Israeli music. All I wanted, all I could think about after that night with Andrew, was Liam. In his arms, I was home, and I was safe. Maybe, through it all, he *was* my person. Maybe I had thrown away something good and real and right. There were such cruel men out there. Was he really one of them?

In Israel, I had longed to be back in America. But now, in New York, I ate dinner alone, curled up on the couch, the Kardashians on TV my only form of company. I thought that moving back would feel like home, and for the first three months with Andrew and then my newfound friendship with Chloe, it almost did. Why couldn't I find contentment in being alone? I wished I were one of those women who knew what happiness was without the comfort of a man, but maybe I just wasn't built that way. Anxiety had me waking up every two hours to check if the front door was locked, and the more vulnerable I felt, the more I needed the sense of safety only Liam could provide. *I will always protect you.*

Being far away from Liam made it easy to remember the good and suppress the bad. When I couldn't fall asleep at night, I'd close my eyes and imagine Liam moving in with me, waking up early, putting on a suit, and going to work while I studied. I pictured his face when we'd walk through Central Park, in awe of the beauty he'd seen only in the movies. I imagined us taking a yellow cab to Times Square, stopping at Ramen Ishida for a warm bowl, snapping selfies in front of the Christmas tree at Rockefeller Center, or walking by the Plaza Hotel pretending to be lost in New York, Kevin McCallister-style. I saw us clinking wine glasses at L'Avenue at Saks and cooking dinner together at home after spending too long picking out fresh ingredients at Citarella. I imagined us spending weekends naked in bed, far away from reality, getting up only to open the door for the Chinese food delivery.

In mid-December, two weeks before winter break, my parents called.

"Are you coming home, sweetheart?" my mother asked, her voice cracking. "We miss you so much." They didn't know I crossed out each day on the calendar, counting the days until I went home.

"I don't think so," I lied. I just wanted to test her, to hear her tell me how much she missed me, how much she wanted me home with her.

"Really? Okay, well, let us know. Our friends are taking a trip to the Maldives, and we were thinking of joining them, but if you're coming home, we won't go. Just let us know, honey," she said.

My heart shattered.

My father called the next day. "I don't give a shit about a trip to the Maldives. We've been waiting for you. I need to see you, *Kapara*; come home," he said.

"I don't know," I said again. What was the point of going back to Tel Aviv for break? As soon as I felt like a burden to my parents, the thought of going back was no longer appealing. Liam and I were no longer in contact, and I'd walk the streets of Tel Aviv nervous about running into him. Being here alone was hard, but staying at my parents' house was suffocating, especially without being able to escape into Liam's arms. Plus, I didn't want them to see me like this. There was nowhere for me to go. Nowhere I belonged. "I'm leaning toward staying here and studying," I lied.

"It's your choice," my father said, "but I would love to see my crown jewel." The tone of his voice revealed a sense of worry he was trying to hide.

That night, completely sober, I texted Liam. "Hey, how have you been? Hope everything's good with you."

I had written and rewritten the text countless times since that night in Martha's Vineyard, but this time, I let my thumb hover over the send button until I thought, *Fuck it*, and clicked.

In a matter of seconds, he texted back.

"Wow, it's so great to hear from you. I've been good. Can I call?"

We spoke on the phone for almost two hours before switching to FaceTime, even though I was in sweatpants with no makeup and dark circles under my eyes.

"Those eyes," he said when I apologized for how I looked. I always fell into a sort of passive mode when Liam was around, apologizing for things I didn't need to, searching for the right words to say. I told him that being in New York wasn't as exciting as I thought it would be, and he nodded, listening.

"What are you cooking?" he asked when I ran to the kitchen to check on the pasta sauce.

"My favorite. Pasta with marinara sauce. With extra parmesan," I said.

"You simple girl, you," he laughed. "I remember that."

I showed him the apartment, bringing the phone with me from room to room, until he said, "I get the picture—your parents are loaded—but I'd rather look at your face."

When we hung up, I took a warm shower, brushed my teeth, applied my skin care routine for the first time since the Martha's Vineyard incident, and slipped into bed. I couldn't stop smiling. I fell asleep in a matter of minutes and didn't wake up once, not even to check if the door was locked.

For the next two days, I waited to hear from Liam again. I had already reached out once; now, it was his turn.

I almost fainted when the doorman buzzed on Saturday morning. "There's a handsome man by the name of Liam here; can I send him up?" he said.

"What the fuck?" I said. I heard Liam in the background laughing.

Instead of freaking out and screaming hysterically, I panicked, cursing myself for not having waxed any part of my body this entire month.

What was I thinking? Whatever, it was too late now. What was he doing here? "Yeah, yeah, sure, send him up."

In the time it took Liam to reach the thirty-fourth floor, I threw my dirty laundry in the closet, brushed my teeth at lightning speed, shaved my bikini line and armpits, and changed out of my oversized T-shirt and into a little pink slip pajama dress.

He waited at the door for a minute before knocking, and I greeted him with a smile, shaking my head. He picked me up and spun me around like he always did, like nothing wrong ever happened between us. I watched as he walked around the apartment, the dissonance growing with each step. Liam had stepped out of my phone screen and into New York. *How did he get my address?*

Liam knew I hated surprises, that there was something about not knowing what was to come that made me anxious. "But after our conversation two days ago," he said, "I could hear it in your voice. I still had a chance. If I have a chance to go after the love of my life, then I'm not going to sit back and let this opportunity slip away. I couldn't sleep without knowing that I gave this relationship everything I have. I didn't even contemplate. I didn't ask anybody. I just went online and bought a ticket, and twelve hours later, here we are," he said, his eyes sincere.

It was weird seeing Liam in the context of New York at first, but my relief at having him next to me, at not being alone, overpowered any doubt in my mind.

"Well, Tiny, are you shocked? Are you happy I'm here?" he asked. Hearing him call me by my nickname brought back a familiar feeling.

"Of course, I'm shocked, but a good kind of shocked. I'm so happy you are here," I said, shaking my head. I really was. "You think we're a couple in a movie, don't you, showing up on my doorstep. You pretend to be tough, but you're such a romantic."

"You bring out this side of me; trust me, I've never been like this with anyone else."

I walked over to the kitchen. "Espresso?" I asked. He nodded. "So what's your plan? Where are you staying?" I said, pressing the little coffee button on the Nespresso machine. Liam was silent for a second.

"I mean, I thought I'd stay here with you, but if that's not cool, I can book a hotel," he said, his mood suddenly changing. I pushed away the little red flags popping up in my mind and let myself bask in the euphoria I was feeling for the first time in months.

"No, no, you're not going anywhere," I said, walking toward him slowly. "Of course. Stay here, with me."

He smiled.

"How did you find me?" I asked.

"I called your mom and asked her for your new address the day you left. Who do you think those welcome flowers were from?" Liam said.

I leaned into him, kissing the space between his ear and his collarbone. I was creeped out and turned on all at once. "God, you're so hot," he said, pulling me into him and picking me up. With my legs wrapped around his waist, Liam sat me down on the kitchen counter, slipping off my silk pajama dress. Hell, I deserved this. Having Liam there with me was like taking a double shot of Clase Azul tequila. I would deal with the consequences later. For now, I was high on love.

————

The next morning, we walked along the avenues all the way to Central Park. We started at the Jacqueline Kennedy Onassis Reservoir and made our way to Shakespeare Garden, and the entire time, I felt like I was playing a character in a play. There we were, two beautiful people, young and seemingly in love, walking through the garden of flowers sprinkled with snow, but deep within me I was questioning the entire situation.

Liam loved grand gestures, and if there was anyone I knew who had the balls to hop on a plane and show up across the globe, it was him. When I let myself think about it, I felt smothered, but as I breathed in the crisp December air and walked by the gardens, I decided I didn't have to make any decisions just yet. Why did I overthink everything? Liam was here, and I was happy. Couldn't I be content with that? It calmed me to remember that I could relax and enjoy the moment, enjoy right now. I would let him take my pain away, and wherever our relationship led, that's where we would go. We strolled along the winding, manicured paths, taking in the acres where rosemary and pansies would bloom—alluded to by Ophelia in *Hamlet*, he explained. He had researched the garden at the airport before the flight, taking screenshots of all the places in the city he wanted us to go to. We walked up the steps toward a white mulberry tree that, Liam said, grew from a graft of a tree planted by Shakespeare himself in 1602. Along the pathways of the garden, quotations from Shakespeare's plays were placed sporadically, and even though Liam hadn't read a book in years, we stopped to read each one, his smile widening each time he looked at me.

Suddenly, seemingly out of nowhere, I saw a band set up right in the middle of the garden playing the same song Liam played that night at the watchtower, John Legend's "All of Me."

"Oh my God, Liam, that's our song!" I said. I couldn't believe the universe had come together so perfectly, that God or whoever was watching over us not only plopped Liam into my lap but also coincidentally brought us to this stunning floral garden *and* brought a band to play our song. I walked over to the band and sat down on the bench across from it, listening and singing along to the song that had snuck into my Taylor Swift playlist, a song I had fallen asleep to on repeat for the past month while drinking wine in my apartment, alone in the city.

"I could cry," I said, looking at Liam.

"Why are you sitting down, Tiny? Here, why don't you stand right over there, and I'll take a picture of you with the band?"

I stood up; even though I didn't care about the picture, I cared about the moment, about remembering it.

"Take off your sunglasses, will you?"

"Take the picture already; I want to listen to him sing!" I said.

Liam knelt down to snap a better photo of me, and as he was just about to take the picture, he slipped his phone into his back pocket and switched it with a little blue box. His hands shaking, he looked up at me and opened the box to reveal a cushion-cut 1.2 carat (at least!) Tiffany diamond ring.

"Ella, you are my best friend. You are the love of my life. You make me a better person. I know we've had our ups and downs, but you've changed me, and I will spend the rest of my life showing you how thankful I am for that. There are moments in life that make you appreciate them while they happen, and every moment I spend with you is like that for me. When I watch a piece of hair fall across your face, when I see your eyes light up when we walk past a puppy . . ." He stopped for a second as if forgetting his lines. "When you look at me, I know you'll always be by my side. Will you make me the happiest man in the world? Will you marry me?"

Immediately a saying my mother always said popped into my mind: "Reality outdoes imagination."

I didn't answer right away. Liam had shown up at my apartment unexpectedly—and frankly, uninvited—merely a day before. One side of me couldn't believe he had the audacity to put me in this position, and the other side of me was melting at his romantic gesture. Only a few minutes before, I was calming myself down by remembering that spending time in the city together didn't mean diving deep into this relationship for good, and now, he was proposing marriage. Had he talked to my parents about this? Did they agree? I couldn't imagine my father giving Liam his blessing.

As I tried to make sense of what was happening, I heard the *click, click, clicking* of a camera. Liam had even hired a photographer. I saw two young women standing near the fountain, their heads bent together, their hands covering their mouths. They caught me looking in their direction and started clapping and *woo-hoo*-ing, as if they had just witnessed the most romantic proposal of all time.

And they had, hadn't they?

If I were one of those girls, peering into my life from the outside, I, too, would rest my hand on my heart and hold back tears of joy or maybe of jealousy. If I were to imagine my perfect proposal, I wouldn't have been able to picture us here at Shakespeare Garden, a place filled with nature and the love of literature. Liam had exceeded my expectations. *Reality outdoes imagination.* When I looked at him, a million thoughts raced through my mind. His face said it all. As he knelt there in front of me, Liam seemed unquestionably, unwaveringly sure that he wanted to spend the rest of his life with me. He had a goal, and he went after it. To him, I was the most precious gift. What more could any girl ask for?

This was what life was all about, wasn't it? Taking chances, risking it all for love. I knelt down to meet Liam at eye level and wrapped my arms around his neck. Even though I wasn't nearly as sure as he was, I took the leap. "Yes," I said, offering my left hand to him. "You're crazy, but I love you." So he wasn't the Prince of Monaco. But he was my Prince Charming, after all.

"I will never let you go, Ella Davidson," he said.

The ring fit my finger like Cinderella's glass slipper, and even though it was new, it felt like it had belonged on my hand all along. Things were going to be different this time around. This was the happily ever after Liam and I deserved. I just hoped our carriage wouldn't turn into a pumpkin when the clock struck midnight.

"It's just you and me now," he whispered as he kissed me. We walked hand in hand down the stairs of Shakespeare Garden, Liam's grip just a little too tight.

Chapter 21

"Mom, I'm engaged," I said, twirling my fingers closer to the camera on FaceTime.

Her eyes widened, but I caught a trace of a smile at the corners of her mouth. "Okaaaay," she said.

Liam popped his head into the frame. "Can you believe it, Maya?" he said, happiness radiating from him.

She shook her head. "I can't believe it. Congratulations, my loves, I'm so happy for you. Truly."

My mom *was* happy for me—for us—I could tell. What mother wouldn't want her daughter to marry the man she loved? Since I was a young girl, twirling around in princess Purim outfits, my mom would talk about my future wedding. "There'll be peonies everywhere; you know I love peonies. And the chuppah—you won't even be able to see it; it'll be so smothered with flowers. Pastels, we'll do pink, lilac, even blue. Do you like baby blue, honey? Okay, we'll see." She would go on and on, painting a picture of my perfect wedding day, the two of us snuggled in my bed as she stroked my hair. As I got older, when I couldn't fall asleep, I used to imagine my wedding until I was lost in my mother's world of peonies, walking down the aisle past the people I loved to the one person who was supposed to love me more than anyone.

Yet, now when I pictured the man standing under the chuppah waiting for me, his face was blurry. It wasn't Liam's face I saw. This was supposed to feel right, but no—it felt off. As we walked down the icy-cold streets of the city, I found myself searching for the one thing that would save me: tequila.

"Let's call your dad," Liam said after we hung up with my mom. It was as if he wanted the world to know we were engaged so it would be official, so I wouldn't be able to change my mind.

"Let's get a drink first," I said. "To celebrate."

We found an old Irish bar, the Dublin House, near the corner of 79th and Broadway, the only place open that early on a Sunday. Liam ordered tequila on the rocks with lime for both of us, and for a second, I felt at ease in the dimly red-lit bar with its worn-out Carlsberg coasters.

"To my future wife," he said as we raised our glasses.

As I sat there on the wooden bar stool, I thought about how the world kept turning. This enormous event happened in my life less than an hour earlier, an experience that was bound to change my future forever, but the bartender in front of us was living his life like he would any other day of the week, watching the foam skim the rim of the beer glass, glancing at the television screen every few minutes. Couldn't he see that my life was spiraling out of control? What did it mean to take control over my life?

"Do you think that this is just how life is?" I asked Liam.

"What do you mean?"

"Like, is this how life works? You just live and then big things happen to you and you go with the flow until you're suddenly married with kids, living in a suburb and driving them to soccer practice while looking for a reason to live?"

"I don't think so," Liam said. "I don't let life happen. I *make* life happen. But it depends on the kind of person you are. A lot of people are like you, letting life happen to them. That's why we fit together. You let life happen, and I make it happen for both of us."

"Yeah," I said.

"I wish I was like you," he said. "It's easier that way. You just get to sit back, relax, and watch me do all the work."

"I didn't used to be like that, though. I used to make life happen, too."

"Another round?" the bartender interrupted. I shook my head. I was already drinking on an empty stomach.

"Hell, yeah," Liam said, ignoring me. "We're getting married!"

When we made it back to the apartment, I called my dad while Liam was in the shower. He had already heard the news.

"Mom told me. I'm getting old, huh? My crown jewel is engaged."

I laughed, but the line was quiet on the other end.

"Dad?"

"What?"

"Are you there?"

"I'm here."

I couldn't get the words out because I didn't know what I was feeling. I could feel only the tears welling up behind my eyes. Getting engaged to the right person wasn't supposed to feel like this, was it?

"Uff, Aba."

"What, sweetie? Talk to me."

"I don't know."

"Of course you know. You know better than anyone else."

"Yeah. I just don't know if I'm ready yet," I whispered.

"If there's a doubt, there is no doubt," he said.

"That's not true; a lot of people get cold feet when they're considering spending the rest of their lives with someone. It's a huge decision, Dad."

"You're not like a lot of people."

"Yeah."

He took a deep breath. "Listen, Ella. Take it easy. Take your time. Don't do anything drastic. An engagement is just an engagement. Think about it until you're ready, until you feel like it's right, if that feeling ever comes. But I can tell you one thing. The day Ima and I got engaged was one of the best days of my life. And hers, too. Is this one of the best days of your life?"

Just two days before, Liam and I were broken up and hadn't spoken for over six months, and now, he was my fiancé. This was how he was, though. His gestures grand, his intentions clear. I had been stressed about school, about accidentally running into Andrew, about being alone in the loneliest city in the world. The nights in my apartment wore me down, and now I had a gift placed in the palm of my hand. The road was bumpy, but from now on, if I wanted it to be, life with Liam would be smooth sailing.

———

For the first few months of our engagement, Liam showered me with love. He couldn't afford any gifts after spending his savings on the ring, but all I wanted was a companion to ease the depression I had sunk into. The better he treated me, the more I started feeling like this engagement could actually be a step in the right direction for us. We decided not to fly back to Tel Aviv for my winter break and instead enjoy Christmas in the city, just the two of us. Tangled in the sheets in the late mornings, Liam and I grew closer with each day. I couldn't bear the thought of him leaving.

"I have a tourist visa, so I can stay here for six months before I have to go back," he said when I asked him to stay. "We'll live off your parents for now. I'd want to get a work visa soon, though, so I can make a living for us."

Liam had left the army on a whim to move here with me, and even if he wanted to, he couldn't go back to serving as an officer. Without giving even a few days' notice, Liam left his uniform on the commander's desk with a note thanking him for a meaningful service. The last sentence read: "I'm going to follow my dreams."

"My Uncle Tom, my dad's brother—you haven't met him yet—he works at Target as a delivery guy and said he could hook me up to work under the radar until I get the work visa. But the plan is for us to get married, and then I can work without needing favors from anybody."

"What do you mean?" I asked.

"When we get married, since you're an American citizen, I'd be able to start the green card process and then be able to work legally as an American resident."

"We literally just got engaged. I haven't even thought about my wedding dress, and you're already talking to me about a wedding? Hold your horses, cowboy." I felt my palms moisten.

"Not a wedding, dummy. Not yet. Just signing the papers."

Winter break ended, and I went back to classes at school. Liam spent days on the couch in his boxers watching *Fauda*. The apartment was a pigsty—Liam's dirty boxers scrunched up on my study chair, his towels littering the floor in the bathroom, the refrigerator empty. Instead of studying when I got home from school, I'd start cleaning the place like a maniac, opening the windows to let in fresh air, vacuuming up the crumbs of whatever Liam had for breakfast that morning in our bed. Liam didn't want the cleaning lady coming anymore because she "disturbed" him, so I took on her role. He insisted I was privileged and could handle cleaning an average-sized New York City apartment, and I couldn't argue with that.

To make matters worse, it turned out that Liam's uncle had "tricked" him. Without a work visa, he couldn't set Liam up with a job after all, which meant we had to sign the marriage papers as soon as possible.

As each week passed, Liam's attitude toward me changed. He was impatient and rude, he wouldn't let me wear shorts, and he called half a dozen times in a row if I didn't answer his call the first time. I made up excuses for his behavior—*He's just upset that he can't work right now, he's still getting used to this new country, he doesn't speak English well*—and spent class breaks looking up recipes online, following them word for word. I knew how to follow directions.

Chapter 22

"Okay, Liam, but really quick," I said as I slid off my jeans and hopped back in bed with him. Liam woke up with my alarm, he was always horniest in the mornings, and I had exactly half an hour to get ready and make it to Ray's class on time.

Make him work for it, but keep him satisfied.

We lost track of time, and, of course, I was running late. When Liam finished, I left the untouched cup of coffee I brewed earlier on the kitchen counter, sprinted to the university, and sped up the stairs to Ray's classroom. He was known to lock it as soon as class started and never let students enter once the lecture began. What made me think I had a prayer of getting into his class that morning? Even though I thought Ray would probably ignore my frantic knocking and laugh me out of the building, I continued to stand outside of his classroom until I saw the doorknob turn.

Ray's bald head peeked out, and I started apologizing. "I'm so sorry, Ray, I had the most hectic morning, and I don't know what hap—"

I felt my cheeks flush. My eyes filled with tears. Why was I crying? I'd just gotten engaged, for God's sake. I looked down at the floor and wished I could just sink through it and disappear.

When we made eye contact, Ray was suddenly, completely focused on me. I could tell by the softness in his eyes that he recognized that my pain came from somewhere deeper than just today, deeper than just this one time being late. He ushered me into the classroom and whispered so none of the other students could hear, "It's okay, Ella. It happens."

As I sat through class and took notes on the last few chapters of the current book, I had to physically stop myself from sobbing. I bit my tongue, recited song lyrics in my mind, and counted the tiles on the ceiling of the classroom—anything to make sure my tears wouldn't start to flow, because if they did, I wasn't sure they would stop. I was sweating, my whole body damp under the light pink sweater I threw on when I was in too much of a rush to realize it was only forty degrees. I closed my eyes and silently repeated Ray's words. *It happens.*

I sat motionless in my chair, but I felt like everything was spinning out of control. Liam had sprung this engagement on me out of nowhere, and now he was on a mission to convince me to sign the marriage papers. If we continued on this path, I would be late to every class. I'd be a failure.

Ray began a review of the books we had studied during the semester. He clicked the next slide and gave us a few minutes to copy down important quotes from *The Prince* that would be on the final. I snapped out of my thoughts and looked up at the screen. "Everyone sees what you appear to be, few experience what you really are."

When class ended, as I organized my belongings, Ray tapped me on the shoulder. "Do you have a minute?"

I nodded, sure that Ray was going to scold me for having the audacity to show up late to his philosophy class. I was ready for it. He was right.

Instead, when all the other students emptied the classroom, he sat me down in front of him.

"What's going on with you, Ella? What happened?"

The room was quiet. All I could hear were the students outside on the lawn and the rhythmic thump of my own heart.

I looked up at Ray, shook my head, and shrugged, my eyes welling up again.

"I'm listening," he said.

I wanted to tell him. I wanted to tell this man I barely knew, and no one else, what had been going on in my life. It was on the tip of my tongue. I wanted to tell him about Liam's surprise visit, about Shakespeare Garden and the cushion-cut diamond ring. About how I felt like I'd never be able to tell Liam how I felt, how confused I was because, even though I loved him, I was scared of him. I wanted to tell Ray how Liam was harassing me to sign the marriage papers, how I felt ugly and shapeless, how my father was against the engagement, how my mother's excitement over wedding planning blinded her from seeing what I was feeling. About how pathetic I felt waiting for something to happen instead of making it happen myself. I pictured Ray resting his chin in his hands and listening to my story, sometimes nodding, sometimes laughing, other times not saying anything at all.

Instead, I took a deep breath, shook my head, and put on my best smile. "I'm fine, Ray. Really."

Chapter 23

One morning in late January as I sat at the dining room table studying, Liam waved his hands in front of my computer screen.

"Na, na, na, na, na," he sang.

"Stop it," I said, the organic chemistry equations that once seemed so easy jumping off the page into an endless tornado of chaos.

"Don't you think you're wasting our time?" Liam asked. There was no more *my* time or *his* time. Our time had merged into one. "Look at me," he said. "You're a star. A fucking star. You shouldn't be wasting hours on chemistry and calculus and whatever the hell this is. You don't need to be taught. You can teach them. Do you hear me? You can teach those professors who think the sun shines out of their ass."

I laughed. "Thank you, baby." I could tell Liam meant what he said. He got this look in his eyes, this crazy look that made his pupils shrink and his eyes open wide.

"I'm serious, Ella. You shouldn't waste your time or your parents' money on some stupid education. Look at Zuckerberg, Bezos, Bill Gates—did they go to school? Education isn't what it used to be. Fuck Columbia. Fuck these books," he said as he pushed the textbook onto the floor, my multicolored MUJI pens scattering across the rug.

"Liam!" I yelled. "What are you doing?" I laughed.

"Are you happy? You don't seem happy, and you and I both know it's because you're spending your days in school. What are you doing? Life is short," he said.

"I know, maybe I'm not happy, but it's not like I can drop out of Columbia and call it a day."

"Why not? You can. You never open your mind. You're always stuck inside this bubble of what you think you're supposed to do. What the world tells you to do. Do what you want to do," he said.

I didn't know what I wanted to do anymore. The voice in my mind I used to listen to had faded until all I could hear was a piercing silence.

"I'm going to make sure you live your life. Not waste it," he said. "Fuck Columbia; you're better than them."

For weeks, Liam etched into my brain this idea that Columbia was taking up all of our time and energy, that I was wasting my life—our life—going to classes. I stopped answering my father's calls and only texted him back when I had to.

"Are you alive?" he asked, half-jokingly. What I didn't know until I talked to my mother was that ever since staying in New York with Liam instead of traveling to Tel Aviv over winter break, my father was so worried about me that it affected his day-to-day life. He left patients sitting on the examination table confused, just to step out and breathe a breath of fresh air, just to call me and hear my voice. He felt, from almost six thousand miles away, that his daughter was in the dark.

Out of the blue, Liam surprised me with a three-day trip to the Catskills during one of the busiest weeks at school. I missed a physics lab that couldn't be made up, but the two of us stayed in a cabin in the woods, isolated from other people and at one with nature. For the first half of the first day, I was stressed until Liam gave me a pep talk that calmed me down.

"Let go, Tiny. This is what life is about," he promised.

I pushed the thought of school aside and spent the next two mornings writing at the cabin while Liam hiked and hunted. In the evenings, we drank red wine and made love until our eyelids were heavy.

One night at dinner at the local hotel, he said the words *drop out* more times than I could count. We met an Israeli couple, and even to them, he made it a point to explain, "My fiancée wants to drop out of Columbia and become a writer full-time. She's gonna write books that are gonna turn into movies, and we're gonna be rich," he joked.

Later at night, when the whispers of our voices echoed deep into the sheets, he said, "I have an idea: You drop out of Columbia, we use the money your parents would have paid for your education to buy ourselves a little house upstate, and we get pregnant."

My heart dropped. I lay in bed, silently looking up at the moonlight reflecting against the ceiling. So this was it? This was my life? The stainless-steel nightstand next to the bed, the gray businesslike chairs around the small cabin table, the yellowed chandelier hanging down from the ceiling, the man lying next to me. Pregnant? I was twenty-one years old. But when Liam wanted something, he chipped away at it like a block of marble until the sculpture he had imagined came to life.

"I'm not ready to have a baby. We're not even married yet," I gathered the courage to say.

"Oh, God, I love you," Liam said. I felt a wave of relief. And then, "You want to marry me already? Let's do it. Let's go to City Hall this weekend and get married. You know how important it is for my work status, and we've been engaged for a while now anyway, so why not? When our family and friends are off work for the summer, we'll have a huge celebration at whatever fancy hotel you choose. But for now, it's us. Me and you. I don't need any more than that. You're enough for me,

Tiny," he said, his hand creeping up my thigh under the covers. "Am I not enough for you?"

"Wait, wait . . . but we said we would wait with the marriage. I want our families to be there; I told you that," I said, my head spinning. I felt a wave of exhaustion wash over me. I just wanted to fall asleep.

"Am I not enough for you?" he said. "I really mean that. Am I not enough for you?"

"I love you! Of course you're enough for me, but I'm not ready to be married."

"But? There shouldn't be any *buts* after you tell someone you love them," he said. "Plus, it's not a real marriage. It's just signing the papers. Then, later, we'll do the whole white dress thing. I know you've always dreamed of that. If we sign the papers now, I can get a green card and work as a resident instead of a foreign worker. I can make more money, and we can move upstate and have a baby. My baby will have a baby," he said. "And she'll be even tinier than you."

"I don't know," I said. Lately, all I knew was that I didn't know. I thought that moving back to New York would be a completely different experience than the army, but now, living in the city with Liam was almost as punishing and confusing.

"What are you thinking? What do you feel?" he asked.

"Darkness," I said. "I feel darkness."

"Okay, well, you're going to think about it," he said. I could sense the impatience bubbling under his skin, the shadow of his eyelashes moving up and down as he blinked. Still, his hand crept up my thigh, higher and higher.

"I'll think about it," I said, "but please, I don't want to talk about it every single day all day. Like you do about dropping out of Columbia. It wears me out."

"As long as you promise to think about it, I won't talk about it again until you bring it up," he said.

I was so tired I couldn't think anymore. I pushed Liam's hand away; sex was the last thing on my mind. I closed my eyes and fell into a faraway sleep, only to be woken up to Liam slipping off my underwear and slipping into me.

———————

The next afternoon, back at our apartment, Liam barged in while I was showering and pulled back the curtain, exposing my naked body. I never told him about what happened with Andrew, knowing that his jealousy would overtake his empathy. He put the top of the toilet seat down and took a seat, as the shampoo bubbles trickled down my neck.

"What are you doing?" I said, half-laughing, half-alarmed.

"We need to talk about our conversation last night," he said. So much for not bringing up the marriage papers. I looked over at him, immediately recognizing the dark atmosphere that surrounded him, and took a deep breath. Another fight? Seriously? Didn't he get tired of fighting? We had just made up from last week's argument—*Why was I flirting with the waiter at Cipriani's? Was that why it was my favorite Italian place?* I reassured Liam that laughing at the waiter's corny joke about tiramisu—*If it isn't delicious, you can tiramiSUE me*—wasn't flirting, but he wouldn't have it. I spent the dinner moving my truffle penne pasta from one side of the plate to the other, while Liam reprimanded me, only lowering his voice when the couple at the table next to us looked over.

"I'm serious—we need to talk," he said.

"Now?" Couldn't it wait? I was in the middle of taking a shower, the only ten minutes of the day I really had to myself.

"We need to sign the marriage papers or else I can't work," he said, brushing his hand through his hair as he stood up and nonchalantly checked himself out in the mirror. "I don't get it. Do you want me to leave you? How would you handle living here by yourself? You don't even know how to pay the bills." Liam helped pay the bills but only in a literal sense. When he filled out the paperwork, he used my parents' credit card.

As I applied conditioner to my hair, letting it soak in, I pulled the shower curtain forward so it would serve as some sort of protective shield. I felt vulnerable and bare standing there stripped down in front of Liam, and even though he'd seen me naked hundreds of times, this time felt different. Immediately, he jerked it back.

"Can you get out?" I said.

"Why? So you can touch yourself? I told you I don't like to think about anybody but me touching your body."

"Are you kidding me?" I said.

For the rest of the afternoon, even while I dried off and brushed my wet hair, even when I walked into the kitchen to make us dinner, even at night when I was getting ready for bed, he followed me. He harassed me about signing the marriage papers and wouldn't stop, even when I begged him to leave me alone. Being engaged to Liam was one thing; I could drag that out for two years if I had to. But marrying someone, even if it was just signing papers, felt heavy to me at twenty-one. I wanted to convince him to wait with the marriage papers, but he wouldn't quit.

For the entire month of March, Liam blamed me for his inability to work. I was starting to fail my classes—chemistry equations swapped with anxious thoughts about what Liam could do, reading homework interrupted by his incessant nagging. One afternoon, just as philosophy class ended and the rest of the students packed up their books, Ray asked, "Ella, can I have a minute with you?"

I waited as the other students left the room. "I've noticed you haven't been yourself lately," he said. "You almost fell asleep today, and you didn't raise your hand once, which means I know you didn't do the reading."

I didn't have the energy to lie. "I'm sorry, Ray. I didn't have time." If only he knew what I was doing instead: washing dishes, folding laundry, sweeping under the table, all while Liam sat on the couch reprimanding me for not signing the marriage papers, the television blaring with another gory action movie.

"You should find the time. Or change your schedule. School should be a priority for you. Especially my class. When you actually study the material, you even understand some of the more profound theories. Don't waste that potential," he said.

When I arrived home that day, without even greeting me, Liam continued his harangue. "I've thought about it. All we have to do is sign marriage papers so I can get a work permit. It's no big deal. You're nuts, you know that? You promised we'd be married soon, so what does it matter? You've put me in a pathetic position, having to beg you to sign papers so I can work. Any girlfriend would do that for her boyfriend, especially one she sees marrying someday. Do you not see me in your future? Is that what it is? Because I can't wrap my head around it."

"I never asked you to come here," I said under my breath, plopping my backpack on the dining room table.

"What did you just say?"

"I'm just saying, you came here on your own. You surprised me. You said your uncle would help you find a job. You moved in with me without any prior notice. Now, in the one place I felt like I was excelling, I'm failing again. I can't study with you constantly nagging me about signing marriage papers." Ray's face flashed through my mind, and the words spilled out of my mouth. I felt my throat dry up.

"A deal's a deal. I only agreed to move in with you because you promised me you'd sign the papers," he said.

"I never promised that."

"Yes, you did."

"When?"

"When we were at that swanky lounge bar with the squeaky-clean leather couches. You don't remember?"

"No, I don't remember."

"You never remember anything."

The following night, I ran into Chloe at the library. At first, we pretended not to notice each other, but it was obvious by the glances we kept sneaking that we had. I organized my books and my laptop and walked over to Chloe's table, where she sat alone, surrounded by piles of books. I plopped my books down and took a deep breath.

"I shut everyone out after Martha's Vineyard," I started. "But still, I expected you to make sure I was okay."

"I tried," Chloe said. "It doesn't matter now. The past is in the past. I'll be here for you no matter what. I'm going to get us coffee. Iced coffee with vanilla sweet cream foam? We deserve it."

We sipped our coffees, the sound of book pages flipping our only form of company. When it was well past dinner, Chloe stayed to keep studying, and I walked home.

When I opened the apartment door, it was as if I had entered into a dream. Liam wore a white T-shirt and sweatpants, his hair wet from the shower, the smell of soap trailing him as he led me into the living room. Hundreds of balloons, candles, and red rose petals decorated the space, our song playing in the background.

"I love you, Tiny. I promise you that. Remember when I told you I'd be there to protect you no matter what? No matter where you would be? You are the most important person in my life, and I don't want to make you feel like you can't be yourself around me. I'm sorry for pressuring you to sign the marriage papers when I said we didn't have to talk about it. I don't deserve you in the first place; we both know that. Since you aren't sure what you want to do yet, I wanted us to cherish the time we have left together. I can't stay here much longer if I don't start the green card process, but I want every minute I have to be spent with you before I leave."

"This . . . it's all beautiful, Liam. I love you, too. I'm sorry. I want you to stay. I can't imagine being here without you." The thought of being alone scared me. What would I do with myself if Liam hopped on a plane to Tel Aviv?

"Then let's just sign the papers. Tomorrow. We don't have to tell anybody. Not your parents, not mine. We can have a big wedding in May; no one will know we already signed the papers. It's just for us. For me to be able to work. Don't even think of it as a wedding. I promise I'll give you the wedding you've always dreamed of. And I promise you I'll stop nagging and you'll be able to study and get on top of your grades again. You trust me, don't you?"

"Of course I do," I said. "Fine, let's get it over with. Tomorrow. And I don't want to hear another request out of your mouth after this, mister. I need to study."

"You are the love of my life," Liam said, shaking his head. "Sit down, relax; everything's going to be okay." He pulled out the dining room chair, poured me a glass of champagne, and served me a warm bowl of pasta in marinara sauce. With extra parmesan.

Chapter 24

The day we went to sign the papers at City Hall, I couldn't find anything to wear. After contemplating several options, I ended up choosing a long-sleeved black ruffled shirt, black jeans, and black boots. Who knew I'd dress to my wedding the way someone dresses to a funeral? Liam wore a white button-down shirt and black dress pants, like a kid at his bar mitzvah. After forcing a croissant down my throat and drinking my morning coffee in bed, my hands cupping the glass to embrace the warmth my body was thirsty for, Liam was in such a rush that we practically ran out of the apartment and hailed a taxi. As I made my way into the cab, ignoring the sudden cold of the blustery March morning, I tried to calm myself down by repeating the words Liam had engraved on my mind for the past few months. "We're not getting married, Tiny—I mean, not *really*—we're just signing the papers so I can stay here with you."

I'll deal with this later, I kept thinking. We were engaged, and now we were signing papers; a part of me wanted to keep us together, but another part was screaming that this was wrong.

Signing the papers. We're only signing fucking papers. This was the mantra I repeated in my mind as the taxi driver sped up Second Avenue, turning up the Miley Cyrus song playing on Z100. I was going to marry the man I loved. He was the man I loved, right? This was love, wasn't it? I looked out the window at busy commuters on their way to work. *The world keeps turning.*

Liam and I shared a dislike for the city's morning traffic, yet as the estimated arrival time on the GPS kept slowly increasing, I felt an indescribable love for the standstill. I could kiss every person behind the wheel, every Uber driver in his black car and housewife in her Range Rover, blocking the way toward a future my heart knew I didn't want.

What I did want was for the universe to intervene. I hoped something would happen and we wouldn't be able to make it to the town hall in time. *Please let us get a flat tire. Please, please, please.* I didn't consider, of course, that if this flat tire fantasy were to hypothetically happen, Liam would, in the blink of an eye, find us another cab to hop into and continue this mission. That's what this was to him—a mission, an operation, something strictly technical.

I held Liam's hand in the cab, and he squeezed it back, leaning in to peck me on the forehead. I felt his tension accumulating with the traffic. I thought maybe it was a sign from God that we shouldn't be doing this. The metal tips of my black boots made monotonous, anxious staccato clicks against the back of the taxi driver's seat.

"Stop it," Liam said as he angled his head higher to get a better look at the traffic, and I watched my foot freeze mid-tap.

In a sense, I was relieved. I had grown so accustomed to going against my desires and putting his first that it seemed almost natural to push this fearful voice down into my stomach until I heard nothing but a muffled cry.

Whenever I got in trouble at home as a young girl, I used to imagine getting physically hurt—breaking my arm, falling down our Connecticut barn-house stairs—so that my parents would forget that

I had done anything wrong in the first place and simply pray for my well-being. When Liam and I fought, I would sometimes go back to being that little girl, imagining that something bad would physically happen to me so he couldn't be angry at me. In this daydream, I would accidentally hurt myself and see Liam's face soften as he magically forgave me for whatever I had done to upset him. It seemed like being hurt physically was better than the emotional pain I felt when he was angry. A broken arm I could bear. A broken heart I could not.

As we stepped out of the cab and entered City Hall, I felt that feeling again—the desire to faint or fall or break something or have a mental collapse—anything really—so we wouldn't have to go through with signing the papers. But here we were, and it was time. There was no turning back now.

The heat of the air in the hall hit me as we walked in, and I felt smothered by it. Around us were couples smiling, most of the women dressed in beautiful white dresses fit for real weddings, their families snapping photos. The first person to greet us was a photographer in an oversized black trench coat. "Need a witness? Photographer? Twenty-five dollas," he said.

Liam nodded. "Shit, we do need a witness. Will you do it for twenty dollars, man?"

"Twenty-five or nothing, fella," the photographer said.

Liam pulled out a twenty-dollar bill and then another ten and handed it to the man.

"I don't have any change on me, man," the man said, probably lying.

"Okay, fine, keep it. Let's go," Liam said, rushing to the line in front of a sign that read "Marriage Ceremony Here."

Behind me was a slim woman dressed in a black Count Dracula dress, wearing black lipstick, heavy black eyeliner, and gold glitter pumps. She had style, I had to admit. The couple in front of us was dressed as if they were going straight from City Hall to their black-tie reception, the man in a fitted tuxedo and the woman in a mermaid dress she could barely walk in, holding the tail up with one hand so it wouldn't sweep up the dust along the dirty floor. She looked beautiful, aside from her horrible perm, but it was the couple's happiness that couldn't be ignored. They kissed each other as they moved forward in line, taking selfies and acting as if nobody else in the world existed.

"You okay, Tiny?" Liam said, relaxed that we had made it on time.

"I'm fine, but this isn't our wedding day, okay? I want a real wedding," I said.

When we neared the front of the line, an elderly City Hall worker handed Liam a ticket: 526C. Liam finally had his golden ticket.

Before the clerk called the numbers, each couple had the chance to take a few pictures against a ridiculous Empire State Building backdrop.

Where am I? What am I doing? How did I let myself get into this situation?

When our number was called, we sat in front of a middle-aged Russian woman who seemed to want nothing more than to go home. Liam handed her our passports, and she looked at each picture and then up at our faces. Who did she see in that picture? Was it the same girl she saw when she looked up at me? In a matter of seconds, the clerk asked that we sign our names below.

"Would you like to take his last name?" she asked me.

"No." I looked at Liam. "Not yet."

"Sign here and go wait in that room over there." She pointed to the waiting room outside of the chapel area. "Mr. Lopez will be with you shortly."

We sat together on a worn-out couch. Liam scrolled through his phone, watching TikToks and chuckling to himself. I looked around me. The wallpaper was slowly coming off of the walls, the chandelier was crooked, and the scent of overperfumed brides filled my nostrils.

A family of four walked into the room to ask me, of all people, to take their picture.

"Let's take a picture, too," Liam said as he leaned in closer to me. We took a few selfies, and he zoomed in on my face in the screen.

"You're beautiful," he said. "You know that?"

After no more than fifteen minutes, Mr. Lopez, a short, tan-skinned man with a buzz cut and a thin mustache, greeted us with a warm smile. He presented us with a marriage speech he'd memorized, alternating his voice tones like he had recited it hundreds of times.

"Do you, Liam Levine, take Ella Davidson to be your wife, to have and to hold from this day forward, for better, for worse, for richer, for poorer, in sickness and in health, to love and to cherish, till death do you part?"

Liam looked at him, not at me, and said, "I do."

"And do you, Ella Davidson, take Liam Levine to be your husband, to have and to hold from this day forward, for better, for worse, for richer, for poorer, in sickness and in health, to love and to cherish, till death do you part?"

I took a deep breath. "I do."

With Liam, I was either in agony or ecstasy. When we fought, I couldn't eat anything; I could barely sip my coffee. This would go on for a few days until I apologized for upsetting him. Following this apology and usually a round or two of makeup sex, I would eat everything in sight like a ravenous child. I thought signing the papers that day meant saving myself from agony. I was wrong.

———

As soon as we were officially married, Liam turned back into the person he'd been in Israel, and I sank even deeper into the depression I felt before he arrived in New York City. What drove me crazy was the more I felt like I was losing myself, the happier Liam was.

After we signed the papers, a smile radiated off his face when he woke up in the mornings. He even started leaving the house to go for long walks, texting me pictures of tulips planted alongside 67th and Park or dogs lounging outside Madison Avenue storefronts while their owners shopped inside. It was as if he were sucking all the energy out of me and stocking up on it himself, and I couldn't even put my finger on what exactly he was doing wrong. Was it just me? Was I the problem? Did I need to take antidepressants like he suggested?

Didn't he see how rapidly I was losing weight? How slumped I was sitting on the couch? Liam treated me like a regular person, when it should have been clear to him that I was losing myself. But I realized, even through the tumult, that I couldn't let life happen to me anymore.

My world was crumbling. I went from acing exams and finishing homework assignments before they were due to skipping classes and watching my grades plummet. School was always the one thing I was good at. Academics had always been easy for me, and of all the subjects I had studied, science and math and, now, philosophy came the easiest. I wanted to keep safe the one thing that made me feel sane: my education. But when I tried to talk to Liam about the failure I felt I had become, he would change the subject.

"We've been arguing nonstop," he said. "Let's wait for things to cool down between us before we talk."

Or, when my tears started coming, he'd say, "We can't talk if you're going to get emotional like this. Pull yourself together."

Still, I couldn't walk ten minutes to campus without at least three calls from Liam. "When you get home tonight, I want to add that GPS app to your phone. I'm worried sick about you every time you leave the house. I'm the only one protecting you in this city, and I take that seriously. Do you know what kind of responsibility that is for me? Especially when you have your head in the clouds half the time."

I was the last person at the library every evening because at home, I couldn't study. Liam needed me, wanted me to cook for him, to suck his dick, to watch idiotic TikToks of people tripping or stunning girls in bikinis dancing, their boobs bobbing up and down while he stared.

When we first started dating, Liam showed me the side of him he knew I wanted to see. He was vulnerable, he cried real tears, and he allowed himself to rest his head on my shoulder. I was his safety in the same way he was mine, until the umbrella was deep up my ass, snug and warm. Now, far away from those I loved, his time had come to open it.

Chapter 25

My parents came to visit us in April, both of them tan and glowing from strolls along the boardwalk in the warm Tel Aviv sun. It was Liam's idea to invite them, even though, since getting the marriage license, he insisted we take a step back from our families. I was excited that he seemed to be warming up to the idea of spending time with my family, to letting them into the bubble that had become our life.

I had been cooking since the morning while Liam worked on the green card paperwork, our tiny apartment full of homey smells of garlic and thyme, paprika and basil. I prepared my signature dish, pasta Bolognese, the only dish I knew how to cook without having to follow a recipe. I imagined that after a twelve-hour flight, a warm bowl of Bolognese would put a smile on their faces. I decided to serve it with steamed Brussels sprouts and brown rice, my mother's favorite. I missed my mother, the comforting way my body fit to hers when we hugged, no matter how thin she had become.

As we waited for my parents to arrive, I put on my father's favorite Marvin Gaye record, and the apartment filled with a sense of lightness. Liam picked me up and spun me around.

"I fucking love you," he said.

The doorbell rang, and I opened the door to welcome my parents, their noses red from the April cold, their smiles bright. They hugged me at the same time, the way they used to when I was a child, and as I nuzzled my face between them, I felt for a second like I was about to cry. They looked so good together, so right, so unlike Liam and me. Liam was thick and heavy. He loved American food and had gained weight eating bacon, egg, and cheese sandwiches we didn't have in Israel, while I was as thin and delicate as a feather the wind could pick up and blow away.

As soon as my parents stepped into our apartment, Liam poured them a glass of our signature Sancerre, pronouncing the French word without a trace of insecurity. He had come a long way since that night at the Pineapple Bar.

"How was your flight?" he asked my father.

"Good, good. Long," my father answered and looked over at me. "You look thin, sweetie." He turned to Liam. "What, you aren't feeding her?" he joked.

Meanwhile my mother walked into the kitchen, humming to herself. "How are you, sweetie? How do you like the apartment? I'm so glad it's getting some good use, but you should brighten it up a bit; everything's black, white, and beige."

I didn't realize that she was nervous for me, worried about her skinny, deflated daughter. That maybe it was too much for her to take in that her recently engaged, twenty-one-year-old daughter was living alone in New York City with her older boyfriend, barely taking the time to return her calls. She was there when I arrived home that morning in Tel Aviv with a bruise on my cheek. She knew.

I had spent the entire day running around the Upper East Side preparing for this evening, hoping the evening was so well put together that it would mask the fact that my life was falling apart. I even made a homemade tiramisu, although I bought the ready-made cream from Citarella; I wanted my culinary efforts to impress my parents so much that by the end of the meal, they'd look over at their eldest daughter and think she was living a lovely, gracious life.

"You know, Mom, I don't need your judgment right now. In fact, it's just about the last thing I need," I barked.

"You're like a porcupine, stabbing anything coming your way. I'm just saying," she said.

"Okay, I like the black and white and beige. It's called style," I said. There was a cruelty in my voice I knew would cut her. *Why am I acting like this when I miss her so deeply? What is wrong with me?*

We sat down, and the music stopped. I immediately noticed because the air filled with the sound of forks clinking against the plates. Just as I was about to get up to change it, Liam cleared his throat.

"We wanted to talk to you about something," he said. "Right, Tiny?"

Talk about something? About what? When did we discuss that we were going to talk about something with my parents? Liam always surprised me with his announcements, but I felt like I had to be on his side to show my parents I was in control.

"Yeah," I said. "Go ahead." I gave Liam permission in front of my parents, as if I had any say in our relationship to begin with, let alone with what was going to come out of his mouth next. I was just as clueless as my parents were, sitting there eating their spaghetti.

"Well," Liam said as he lifted his wine glass and took a large swig. "We're married!"

My father stopped mid-bite and looked up at me from his plate. He didn't even look in Liam's direction, as if Liam didn't exist in this situation. My father closed his eyes, scrunched his eyebrows together, and tilted his head, as if he hadn't heard correctly.

"What is he talking about, Ella?" my father asked me.

How could Liam drop a bomb like this right now? We had agreed not to tell anybody about the ceremony, not until after the actual wedding. I knew how hurt my parents would be if they knew we had eloped behind their backs without their approval.

Liam continued, "We decided as a couple that this was the right st—"

"Will you shut up?" my father snapped. "I want to hear what my daughter has to say." He sat there in silence, his eyes and his mind calculating the situation. My mother stared at me.

"Daddy, we're going to have a real wedding, and you and Mom will be there—don't worry. We decided to sign the papers on a whim, really, so Liam would be able to start the green card process and work here," I explained. "I'm sorry we didn't tell you before." I felt near tears.

Liam cleared his throat. "With all due respect, Ben, your opinion is extremely important to us, don't get me wrong, but your daughter isn't a child anymore; she can make her own decisions," Liam said matter-of-factly.

I took a large swig of my wine.

"Liam's right, Ben. They're big kids. We should be happy for them," my mother said, speaking for what felt like the first time since we'd begun eating. "Plus, now we get to plan a wedding!"

My father scratched his chin, the peppered stubble making a scratching sound I could hear from across the table.

"This isn't something you just do, Ella," my father said, ignoring Liam and my mother. "You talk it over with your family."

"Ella and I are family now," Liam said under his breath.

"It just sort of happened," I lied, watching Liam pour himself another glass of wine.

How could my father just sit there like that? Part of me wanted him to kick Liam out of the apartment; my parents were the ones paying for it, anyway. Another part of me wanted my father to pick me up and fling me over his shoulder as I kicked and screamed all the way to the airport. Deep down I wished they'd reprimand me; I wished they would bring me back to their hotel room, order Chinese food for me, and tell me everything was going to be okay. I wanted to start my life over again, to leave this entire situation, but I didn't know how. I felt stuck, like my feet were glued to the floor and I couldn't take a step.

For the entire evening, I had been on the verge of tears, but at that moment I felt like I was going to cry uncontrollably if I didn't do something, so I stood up and went to the bathroom. I patted my face with a wet cloth, making sure my mascara didn't run. Why hadn't I predicted this happening? Why was everything with Liam a surprise I wasn't ready for? What did I expect my parents to do? I was an adult, right? They couldn't save me anymore. I thought I wanted my parents to ignore my misery, and now they were. So why was I even more miserable?

I felt so alone that I thought about locking myself in the bathroom and never coming out. Why were they playing along in this game with me and Liam? How could they have pretended that this was a normal family moment? Couldn't they see that my life was falling to pieces?

When I stepped out of the bathroom, Liam caught my gaze. He winked at me. *Winked.*

I had given up on myself, and now, it felt like my parents were giving up on me, too. Could I really blame them? Under the table, Liam put his hand on my knee. His touch repulsed me. My father wasn't eating anymore. My mother wouldn't stop blabbing on and on about the wedding. As the conversation veered to small talk, I felt Liam slide his hand up my inner thigh. I pushed him away.

Chapter 26

My parents rented an Airbnb on the Upper West Side for a week, but I barely spent any time with them. I grew distant from my father again, ignoring his attempts to reach me. Liam couldn't forgive my father for speaking to him disrespectfully, telling him to shut up at the kitchen table "in his own home." I didn't bother to remind Liam that although he and I lived there together, the apartment technically belonged to my parents.

"You father isn't welcome in our home anymore," Liam said. "I don't want you seeing him; he only brings you down."

I met up with my mother to talk but only when Liam was sleeping or busy, and only to talk about the wedding.

"We'll have it in the city, right? And I'll have Grandma and Grandpa and Anna fly over. There won't be that many guests because who can afford to fly all the way to New York from Tel Aviv on such short notice? But it'll be classy, sweetie. Stunning," she said as we drank coffee on 90th and Madison at a gluten-free cafe with '80s love songs playing in the background. "If we had more time to plan, I'd be less stressed. Two months?"

"I don't want anything too fancy," I said, too tired to think.

"Help me!" I wanted to scream. I wanted to blurt it out a dozen times since seeing my mother, especially when I walked toward her from a street away and saw her fragile frame and her big, brown, comforting eyes. I wanted to hug her tightly and cry, without having to explain.

Liam's anger toward me became more frequent, my mistakes more drastic. When I accidentally dropped a plate on the floor as I was unloading the dishwasher and it broke into pieces, Liam insisted I did it on purpose, since it was part of a set his mother had bought us. When I threw his T-shirts into the dryer and they shrank, he didn't talk to me for two days. When I told him in the cab on the way to the doctor that I didn't think I needed antidepressants, he screamed at me in front of the driver, saying he was done with my shit. I stopped answering phone calls from friends and didn't meet up with any of them, not even Chloe, who called me at least twice a day. Liam and I were alone, and while he was the only person I felt like I could turn to, he was also the only person I was failing over and over again.

One Friday morning when Liam took the train down to Soho to meet his uncle, Chloe showed up at my apartment.

"What are you doing here? The doorman didn't call me."

"You think he could say no to this innocent face?" She tilted her chin up and cupped it in her hands, her soft blonde hair swaying. She sat on the couch, and I sat down beside her.

"Where have you been?" she asked. "What's up with you? You never answer when I call."

Chloe hadn't been a confidant after the situation with Andrew, not that I ever tried talking to her about it. She wasn't there for me when she saw me walking down the stairs of the Martha's Vineyard villa with a bag strung over my shoulder and mascara running down my cheeks, waiting for the Uber. Any sane person could tell that something was wrong, but she chose to sit back and watch.

"I've been busy," I said.

"Yeah, pretty busy considering you've skipped like a fourth of all of our classes lately," she said.

I laughed. "What do you want? Why did you really come here? It's not like you cared to check in on me after what happened in Martha's Vineyard."

She scoffed, playing with the strap. "Oh, Ella, grow up. You didn't talk to me about it, so I figured you didn't want to. You always wait for everyone to pick up the pieces for you, but you don't give yourself any of the responsibility. I'm not saying you're to blame for what Andrew did—you are absolutely not; he's an asshole. I don't even know what he did exactly, but I know it wasn't just pranking you in the shower like he told me. But either way, you expect the world to swoop in and make your life better. Stop being so passive. This is your life. We have one life to live. I don't mean to be harsh with you. I know this hasn't been the best time for you; I can tell by the black circles under your eyes."

I sat there silently.

"Will you talk? Say something? You have a lot to say. I know it. Say it," she said.

That's when the words started pouring out—to Chloe, this friend I didn't know that well anymore, a model who was probably bored on her way back from lunch and decided to stop by to see if I was home, to fill up her afternoon for an hour or two. Or maybe she was lonely too; she must have been, the way everybody in this cruel city was.

I talked to her the way I used to talk to Julia. Real and raw. "I'm not myself anymore. I'm in a situation where I don't feel emotionally safe. I feel confused about everything, Chloe, from what I'm going to eat in the morning to what I'm going to watch before I go to sleep. I can't make any decisions anymore, and I look to Liam to make them for me. When he does, I feel small, and when he doesn't, I feel lost. When he's around, I'm scared he's going to flip, and when he's not around, I'm scared to listen to the thoughts in my mind, to let myself feel. I used to have a spark, and now it's gone. I let it go. I let him have it, and now I'm stuck like this. With him. Forever."

It was the first time I said those words out loud. *I was stuck.* That meant I didn't want to be with Liam, didn't it? But just the thought of leaving him scared me. I loved him. I loved the way his eyes slanted upward when he smiled. I loved the man he was when we first got engaged, the man he was in the beginning of my army service when he protected me from Commander Mia, from myself. I loved this man who had, over time, become my entire life.

"You're not stuck," she said.

"I am stuck, Chloe," I said. "I married him."

She turned and stared at me. Her perfect pink lips parted. "You did? When? Why the hell would you do that?"

I didn't take the time to ask myself that question. With Liam, I was going through the motions.

"Because he wanted a work visa. Because I don't know how to say no to him. Because I'm too pathetic and dumb and scared to be alone."

"So you married him. So what? You're young and beautiful and smart, and you don't even lean on him financially. Do you know how lucky you are? How privileged? I live in a studio apartment with Kamila; the only thing granting us privacy is a curtain we put up in the middle of the room. When she cooks, my bed smells like garlic and onions, and that's how I go to sleep. No, seriously, smell my hair," she said, leaning in for me to smell it. It smelled like onion rings. "Stop feeling sorry for yourself and start changing your life."

We left the apartment to take a walk along the East River, and we talked until the sun went down and the city lights sparkled.

"You know the East River is like super special, right?" Chloe asked.

"Why is that?"

"Well, inland rivers usually travel only in one direction. No matter what's going on, they just keep traveling straight. But the East River's current changes with the time of day. Sometimes it heads northeast toward Connecticut, and other times it flows south to New Jersey."

"Really?" I said.

"Yeah," she said. "If you come here at exactly the right time, you might catch it. It's amazing. The water just switches its entire direction."

From that moment forward, I realized I had somebody physically close to me who cared. Someone far enough away from the situation but close enough for me to reach out to. Her words were enough to trigger my own thoughts, thoughts that had been there all along, and when we came back to my apartment, we sat on my couch drinking instant coffee and laughing at the ridiculous catfights on *The Real Housewives of Beverly Hills*. I realized I hadn't felt this sense of freedom in what seemed like a century.

I couldn't believe my wedding to Liam was less than two months away.

––––––––

In early May, on an afternoon that paled with heat, my father and I walked to 80th and 1st Avenue for breakfast at the Gracie Mews Diner. He had arrived at 5:00 a.m. that morning on the same United flight from Tel Aviv he always took.

"I know we haven't been speaking, but I'm coming to New York for the day, before my meeting in Salt Lake City," he said when I answered the phone. "Can I take you to breakfast?"

My father insisted he was coming for business, but his meetings were all over the country: Salt Lake City, Chicago, New Orleans. Yet he had stopped in New York first, lugging his bags onto an Uber and making his way all the way up to the Upper East Side, to our faded front door.

That morning, I woke up before my alarm, like always, the sheets drenched in sweat. Since signing the papers, I was waking up between 3:00 and 4:00 a.m., thinking about the wedding and watching *90 Day Fiancé* silently on my phone as I read the subtitles. Liam was my real-life ninety-day fiancé, pressuring me to sign papers until I agreed, living in America thanks to my citizenship, promising to find a job but instead lying around the apartment complaining of boredom.

Sometimes, as he slept beside me, I'd just stare out the window at the building across from ours, making up stories about the tenants. I already knew the people's schedules. The couple on the top floor woke up at 5:55 a.m. each day, the light flickering on as soon as their alarm went off. I wondered if they, too, believed in the Israeli superstition that the number five protected from the evil eye. Five was the number of fingers on a hand, and a hand was a *hamsa*, the ultimate repellant of evil. Did they know they were starting their day with a blessing? I imagined they started the day making slow, passionate love, the husband bringing his wife coffee in bed when they were finished. On the tenth floor, I saw the reflection of an old woman sitting in a rocking chair, her television glaring all night. I had no story for her, just the sad truth of aging alone.

My own insomnia was lonesome, keeping me up at night and making me feel like I was alone in the world in spite of Liam's deep breathing beside me. More than anything, Liam was frustrated with it.

"You don't sleep, and then you're tired all day. I have nobody to talk to anymore. Knock, knock, is anyone home in there?"

The Columbia general practitioner advised me to take antidepressants, the eternal solution for all problems in America. After countless calls from Duane Reade insisting I pick up the prescription, I almost did, desperate to feel something other than the lingering anxiety I felt in Liam's presence—until my father warned me of the side effects of antidepressants, one of which was weight gain. That saga ended before it began.

That particular May day, my father arrived before the sun rose, still wearing the United Polaris pajama shirt they gave him on the plane. I was already dressed, teeth brushed, hair up. When I heard his knock on the door, I could breathe. My world with Liam was foggy and faded, the couch blurred with the pictures on the walls, the floor unsteady beneath my feet. But when I opened the door to my father's smiling face, to his bright eyes that contrasted with Liam's dark ones, the fog cleared. When I jumped into his arms and felt the weight of them wrap around me, when he kissed my forehead the same way he'd done all my life, when he looked into my eyes and saw the darkness, I knew I wasn't alone.

With one inhale of my father's scent, I could breathe again. Before I could stop myself, I let the weeks of stress explode, sobbing into his shirt.

"Oh, my crown jewel," he said, his voice breaking.

I stood there with him at the entrance to the apartment I shared with Liam, one foot out the door, the other stuck inside. I was straddling the line between freedom and fear—my father pulling me in one direction and Liam pulling me in the other.

I slipped out of the house, leaving the world I shared with Liam behind, even if only for a few hours.

We walked silently down the street, the sunrise casting a pink glow on the townhouses, the tulips planted in the miniature gardens still tight, hugging themselves in the morning, not yet ready for the day.

"What, Dad?" He was biting the space between his forefinger and his thumb again, the thin skin turning white between his teeth.

He shook his head and stopped biting. "Do you know how much I love you?"

I laughed. "Of course I know, Dad."

We walked silently until we reached the diner, my heart too drained to continue the conversation. I was tired. I didn't feel like telling him what I was feeling, and I didn't need to because he knew. He had always known. It was as if I were looking up from the bottom of a well, the world around me continuing, business as usual, but I couldn't climb out, and nobody but Liam knew I was in there. The world kept turning. Once in a while, Liam would come check on me, tell me to get up, get ahold of myself, but I couldn't pull myself out of the well. The walls were too high, the weight of my body too heavy. Thinking was no longer part of my daily life. I felt like I was constantly daydreaming.

It reminded me of a quote Ray came across and read to us the week before, from Patrick Hamilton's 1938 play *Angel Street*: "Your mind indeed is tired. Your mind so tired that it can no longer work at all. You do not think. You dream. Dream all day long. Dream everything. Dream maliciously and incessantly. Don't you know that by now?"

Inside the diner, my father ordered a house salad with two eggs over easy on top, no dressing.

"Salad in the morning?" the waitress asked. "And for you, miss?"

"I'll have a coffee, please, with milk."

"You have to eat something; look at you," my father said. I weighed 109 pounds, the thinnest I had been since middle school, but just thinking about food made me nauseous.

"I'm not hungry."

"Something, sweetie—you need to eat," he insisted.

I ordered a plain waffle—no butter or syrup. It arrived dry and pathetic, sliding to the edge of the plate when the waitress put it down in front of me. I nibbled on the corners, the sweet, warm dough dissolving into my mouth. I couldn't remember the last time I ate something and enjoyed it. I took a large swig of coffee to wash it down.

"Look at you," my father said again, gesturing toward me, the green neon "Open" sign flickering on and off behind him.

"You used to be a flower. Blossoming. Blooming. Laughing. Now look at you. Wilted. Sitting here like this." He hunched forward and scrunched himself into half a ball, his elbows tight against his ribcage, his fists touching his forehead. "Where did my daughter go? Where is my crown jewel? I can't sit here and watch you go through with the wedding. I won't let you."

I saw in his eyes the yearning to find me, but the anger inside of me started bubbling up again.

"Dad, stop trying to control everything all the time. You screwed up my life in the first place by moving me to Israel and making me join the army. You can't see me like this? Well, it's practically your fault. I never would have met Liam in the first place," I said.

"I thought in the long run moving to Israel would make you happy. I thought you'd become part of the culture. It was so important for me to watch you grow up in the country I grew up in. But maybe I was wrong; maybe I was wrong.

"I could have gotten you out of the army," he said, talking to himself now. "I could have waited a year before moving, waited for you to go to college, and then moved. I know I could have, but I thought this was best for you." He looked out the diner window at the streetwalkers. "I regret it now. Is that what you want to hear? I regret it. You were right; I never should have moved you to Israel to begin with. But it doesn't matter where you are; it matters who you are with, and you shouldn't be here alone. Come back to Tel Aviv with Ima and me, at least until you get stronger."

"After all of this, that's your solution? To run back home to Mommy and Daddy like a child? I'm not a child anymore, Dad. I'm married. I'm having a wedding. I have to stay here in New York—don't you see that? I've failed in so many things in my life, and I keep failing over and over again. I can't fail this relationship. I can't bear to fail again."

We paid the check and walked down to Central Park, dogs running loose before 9:00 a.m. I focused on taking one step and then another, moving slowly. The trees swayed in the brisk wind—a picture-perfect view able to deceive the darkest reality. An ice-cream truck was selling snow cones.

"I'll get you one," my father said, even though I didn't ask for one. He bought himself a water bottle and sunflower seeds, like he always did. We sat down on a bench overlooking the Jackie Kennedy Onassis Reservoir while the red, white, and blue dye stained my lips. This was the country I had called home for fourteen years, but I didn't feel like I belonged.

I grew up absorbing my father's optimism without knowing where it came from. He had grown up barely able to afford a slice of pizza, yet he lived his days appreciating every moment as it happened. As a father, he directed that optimism toward us. Even when the car rides were long, when the house didn't sell, when it rained on Sunday mornings at the East Hampton beach, he found a way to make us feel like everything was going to be okay, like this was how the day was supposed to turn out. "If the door closes on you, you go in through the window," he'd say.

But today, in the same way he was deflated and disconnected when we saw the red swastika on the door of the beach house, he disappeared. Even with his hand on my shoulder, I felt him fading, as if it was too much for him, for all of him, to really be there with me. He sat on the bench pushing his glasses up the bridge of his nose, and I watched as his eyes went vacant. He stared off into the reservoir, and while I tried to follow his gaze, I knew he was lost in his thoughts. I knew what was making him so sad. There was a defeat I didn't recognize in the stoop of my father's back, in the way he sipped the water from the bottle, in the way he shook the sunflower seeds in the palm of his hands before cracking them with his two front teeth.

"I didn't ask you to come and save me," I said. "You did this for yourself. For your own reasons. So you could be the hero."

He scoffed. "I've sold companies. I fought in the Lebanon War. I helped deliver Jake, unhooking him from the umbilical cord that was wrapped around his neck." He took a deep breath. "And still, saving you from yourself is the hardest thing I've ever had to do."

"Get it through your head, Dad. I don't need you to save me. I don't want you to save me. Give me some fucking credit. Why can't you just let it be?" I asked.

"Because," he said, his hand gripping the side of the bench, "nothing I've done in this life will be worth it if my daughter isn't happy."

There was a long silence.

"Look around you," he said. "There's something about New York. Something about this city, don't you think? It makes you feel so small. Even the bathroom in this park, it was probably built more than one hundred years ago. We're just a speck in this life. This small." He made an inch with his forefinger and thumb. "Is this how you want to spend the rest of your life? Scrunched up like a crumpled piece of paper?"

He gestured to the park around us. "The world is your oyster. Don't you see that?"

That's when my father pulled a business card out of his wallet. "Have your wedding next month. Do what you want. I will be there to support you, even if I think you're making a big mistake. But promise me you'll hold on to this," he said as he pressed the card into my hand.

I looked down and read the text, small and clear.

TEDDY D. GOLDBERG

DIVORCE ATTORNEY-AT-LAW

BY YOUR SIDE WITH PRACTICAL SUPPORT

AT A REASONABLE PRICE

TEL: (126) 224 9764

Chapter 27

Logistically, I thought it would be more difficult to take a leave of absence from Columbia. In reality, all I had to do was email the dean stating the request, and that was that. I had already come up with another lie for when they'd ask why I was taking a break; *I didn't have the funds, I landed a job I simply couldn't give up*, but the admissions secretary didn't even ask me. Why was I always expecting someone else to care? Once May came around and the semester ended, so did my affiliation with the school, until further notice. I kept telling myself I needed this time to recover, to take a mental health year. If I could just take some pressure off, I would be able to handle the situation with Liam lucidly. I could devote my time to building our life together and taking care of myself until I had enough energy to go back. This was the right thing to do, and Liam's affection since giving in only made that clearer to me.

I was drinking a cortado at Starbucks with Liam when I received an email from the school: "Your Columbia University email account has been deactivated."

And that was that.

Maybe Liam was right. I let life happen to me. Somewhere inside me, I expected a Columbia professor, or even one of the guidance counselors at the Student Life office, to reach out and ask if I was okay. But on the other end was always silence. I couldn't trust anybody to save me, and I wouldn't have let anybody save me if they tried.

Since officially taking a leave of absence, I lived in euphoria with Liam. We planned the wedding, agreeing to have it at Uncle Tom's beach house in Montauk because he would let us rent the place out for the night for free. Liam stopped yelling at me, stopped telling me he was sick of my shit, and instead showed me a patience I forgot existed. After I accidentally plugged our credit card information into a fraudulent website and almost had an anxiety attack when I had to tell him, he stroked my arm and promised he wasn't mad. "Why are you so upset? You're making me out to be some sort of monster. It happens, Tiny. I'll just cancel the card."

Liam rewarded me when I gave into his requests, and I basked in his acceptance every time. Surprise flowers on the dining room table when I came home from Trader Joe's, the smell of *arisa* encompassing our apartment when he was in the mood to make my favorite spicy tuna sandwich. This was the life I had dreamed about, wasn't it? This was what was important in life. Health. Love. I had to stop and appreciate the small moments, Liam would always say. But, like an hourglass, I knew the flow of sand would come to an end, the world would turn upside down, and it would start all over again.

"You don't do anything all day but can't even put food on the table when your fiancé gets home?" he said.

Here we go, I thought. *He's back.*

Liam insisted I get a job to help pay the expenses. I could be a waitress or a hostess or a bartender, but I needed to contribute to this relationship financially. When did I go from a Columbia University student with a future to an unemployed college dropout? When did I go from being financially supported by my parents to having to text Liam for permission to buy a slice of pizza?

"Your name shouldn't be on our bank account anymore," he said one evening as I was folding laundry.

"Why?"

"It's better for our credit score if my name is the only name on the account," he explained.

I looked at him blankly.

He laughed. "You don't even know what a credit score is, do you?" he said, shaking his head.

"Yes, I do," I said, folding a pink lace Victoria's Secret thong.

The days turned to weeks. I spent mornings lingering in bed, too exhausted to get up.

"What's wrong with you? Get out of bed already. Ella, Ella, Ella," Liam chanted in my ear like an annoying little sibling, but my exhaustion was too great.

"Talk to me. What are you feeling?" Liam asked.

"I don't know . . . darkness," I said.

Writing seemed like an impossible task. I made grocery lists and planned each evening meal in advance, sure to switch up the menus so Liam was satisfied, but soon, even that seemed like too great a duty. When I served him a bowl of *cacio e pepe* pasta, he looked at it, disgusted, and then at me.

"Are you cheating on me?" he asked.

"Are you crazy?" I answered, quickly adding, "I didn't mean that. I'm sorry. I'm just tired."

Liam cleared his throat. "My father says *cacio e pepe* is called 'the cheating wives' pasta.' He spent a summer in Sicily with his Italian friend from the army. Since there are only two ingredients, pecorino cheese and crushed black pepper, it's known that women who make this pasta for their husbands do it quickly so they can get back to more important things, like cheating on their husbands."

I wasn't sure if he was joking or not, and neither was he. Liam hadn't yet decided how he wanted the evening to go.

"Interesting," I said, sitting down beside him. I tried to keep my eyes bright and my lips slightly parted, like nothing was bothering me. I tried to smile, but after a few seconds, I felt like I'd been smiling for too long, and I didn't want to look anymore at Liam's raggedy white T-shirt and his dirty, unkempt fingernails.

I couldn't eat at all that month. Each time I looked at the food on my plate, it would somehow rearrange itself into a pile of wet, ominous-looking worms. I knew there were no creatures in my food, but once the image was stuck in my head, there was no way I could eat.

"Why are you doing this to us?" he asked, the creamy cheese sauce piling up around the corners of his mouth.

"Doing what? What am I doing?" I said.

"Your energy is ruining the evening," he said.

"It's not my energy. It's not me. I mean, is it me?"

"Never, Ella. Never you."

We were both silent, and I realized something real was happening. This was my life now. Happening to me. But if I could wake up and make the right choice, I could turn the story around.

When I wiped a tear from my eye, he said, "Do you want to make this work, or should we just end it now?"

Why did every mistake I made have to jeopardize our entire relationship?

"I do," I said.

Do I?

"Well, it doesn't sound like it," he said.

We sat silently until Liam finished eating. He left his plate on the table with the scrunched-up napkin beside it and went into the bedroom.

I fell deeper into the abyss.

———————

It was a week before the wedding.

"We're so excited, sweetie!" my mother said over the phone. "I have your dress—I hope it fits. And mine . . . I mean, it isn't as stunning as yours, but it's up there. Light pink silk with crystal straps. Anna's flying with Aba and me—we paid for her ticket, don't worry—and Grandma and Grandpa are coming two days after us. We paid for their tickets, too, but don't tell your father. I can't wait to see you all dolled up. My baby is going to be a bride in a week!"

I'd trusted my mother with choosing my wedding dress, considering she cared more about it than I did, and after contemplating between a floral princess gown and a collared, backless plain white dress, I went with the flowers to match the chuppah. Who would have thought, all those years ago, that while planning my wedding, I wouldn't even have the energy to choose my own dress?

The night before my parents arrived, five days before the big day, Liam took me to the Polo Bar, an expensive, exclusive restaurant on the Upper East Side where taking photos was forbidden and celebrity spotting was obvious. It wasn't until the bartender served us dirty martinis that I tried to enjoy the evening and forget about the sharp fear that contracted my stomach muscles. I lived with the constant worry that I would do something to set Liam off.

It was unlike Liam to reserve a spot for us at a high-end restaurant in the city. Liam preferred hamburgers and beer, not caviar and champagne. He was down-to-earth and real, he liked to remind me, and I was materialistic, privileged, and spoiled. He was wearing the same light-blue shirt he wore when he proposed, but now it pulled at the buttons. I knew by the way his eyes scanned the room that he was stepping out of his comfort zone for me. I squeezed his hand as the hostess led us to a corner table with a white candle flickering next to a small vase of daisies.

"You have to work on yourself," he said after we ordered.

"Work on what about myself?" I asked.

"Come on, Ella. We've been through this. We've done this a hundred times. You really want me to get into it again right now?"

I nodded.

"First of all, you're wearing too much makeup. It looks cheap with the black on the eyelids. And why did you do your hair like that? You know I don't like curly, all ratty in the back. You're a woman, my future wife. You need to look more put together. Now, if you really want me to be honest, the bones in your face have been sticking out lately. You kind of look like a skeleton. But then, the other night when we were having sex, I noticed the baby fat around the waist and almost went limp. You know you can get rid of that with crunches, right?"

I looked at Liam blankly. While he talked, I counted the hairs sticking out of his nose. Two of them were white. How could he let himself criticize me? Had he looked in the mirror lately? From the moment he took off his uniform, he went from sexy officer to unemployed loser. I knew it, and so did he. While he spoke, his eyebrows kept moving up and down, and he started using his hands to explain, like his father did. Like he used to tell me he never wanted to do. His nature was stronger than he was.

Yet for the first time in the years we'd spent together, I felt protected by a wall I had built. It was as if I had muted my surroundings, as if Liam were just mouthing the words, as if the restaurant were silent, and I could hear my own thoughts. I'd heard his countless versions of these words, the lists of what was wrong with me, of what I needed to do better, of how easy it was for me to change, and they used to break me down. Not tonight. I wasn't just numb to it. I was over it.

Liam kept going. "And you know the other night when we were watching *Inglourious Basterds* how you kept talking in between every scene? It was a turnoff for me, a huge turnoff. I kept thinking that sometimes I can't stand you. You've become aggressive, always talking about yourself. Talking about missing school. Most of the time it isn't even talking; it's complaining.

"Don't get me started on how much you complain. You really need to work on that. Not for me—for yourself. Who's going to want to be around somebody that complains all the time? Complaining about the laundry, the cooking. Just the bare minimum. Keep the house clean, for God's sake. Is it really that hard? Look around us. Every woman here has a clean house except for you. Fold the laundry once in a blue moon. Cook a meal here and there. Is that so much of me to ask? Really, I'm wondering. Is it?

"You only think about yourself. I try to satisfy you, taking you to a nice place like this, but you don't deserve it. You don't ever think about satisfying me. And I'm not talking just around the house." He lowered his voice. "I'm talking about sex, too. It's all or nothing with you, either you're silent as a fucking fish or moaning like a whore. I don't like either of them. I'm getting bored. Make me work for it, you know what I mean?"

I lowered my head in my arms on the table. When I looked up, Liam was smiling. A sad smile.

"I know you're upset," he said. "But you asked. Don't cry. Everything is going to be okay. You've just lost it a little bit, but I'm here. I love you. I'll help you. Come on, Tiny, stop crying."

"I'm not crying," I said, and I wasn't.

Tomorrow, I thought, *I'll go see the lawyer.*

Chapter 28

On the way to the lawyer's office, I stopped for a blowout. My hair was messy, the knots I hadn't had the energy to brush out tight against my scalp. Even though I was going only to find out what my options were, I knew that on this day, I was doing something worthwhile, and I decided I had to look the part. Yes, I was strong and all, and yes, no one was stronger than me, but I was also feeling horribly anxious. My mouth was so dry I needed coffee to wash down the croissant the hairstylist offered me. I heard my mother's voice in my mind: *When you look good, you feel good.*

Liam had called seventeen times, and it wasn't even noon yet. Did he know where I was going? I turned off the GPS on my phone and hoped he wouldn't notice.

As I walked out of the salon, my hair looked familiar to me. *I know this girl*, I thought as I brushed my hand through the silky strands. When I was a teenager, I straightened my hair every morning, the sizzling sound of each strand burning in my ear. My father used to ask me why I was ruining my beauty, burning and thinning the golden waves. Wasn't I smarter than that? But for the past few months, I hadn't taken care of myself at all. It was good to feel like this—beautiful.

As I crossed 79th Street, I passed hurried, purposeful people. I had this sudden urge to walk up to them on the street and tell them that I had a purpose, too. That I had somewhere to be, that I was planning my wedding one day and going to a divorce lawyer to see what my options were the next, in spite of Liam's warnings. I wondered if they could see it on me—the fear, the guilt, the newfound strength, all of it—whether I was wearing it on my face or hiding it behind my fresh blowout and button-down shirt. I felt naked and raw among the crowd of businesspeople heading out for their lunch breaks. I imagined accidentally running into one of Liam's uncles. I pictured Liam's face and, like a tidal wave, terror washed over me. A thought skittered across my mind: *You can't do this.*

I had arrived at the lawyer's office. I looked up at the enormous skyscraper, the visual illusion that it was going to topple over on me seeming more real than ever, and considered my options. I could turn around and forget I wanted to learn anything about divorce.

Or I could do what I knew I needed to do.

I smiled on my way past the guards and picked up a pass to Teddy Goldberg's office on the thirty-second floor. I was by far the youngest person in that lobby, and I was alone. What would this lawyer think when he saw me standing in front of him? Did he know by my shaky voice on the phone when I called to schedule the appointment that I had no idea what I was doing?

I took some short, deep breaths, the tightness in my chest overwhelming, and tried to relax as I walked into the elevator. *When you pretend to be something, you become it.*

But then, when the elevator doors opened, I couldn't move. I leaned back against the elevator wall and gripped the rail. I wanted to give up, turn off my brain, and fall away in that elevator, watching the floors light up with a *ding* as it ascended and descended, but something wouldn't let me. I forced myself out of the elevator and stared at the gold engraved sign in front of me:

TEDDY D. GOLDBERG
DIVORCE LAWYER

I rang the buzzer outside the office, and the red dot beside the keypad turned green as the door opened automatically. An overweight secretary ushered me in, her desk overflowing with snow globes. When I sat down to wait, I realized that her entire area was covered in snow globes—on every shelf, all over her desk, and even neatly organized around her feet on the floor.

After a few minutes, a slim, middle-aged man in a plaid jacket and dark jeans opened the door to his office and waved for me to come in. Teddy. He looked nothing like the big-shot lawyer my father insisted he was. I sat down in front of him, examining his shiny bald head and dark fleshy under-eye pockets. He clearly hadn't slept much the night before. He sat down in front of me. His small office was furnished with two uncomfortable leather chairs.

Not unkindly, he began speaking. "Ms. Davidson, I understand that you're here to learn what your options are regarding a divorce from Mr. Liam Levine?" he said as he looked through the papers and piles of magazines covering the surface of his desk.

"No, I don't want to get divorced. I love him, and we're getting married in a few days," I explained. "I'm just here to get some information. I want to understand what would happen if I decided to divorce Liam, in terms of his green card process and everything."

The lawyer tilted his head questioningly and then shrugged. "Well, Ms. Davidson, I've been a divorce lawyer for more than twenty-two years. You love him; you don't love him—I don't really care. Let me break it down for you. You got married at City Hall. Now, you're here, which means you want to hear about divorce. If you decide to get a divorce, Mr. Levine's green card process will be immediately stopped. He'll no longer be eligible to apply for residency, and you'll be sending him out of the country, ASAP. Even if he decides he doesn't want to sign the divorce papers, it doesn't matter. Once you sign them and serve them to him, he can wave bye-bye to America."

If I went through with divorcing Liam, I would ruin his life. He quit the army to follow me here and left his sick mother behind. I could tell that as much as he wanted to be in America, it wasn't easy for him. I knew he missed home, missed grabbing beers with his friends at the local bar, missed his mother's cooking. I couldn't take on the responsibility of destroying him.

Liam's raging face floated before my eyes, and I imagined how angry he would be if he knew where I was at that moment. He would kill me. The thumping of my heart in the lawyer's office was suddenly the only sound I could hear. I asked Teddy for a glass of water, and as I steadied myself against the chair to calm down, I realized I couldn't go through with this.

"If you don't want to be with this guy, we'll open a report and file for divorce. He'll have to leave the country in a matter of days, unless he's willing to stay here illegally, which will be his problem, not yours," Teddy said.

"Thanks, Teddy; I'll think about it," I said, rushing out of his office.

I raced out, past the hundreds of snow globes and into the elevator. I felt like somebody had picked up my own world and shaken it. I walked through the lobby past the guards, my mind a cacophony of voices. As I stepped out onto the street, the New York City air engulfed me, and I breathed it in deeply, hoping its warmth would melt my panic. I heard my father's voice pushing me to divorce Liam, my mother's voice debating on which wine to serve at the wedding cocktail hour, Liam's voice reprimanding me. But of all the voices, there was only one I knew I had to listen to. There was always only one.

My own.

Chapter 29

I checked my email. In between unsubscribing from Victoria's Secret newsletters and reviewing my credit score, an email popped up from a Columbia email address I didn't have saved in my contacts.

> Hi Ella,
>
> I hope all is well. Dean Baldwin informed me of your decision to leave Columbia. What a shame. If I hadn't made it clear up until now, I believe in you.
>
> 126-900-3487 if you change your mind.
>
> Best regards,
> Professor Ray Douglass

Almost instinctively, I picked up my phone and dialed the number.

"Hello," Ray answered.

"Ray? It's Ella Davidson," I said. My name felt foreign to me.

"Ella, how are you?" he asked sincerely.

"I'm okay," I said.

"Well, what's going on?" he said. "You got my email, then."

I took a deep breath and closed my eyes. "I changed my mind," I said. "I want to come back."

I didn't know I wanted to come back until I said it out loud to him. To believe that I was worthy enough to go back to school, even though I had already made the mistake of taking a leave of absence. When I left, I thought there was no going back. There were some mistakes you couldn't undo, and I thought this was one of them.

"Good," Ray said, matter-of-factly. "I'll talk to Dean Baldwin and have his secretary send over the application materials. You want to start this coming year, right?"

"Yes," I said, although I hadn't thought that far.

"Good, good," he repeated. "On one condition."

I knew it was too good to be true.

"I'm teaching a few more writing workshops in the summer semester that I'd like you to sit in on. If you're up for it, you can write a few pieces and edit them with the class."

I wasn't going to say a word to Liam. I'd deal with his anger when I had to. This was it. I was going back to school. As Ray gave me the class schedule times and locations, I realized that this was the first time in a long time I felt like what I was doing actually made sense.

Chapter 30

It was the night before our wedding, and I was sitting cross-legged on the gray IKEA couch in our apartment drinking Sancerre, waiting for Liam to come home from hanging out with a friend he met at the Israeli restaurant downtown. Since I was already done up and wearing sexy lingerie under my dress for our anniversary, I figured this was an ideal opportunity to send him some naked pictures and get him fired up for the celebratory evening I was planning.

When I reviewed the photos, the black lace baby doll I was wearing with the pink bows on the nipples suddenly looked ridiculous. I zoomed in on the frame and noticed my love handles hanging over the matching underwear. I tilted my head and squinted my eyes, but all I could see was the baby fat Liam had mentioned at the Polo Bar. I ran to the bedroom to change quickly. I wanted to wear something that hid the flaws. I wanted to be in control of how Liam saw my body, the body I starved anytime we argued and overfed every time we made up. After trying on my entire collection of Victoria's Secret lingerie, I decided on a two-piece red silk set, similar to one I caught Liam looking at on some influencer's Instagram page.

After I finished taking a few photos against the kitchen counter, I kept the lingerie on and set the table in hopes that Liam would walk through the door at that same moment to see me nonchalantly leaning over to place the utensils. I imagined him walking into our dimly lit apartment and smiling at the candlelight casting a glow on the framed pictures of us on the beach in Tel Aviv. I felt immense guilt for sneaking off to the lawyer's office, like I had betrayed Liam's trust, and I wanted to feel his arms wrapped around me, to hear his voice thanking me for planning this night.

The smell of lasagna lingered in the air. I was proud that I'd succeeded in preparing Liam's favorite food, and as I checked on the lasagna in the oven, it didn't look half bad.

"And he says I can't cook," I murmured to myself.

I glanced at the clock. 9:11 p.m. 911. 9/11. I pushed the familiar voice in my head telling me something was wrong deep down into my stomach and suffocated it. *Where the hell is he?* Last week while grocery shopping, Liam thought I hadn't noticed him eyeing some perfectly bronzed Brazilian model-looking girl. Images of him caressing her body flashed through my mind.

He was late. He often got held up strolling Central Park or shopping around Soho. Even though we had signed the marriage papers already, Liam still wasn't working, and it didn't seem to me like he was looking for a job, based on the fact that he watched shows at home and left his computer when he went out. Still, he was impossibly busy, unable to answer my calls or clicking over to the other line mid-conversation. When I asked him what he was doing or where he was, he said I needed to get a life and let go, even though I couldn't walk from First to Second Avenue without a text from him asking where I was going or when I would be back. He had convinced me that the real world operated above my head—and that the only way I would be able to survive it was by trusting him.

I paced the apartment, made the bed, finished the assigned Plato

Symposium reading, which was a breath of fresh air compared to the calculus and chemistry equations I was solving in my sleep, folded the blanket I snuggled in, and waited for Liam. The clock hit 10:00 p.m., and although I promised myself I wouldn't nag him, I felt my fingers punch in his number and heard the familiar ring in my ear.

No answer. My heartbeat accelerated, and pangs of anxiety pinched my chest. I felt the tingling sensation of a cold sore forming around my upper lip and made myself close my eyes and replay the nonchalant kiss he'd given me before leaving to go for a walk. Liam had been in a good mood that morning. He hummed while brewing our coffee. Check. He smiled at me. Check. He kissed me goodbye. Check. But of course, I knew Liam could love me one moment and hate me the next.

Another hour went by, and images of Liam undressing that stupid supermarket model crept into my mind again. *She was for sure skinnier and hotter than me.* If beforehand I was angry with Liam for being late to our night-before-the-wedding celebratory dinner, all I wanted now was to hear his voice through the phone line, soothing me and telling me he'd gotten caught up and was on his way home to me. I looked wildly around my apartment, at the elegant candle-lit anniversary dinner, the lacquered dining table my parents bought for us, set with our most expensive cutlery, and felt, for a moment, that I would be sitting here alone for the rest of my life.

My father used to tell me that he knew my happiness level based solely on my weight. If I gained an extra pound here or there, he knew I was happy. If I was on the skinnier side, he knew I was stressed.

Whenever my hips or collarbone stuck out just a millimeter more than usual, Liam would pull me close to him, inhale my scent, and lead me into the bedroom. During final exams, when I was 5′9″ and 112 pounds, he once said, "God, it turns me on when you're bony like this."

To distract myself from thoughts of Liam, I turned on the TV and began watching *Say Yes to the Dress*. A bride was crying at Kleinfeld, fanning her tears so they wouldn't ruin her makeup. Her mother and sisters stood up to hug her, and Randy asked the ultimate question: "Are you saying yes to the dress?"

I didn't have those moments to share with my family, and now, with our wedding only hours away, I realized I might never have them. At the commercial break, I sat on the edge of the couch and dialed Liam's number for the third time. He didn't answer, so I called my mom like I always did when I needed someone to listen. It was already close to midnight, and I knew she was sleeping at the Airbnb she and my dad had rented, catching up on her beauty sleep for the wedding, but this was an emergency, wasn't it?

"Mom, something bad is happening with Liam."

"What?"

I could almost hear her mentally running through the different possibilities. What could "something bad" mean? Was he calling off the wedding? Drugs? Police? Her usually relaxed voice tensed up.

The words came in gulps of breaths, and I realized I had lost my compass. I'd lost my sense of what was appropriate and rational and what wasn't. I'd been feeling lately as if I was going crazy, as if I didn't really trust my own instincts. Saying out loud "Liam is late to our celebratory dinner, so I think he's cheating on me a night before the wedding" was so ridiculous that I suddenly felt shame for blowing things out of proportion the way I always did when it came to Liam. I started panting uncontrollably.

"Ella, get a bag, any sort of bag," my mom said. "Put it over your mouth and nose and take deep breaths, sweetie—deep, slow breaths. Everything is going to be okay, my love. He's fine. You're fine."

I held a plastic Whole Foods bag over my mouth, the receipt for the lasagna ingredients still clinging to it.

As I continued to send Liam paragraph-long hysterical text messages asking him where he was while my mom tried to get me to relax over speakerphone, I heard the sound of the key turning in the lock. Liam walked in, his face sour and disappointed. He dropped his bag on the floor with a bang, walked past the lasagna, past the half-melted candles, and past me—as if I were air, as if I were just another object on the set of the movie I was playing a character in. Once in the bedroom, he closed the door behind him.

I hung up on my mother without saying a word and, with my eyes closed, leaned back on the couch and tried to count to ten.

I made it to six before I lifted myself off the couch and stormed into the bedroom, swinging the door open as hard as I could.

Liam was sitting at my computer scrolling through Facebook. The bright screen reflected on Liam's face, and as he turned around to look at me standing in the doorway, it hit me. Liam was angry. With me.

"Liam? What the hell? You're four hours late, and you walk in here and past me and start scrolling through *Facebook*? You know I planned this dinner; I made food. Like, real homemade food!" I yelled, pretending to be strong.

He said nothing. I felt my eyes fill with tears and the lump in my throat grow solid. *This again.* For some reason that thought kept repeating itself in my mind. *This again. This again. This again.* It was always the same thing; this was nothing new. It didn't matter that our wedding was tomorrow. This was Liam. This was the feeling I had become accustomed to. Worrying. Wanting to make it right. Waiting for it to be over. *This again.*

I grew up watching my mother roll her eyes behind my father's back while smiling to his face, doing everything and anything to keep the harmony in our home. It was her job, her responsibility, to calm him down, no matter his mood. It was my duty to do the same, to take a deep breath and let it go. Right?

Liam's stare pierced through me.

"I have one question for you," he said, his jawbone sticking out as he bit down on his back teeth. "Do you think I'm stupid?"

My mind raced. "Stupid? No, why would I think you're stupid?"

Calmly, he turned back to face the computer screen and clicked on my ex-boyfriend's picture. Ethan, from years ago, back in Greenwich, in high school—from before the army, from before my life spiraled into this. He dragged the mouse toward the message icon on the right corner of the Facebook page. Click. A list of messages filled the screen.

And that's when I realized it was *my* Facebook he was scrolling through and *my* private messages he was displaying—specifically one short conversation between Ethan and me, when I wished him a happy birthday a month ago and he replied asking me what I had been up to lately. I stood behind Liam and leaned into the screen, reading and rereading the messages hysterically. Liam's familiar scent of burning wood mixed with mint Burberry cologne made its way into my nostrils, and it repulsed me. A thought formed in my mind at that moment: *No matter what you say, nothing is going to convince him that these conversations meant nothing.* Liam always knew better than everyone, especially me.

"Liam, really? This is just a harmless conversation. It was his birthday! Look, look." I pointed at the screen in a panic. "Look, right here, I told him how happy I am with *you*. How great my life has been lately!"

"You know, it just blows my mind," Liam said. "Our wedding is tomorrow. You think I want to go through with it after this? I do so much for you. God damn it. You make me feel like shit."

Liam stood and hovered over me. "I do whatever you want. Anything! You wanted me to stay in New York so you wouldn't be here alone—I did it. You wanted a fancy wedding at Tom's house—I chased him down until he agreed. And now, you have the nerve to go behind my back and flirt with your ex? Don't humiliate me. Please."

We were waking up in less than five hours to drive to Montauk and get ready at the beach house, but all I wanted to do was slip into bed and never leave. Liam looked at me and seemed disgusted, as though he'd just walked into a dirty stall in a public bathroom. His eyes went dark as he left the bedroom, walked into the dining room, picked up the aluminum tray of lasagna, and brought it into the kitchen. I followed him, yelling and crying and still trying to explain myself, although we both knew there was no point. He held the tray with one hand, opened the lid of the trashcan with the other, and threw the freshly baked lasagna right into it with a plop.

We were both silent for a moment, and I could hear faint laughter from the bride on *Say Yes to the Dress*. She'd found her after-party dress.

I wanted to scream at Liam, to tell him to stop ruining what we spent years building. I wanted to smack him, to wake him up. I wanted to remind him that I was his *fiancée*, not a child. I wanted to cry out for him to help me—to tell him that I was only pretending to know how to handle this situation.

I wanted to turn to him for security, when he was the one making me feel insecure all along.

I didn't know who I was anymore. The smart young woman who graduated from the Israeli army who'd gotten straight As at Columbia University studying premed—what happened to her? She'd fallen in love with a man who put out her spark.

She should have turned around, zipped up her coat, and walked out of that apartment, without ever looking back. She should have told him that he'd never find another woman like her, someone who loved him more than she loved herself. She should have told him to get out, that this was her apartment. She should have told him never to speak to her again.

I should have. But I didn't.

I stood in the kitchen with Liam, begging him with my eyes to forgive me for messaging Ethan. But at that moment, he didn't want anything to do with me. He pushed me off of him and turned his head to the side. So I did what I always did after we fought. I used sex to spark his attention, even if only for a moment.

I started kissing Liam's neck, and as his lips met mine, I tasted the saltiness of my own tears streaming down my cheeks. I felt him grab my ass with both hands, hard. Liam pulled off my silk lingerie set, literally ripping it apart, and lifted me up onto the kitchen sink.

I felt like my head was going to explode, like everything around me was falling apart, like the world was spinning. All I could hear was the clunk of Liam's belt buckle falling to the kitchen floor.

We had sex on the sink and then against the oven, and as he thrust deep into me from the back, I stared at the empty aluminum tray of what used to be the lasagna, and instead of being furious, I pathetically wondered if Liam was going to stay after this to talk or go to a bar to "clear his head" like he often did. How was I going to fall asleep tonight? How was the makeup artist going to cover the dark circles under my eyes?

When Liam was close to finishing, I felt him lean into my cheek, his warm breath in my ear.

"Don't ever disobey me like that again, Ella," he said excitedly, and the sound of my name made me feel like he was finally acknowledging me for the first time that night.

His lips against my cheek again, he kissed me softly. Then, out of nowhere, I felt a deep pain cutting through my flesh. I pushed him away, holding my cheek with both hands, blood gushing down my palms.

"You bit me!" I cried, but Liam was in a trance, finishing himself off. Semen dripped down his hand onto the floor as he leaned back against the kitchen counter to steady himself. I knelt beside him, naked and bloody, the sour scent of cum lingering in the air.

"What happened?" he asked when he looked at me. "Oh, shit, what the fuck? I thought I was just giving you a little love bite. Damn. You're so sensitive. Let me see; let me take a look," he said, trying to move my hand away from the bite. I pushed it away and ran to the bathroom, locking the door behind me.

When I stared into the mirror, I didn't recognize the girl looking back at me. I slowly moved my hand from my cheek, afraid to see what he had done. On the side of my cheek was a doughnut-shaped bite mark recording the specific characteristics of Liam's teeth—an imprint of his four top and bottom teeth engraved in my skin, blood still gushing. He had branded me, on purpose or accidentally, but the abrasion was deep. *Do I need stitches? How am I going to show up to* the *wedding tomorrow like this? Everyone will see.*

Liam knocked on the door. "Tiny? Let me in. Are you okay? I'm sorry, I didn't mean to. You get me so excited that I turn into a sex animal—what can I say? I snagged the hottest girl in town."

"Get away. Leave me alone." I didn't want to feel his hands on my face or see the look of sorrow on his. I needed time away from Liam. A minute. Or a lifetime.

I leaned against the bathroom wall and sat on the floor, my cheek pulsing. Liam had once bruised my cheek with his kiss, and now this.

Fifteen minutes later, Liam knocked again.

"Come on, don't be dramatic. Take a shower; you'll feel better," he said through the door. "I'm going out for a drink. I need one. We'll talk about all of this tomorrow."

Tomorrow? When? While we're welcoming our guests and reading our wedding vows?

I didn't answer him, but when I heard the sound of the front door closing, I was relieved he was gone.

I decided to run a bath. Maybe the steam would help the cut heal faster for tomorrow. When the bath was ready, I stepped into the hot water, the bubbles moving aside as if making room for me. I cleaned the blood from my face and arms and watched as the water turned a light pink. My favorite color. I dropped a bath bomb into the tub and held my breath, sinking my head under the water. The sting of the cut hurt at first, but when I came up for air, I already felt better. As I lay there surrounded by the warm water, watching the bath bomb explode into clouds of pink, the mirror surrounding the bath steamed up like it usually did. I always wrote *something* on a steamed mirror, because you can't not, but for a minute, I couldn't think of anything to write.

So I just sat there, the steam rising, and let my finger wander. I closed my eyes and wrote my own name, over and over again.

I opened the bathroom drawer and applied two princess decorated bandages to the bite mark, hoping it wouldn't be as noticeable by tomorrow. What would my father say? When I stepped out of the bathroom in a towel, the apartment was empty, but I felt calm. It was just me and the candles; we were all a little bit smaller than when the night began.

For a long time, I believed Liam when he told me I was wrong. When he told me I was a privileged young woman, a spoiled American brat. Liam always said one day I'd learn that real life wasn't easy. It was a lesson he'd absorbed early, growing up in one of the poorest neighborhoods in Northern Israel. His mother was sick. His father couldn't find a steady job. He paid his grandmother's rent. Left everything behind. All because he'd moved to New York to be with me.

But tonight, my thoughts shifted. Did I dream of showing up to the altar with a bite mark on the side of my cheek, afraid to sleep next to my future husband? Did I imagine sleeping alone in bed the night before the wedding, the smell of cum still lingering in the air, while my groom-to-be barhopped without me? Was this what I truly thought I deserved? *Reality outdoes imagination.*

Tomorrow was the big day. In two hours, my parents would pick me up in the SUV they rented, and we'd drive to Montauk to celebrate the marriage of two young people from opposite sides of the world, both physically and mentally. The makeup artist would be waiting for me there, and my mother would make sure the food caterer had everything right. My parents, grandparents, and Anna had already flown in from Israel; Liam's parents, his brother and sister, and his two best friends flew in last minute, too. Julia was driving in early from Connecticut, and Chloe postponed her flight to Norway to be there for me.

Lying alone in bed in the dark, I unhooked the heart necklace Liam gave me for my twentieth birthday, that night in the army at the watchtower. I held the necklace in my hands, the dim light of the moon revealing the outline of the charms, but inside the intertwined hearts was nothing, only empty space.

Chapter 31

Liam must have snuck into bed during the forty minutes I was actually asleep, because I didn't hear him walk into the apartment. I woke up to my alarm at 5:00 a.m., adrenaline rushing through my body. Today was the day: my wedding day. The day I'd dreamed of since I was a little girl in that Connecticut barn. I washed my face and brushed my teeth in the bathroom, and when I leaned in to the mirror to get a better look at the bite mark Liam left, I was relieved to see it didn't look as bad as I expected it to. I closed my eyes and took a deep breath. "No one is stronger than me," I said, but as I repeated my mantra, my mind transported me to the night before, to Liam sinking his teeth into my flesh, to feeling, for the flash of an instant, like I deserved it.

Liam knocking on the bathroom door interrupted my thoughts.

"Good morning, beautiful," he said when I opened it. "I can't wait to marry you."

"Good morning, my love," I said. The part of me that loved him couldn't wait to marry him either.

He kissed my neck and put the intertwined heart necklace around it. "You almost forgot to put this on," he said.

My parents picked me up at a quarter past six, and when I got into the back seat of the car, a grande soy cappuccino and a spinach egg wrap were already waiting for me. Liam could arrive later, considering all he had to do was hop in the shower and put on a suit. I hugged my father and felt comfort in the familiarity of his smell, even though I could tell by the look on his face he was nervous about the day to come. I had parted my hair on the side to hide the bite mark, and I couldn't bring myself to look him in the eye. If I did, he would know what I was feeling without words. My mother, on the other hand, glowed with excitement.

"Honey! Look at you! Let's do this! I've already called the caterer to make sure they're on the way to the beach house, and guess what? They're already there! Champagne, caviar, and all! I can't wait for you to try on your dress; you're going to look like a princess." She squeezed my hand.

"Maya, relax," my father said, his eyes on the road. "It's only a wedding, not some sort of hard-earned accomplishment."

As we drove into Montauk, past the white-picket fences and clear blue sky, I couldn't believe how picture-perfect my life seemed on the outside but how destroyed I felt on the inside. Yet when the SUV glided into Liam's uncle's driveway, I couldn't help but feel I was being transported into a dream. It wasn't just a beach house—it was an eleven-bedroom mansion with the stylistic combination of a '60s Florida home and the laid-back, gray-stoned feel of a Montauk beach house. I stepped out of the car to catering waiters bustling back and forth, gardeners putting the finishing touches on the lawn, and three pool boys cleaning a turquoise infinity pool. The charming outdoor woven-wicker finish blended perfectly with the pastel flowers my mother had chosen, but no amount of money could buy my happiness.

It was already past 8:00 a.m.; relaxing cocktail music played in the background, creating a contemporary garden-party feel, the crisp whites and fresh greenery complementing the white stools and market umbrellas. A long wooden table with white dining chairs sprawled across the back area of the lawn, and I couldn't help but smile at the blue and white hydrangeas dressing the table, reminding me of Liam's proposal at the Shakespeare Garden. The outdoor sofas were decorated with navy and white stripes, creating an authentic nautical feel that exceeded even my most extravagant expectations.

But all of this was nothing compared to the moment I laid eyes on the chuppah. I stopped in my tracks. It took my breath away. All those nights dreaming about my wedding, dreaming about the perfect princess day, hadn't prepared me for the feeling rushing through me as I walked closer and closer to the chuppah. Symbolizing the new home to which the groom would officially accept his bride, this wedding canopy was lined with pastel flowers so dense I could barely see the four poles holding it up. Draped across the top was a stunning, soft white cloth, held up by flowers on each corner. I couldn't believe this was mine. Mine and Liam's.

I got ready with my mother, Natalie, and Emma in the master bedroom on the third floor, our hair in curlers, looking out the window at the wedding preparations. My father stayed downstairs making small talk with the workers, offering them wine and whiskey without realizing Americans didn't usually drink on the job. The makeup artist, a young, chubby woman in her late thirties, promised to give me a natural look, the way Liam liked, and when my mother was busy with my sisters, I pointed to the bite mark and mouthed, *Please make sure you cover this.*

When my mother came in with the dress, it was more beautiful than when I saw it on FaceTime, and I started to cry. I slipped it on, the white floral print blending in with the decorations, with the energy, with the entire day. I had officially embraced this fairy-tale dream, each hair in place, each nail flawlessly manicured, each smile perfectly crafted. Why couldn't I put my feelings aside? I wanted to enjoy this moment as it happened and lean in to the side of myself that was head over heels in love with Liam. The side of myself that knew he was only human, that he, too, made mistakes. The side that believed him when he promised to change, when he told me he loved me, when he lifted me up and spun me around, protecting me from any danger. This wedding was everything I could have dreamed of and nothing I ever dreamed of, and while on the outside the birds kept chirping, inside my soul was turmoil.

A few drinks later, guests started to arrive. The traditional Jewish wedding expected the bride to stay upstairs before the ceremony so that when she arrived for the first time to walk down the aisle, her entrance had more impact, and that's what Liam and I agreed we would do. As the clock inched toward twelve, I watched the guests from upstairs, alone. Chloe and Julia laughed with each other while sipping champagne, and Liam's parents looked uncomfortable and out of place on the white barstools. My mother trailed behind my grandparents, making sure they had enough food to eat and a place to sit, and my sisters and brother trailed behind her. My father sat alone on the navy-and-white-striped couch drinking whiskey on the rocks, taking it all in.

And then, there he was. Liam. Beaming with an enormous smile, he greeted each guest, kissing them on each cheek, his eyes squinting from smiling so wide. Charisma radiated off of him, and the suit he wore accentuated his muscular chest. I knew any woman who didn't know Liam could have fallen in love with him in that moment. When he wanted to be, he was magic.

When it was time, my mother came upstairs to bring me down, and I hid to the left of the ceremony with her on one arm and my father holding the other. The guests sat in the chairs facing the chuppah, and although I hadn't seen him yet, Liam was waiting for me underneath it, standing beside his parents. "All of Me" started playing, the familiar notes taking me back to that night at the watchtower, that night when I believed Liam and I were meant to live happily ever after, that night when I thought it was us against the world.

As I walked down the aisle toward Liam, I started to shake. After all these years, the face that was blurry up until now came into focus. Liam watched as my parents and I stopped in front of the chuppah. My father kissed me swiftly and waited for my mother, but when she leaned in to kiss me, I saw tears streaming down her cheeks. From the outside, they looked like tears of happiness, but I saw the sorrow in them.

"You don't have to do this," she whispered in my ear, and I knew I hadn't misheard her.

They left me there alone and walked toward Liam, hand in hand, waiting for me beside him.

Finally, I was standing in the aisle alone. I looked at Julia and Chloe, their phones videotaping these moments, and then I looked at my little sisters, giddy with excitement, their dresses flowing behind them. Last, I looked at Liam. I watched as he wiped tears from his eyes—watched as he realized he'd succeeded. He had a look of disbelief on his face that he was actually going to marry me, right here, right now, in front of everyone we loved, and deep inside, I was in disbelief, too.

"You are stunning," Liam said when I walked up to meet him. We stood under the chuppah, the rabbi reading the Hebrew prayers before it was our turn to read our vows to one another.

Liam started. "Ella, love of my life—thank you for it all. I'll never know how two completely different people from opposite sides of the world fell in love the way we have. I never thought my wife would be an American princess, but I hope I can continue to provide that for you as we move forward in our lives. And if it takes time, be easy on me. I know I'm not perfect; I never have been. But you make me want to change. You make me want to be a better person. When I was growing up, I didn't ever feel like I had a normal family like everybody else, but now, standing here with you, I know you will give me all of you. You are my family now. We belong to each other. You're a piece of work, but you're my piece of work, and I know I love you. That's what matters. Love conquers all. I promise to love you and to protect you until death do us part."

Liam wiped the sweat from his forehead, the Hamptons breeze no longer as refreshing as it was in the early hours of the morning. I unfolded the paper scrunched up in my fist, the vows I wrote two weeks before when things between us were better. Two weeks before Liam sank his teeth into my flesh.

For a brief moment, when he was done, I felt sorry for him. But when he leaned in to kiss me on the cheek, the same cheek he bit last night, causing me to feel a sting that traveled through my bones, my empathy for him diminished. I looked into Liam's eyes, and it seemed like he'd aged a decade since the day I met him that night two and a half years before on the beach. Even standing at the altar in his black suit with his hair slicked back, I saw the bags under his eyes, the sunken posture. He might have looked like he had it all together, but inside, he was tired, too.

I started reading: "Liam, thank you for teaching me that love has no boundaries. That love forgives everything. That love really means for better or for worse. Before I met you, I was different. I didn't know what it meant to give yourself fully to someone else. To put yourself last, to love somebody more than you love yourself. I've always been in love with love, and I've always thought that love could overcome anything, that love was first and foremost, and any problems that came afterward could be solved if the love was strong enough."

I stopped reading. I looked up at Liam. I couldn't continue. I crumpled the vows in my fist and threw them on the floor. I heard my mother's voice in my head. *You don't have to do this.*

"But you know what, Liam? I don't believe that anymore. I don't believe love conquers all. I don't believe love comes first. I don't believe it's healthy to love somebody more than you love yourself. I think dignity comes before love. And how about self-appreciation? How about respect? Shouldn't those things come before love, too? What about trust? Don't you think trusting the man you sleep next to and not being afraid he'll sink his teeth into your flesh again is more important than love?"

I continued, "Don't you think love is minimized if the man you love spends evenings degrading you, listing everything that's wrong with how you look and act and feel? If he spends his life belittling you to make himself feel better? What kind of love is that?"

Liam coughed into his hand and cleared his throat. "Are you really going to do this right now?" he said under his breath. "In front of everybody?"

The words spilled out. "I loved you so much in the beginning, with your grand gestures, your endless charisma. You scooped me up when I was down and pretended like you were going to protect me, when you were the one I was supposed to be afraid of all along. You isolated me from the people who loved me most, and you made me believe I was going insane."

I could feel the guests starting to fidget in their chairs.

Liam spoke. "How dare you embarrass me like this? How can you do this to me? You self-centered, privileged brat. You have no idea what I've been through."

"No idea what *you've* been through?" I said. "*You* have no idea, Liam. I used to have a light inside of me, but you . . . you put it out. I'm not the girl I was before the army. She's gone. You don't know what it's like to feel this small, to feel like I'm not enough, like whatever I do will never satisfy you. Why do I have to beg you to talk to me after I make a normal, human mistake? I'm not supposed to fear for my safety at the hands of the man I love. What you did last night . . . it makes me sick, physically sick, just thinking about it. I'm not going to live like that, Liam. I can't start a family with you; I can't bring a baby into this world just to watch you break me down. I don't deserve it. I can't do this. *Fuck you.* Fuck you for thinking you could do this to me for the rest of my life."

After months of pushing it down, the anger was spilling out of me.

"Ella, please, I'm sorry," Liam said. He reached for my hand.

But all I could think was, *I'm lying at the bottom of the stairs, and all I can hear is Liam saying, "I'm sorry, I'm sorry, I'm sorry."*

"Don't do this to us," Liam said. "I love you."

But all I could think was, *I'm at the Polo Bar, anxiety infecting my every move, listening to Liam list everything that's wrong with me before saying, "I love you."*

I looked up at him, my white floral dress feeling as heavy and uncomfortable as the army uniform felt the first time I put it on. I didn't have to say anything else for Liam to know that it was over between us, forever. That straight from this ceremony, I was going to drive to the lawyer's office and file for divorce.

I pulled my hand away from his and met my mother's gaze. She wasn't disappointed or angry or afraid. She was ready to stand behind me, whatever decision I made. A mother's unconditional love. Turning away from the chuppah, I pulled the heart pendant necklace off of my neck, tearing the chain. I held the back of my dress in both hands and ran.

Love conquers all?
Love forgives everything?
Love has no boundaries?
Not on my watch.

———

Liam sent me a pink balloon every day for three months and ten days after I left him at the altar. I wondered when they would stop showing up, but day after day, the same delivery man tied the light pink satin string of the balloon to the door handle of my apartment, and each morning when I'd open the door on my way to Pilates or breakfast with Chloe, the balloon lingered in my face until I pushed it aside and headed out the door. The balloons were a constant reminder that Liam was thinking about me, and for the first month I even looked forward to seeing them. Then, the texts started blowing up my phone, from never-ending messages confessing his love—"You've broken me, but I will never stop loving you"—to angry, one-sentence texts that kept me up at night: "You're a cunt, you know that?"

Months after the balloons stopped coming, my phone would light up every so often with a text from Liam—sometimes in the middle of the night, when I knew he was drunk or high, sometimes in the mornings when his heartbreak was aching deep in his soul. But I never answered him, not once.

As soon as I signed the divorce papers, Liam could no longer stay in the United States legally, and I knew one of the reasons he wouldn't stop messaging me was for the chance to change my mind so he could move back to New York and build his future in America—to pursue his own American Dream.

It took a while, but Liam finally realized that this time, I would stand behind my words.

Chapter 32

THREE YEARS LATER. It is unusually windy on graduation day. The sun beats down on the thousands of Columbia graduates, all dressed in light blue robes, the black tassels of their caps swinging as they applaud. My legs are sticking to each other underneath the heavy gown, and I feel drops of sweat trickling down the backs of my knees. We sit patiently, listening to the keynote speaker recite the speech she must have practiced hundreds of times. My mind is somewhere else, but her last few words jump out at me. "Remember what Oscar Wilde once said: 'Some cause happiness wherever they go; others, whenever they go.'"

My parents flew in from Tel Aviv last week and arrived early on campus with me, so they're sitting in the front row of the guest section. This is what they have always imagined for me. This is what they raised me to believe I could accomplish. A perfect blowout was necessary, of course, but what lingers inside our minds is what matters most. I close my eyes when they play "Pomp and Circumstance." I'd almost let this experience slip out of my fingers but somehow caught it with my other hand before it was too late.

The sun glistens against my cheek, and if anyone were to look at me at this exact moment, they would notice the slightest scar, the outline of a bite mark. My life could have taken a different turn.

When Dean Baldwin calls my name to collect the diploma, the wind has calmed down, and the air is clear. I hear applause and walk fast across the stage, desperate not to be the center of attention. As I walk off, I scan the audience for my parents. They're standing up, applauding, shouting and beaming with pride. I watch as my father holds my mother's face, leans in, and kisses her. *We did it*, I imagine they're thinking.

We throw our caps up into the sky, and they float back down, an ocean of blue confetti. When the ceremony is over, Professor Ray Douglass somehow finds me among the identically dressed students and squeezes me into a hug. "This is just the beginning, you know," he whispers.

I don't have a career or a husband or a plan, but I know he's right.

Standing beside him is a tall, curly-haired young man in a cap and gown, with a bright smile and sparkly blue eyes. Kind eyes.

"This is my son, Aiden. Actually, Doctor Douglass from now on. He just graduated from the medical school," Ray says, unapologetically proud.

"Congratulations," I say.

"Congrats to you," Aiden says, the atmosphere surrounding him easy and calm.

I introduce Professor Douglass and Aiden to my parents, and we make small talk. Before they leave, Aiden turns to me. "Hey, it was really great to meet you, Ella."

My mother opens her purse, inviting me to throw my diploma inside, but I hold on to it instead. On our way to lunch at San Ambroeus to celebrate, we walk past other Columbia students, their gowns tucked under their arms. Even as we sit in the restaurant and toast with glasses full of champagne, I keep my gown on. I earned it.

At sunset, I go for a jog along the East River. Runners race by, dogs bark, the air is crisp and warm. When I finish, I stop to look out at the water, to take it all in. And right there, before my eyes, the current shifts direction. I watch as the water gleams and ripples in a way I've never witnessed before. In a way that makes me stop and stare and think: *Sometimes, taking control of your life means changing direction.*

Acknowledgments

Endless thanks go to the remarkable writers and editors who supported me as I wrote this book: Dorie Chevlen, Eyal Cohen, Harold Rogers, Rebecca Logan, Leah Krumholz, Cassie Mannes Murray, and Claudia Volkman. Thank you to Leigh Stein; you have read more drafts of this novel than anyone should have to, and I am eternally grateful for your unwavering enthusiasm.

Thank you to my professors at Columbia University: Lis Harris, Leslie Jamison, Richard Ford, Phillipe Lopate, Margo Jefferson, Gary Shteyngart, Lara Vapnyar, and Samuel Freedman. Thank you, especially, to Jay Shuttleworth.

To my first reader and forever cheerleader, Jessica Sponheimer, thank you for your indispensable feedback and love. Shani Blatt and Adi Blatt, thank you for keeping me sane between writing sessions.

To my mother and father, thank you for bringing the world to my fingertips. I could never find the words to explain how much I love and appreciate you. Leelee, Abby, and Ben, forever and always, thank you for making me laugh until my stomach hurts.

Of course, my babies. Thank you for choosing me. You are magic. The world belongs to you, and so does my soul.

Finally, to Joni, the light of my life—thank you for making my dreams come true.

About the Author

RAZ TAL SCHENIRER holds an MFA from Columbia University. She is founder of the dating advice column *Smart Girl Knows*. Her work has appeared in *Elite Daily*, the *Rumpus*, and *Betches*, among other publications. *Where Love Lies* is her first novel. Visit her online at smartgirlknows.com or on Instagram: @razschenirer.